"How long have you been looking at me?" Lily asked, blushing.

"Just a second. Why?" Brady's smile turned to a grin. "How long have you been looking at me?"

She shook her head. "I wasn't really looking. I was thinking. Just sitting here."

"You look—nice," he said. His eyes strayed down to her cleavage and hung there long enough for Lily to feel like squirming.

She scoffed. "Just nice?"

He drew his eyes back up to hers, their expression serious. "Well, yeah. What were you hoping for? Bad? Sloppy? Ugly?" He shook his head and smiled. "Sorry, doll."

She laughed.

"I was going for sexy," she admitted, for no reason she could fathom.

He crossed his arms over his chest. "You're always sexy," he said.

By Elaine Fox

Elaine Fox

Beware Of Doug

AVON BOOKS
An Imprint of HarperCollins*Publishers*

This is a work of fiction. Names, characters, places, and incidents are products of the author's imagination or are used fictitiously and are not to be construed as real. Any resemblance to actual events, locales, organizations, or persons, living or dead, is entirely coincidental.

AVON BOOKS
An Imprint of HarperCollins*Publishers*
10 East 53rd Street
New York, New York 10022-5299

Copyright © 2007 by Elaine McShulskis
ISBN: 978-0-06-117568-8
ISBN-10: 0-06-117568-4
www.avonromance.com

First Avon Books paperback printing: February 2007

Avon Trademark Reg. U.S. Pat. Off. and in Other Countries, Marca Registrada, Hecho en U.S.A.
HarperCollins® is a registered trademark of HarperCollins Publishers.

Printed in the U.S.A.

10 9 8 7 6 5 4 3 2 1

For David Voorhies,
who encouraged me
to let my writing go to the dogs.
Thank you for being
the best champion a girl could have.

Acknowledgments

I would like to thank Captain Jeff Smith, pilot-extraordinaire, for his generous help with the duties of a private jet pilot. I only wish I could have used more of the fascinating and informative details he gave me. If there are any mistakes in the story, they are entirely mine.

One

"Someone's moving in."

Nathan made the statement as if he and Lily were parked in a dark alley, wearing night-vision goggles and staking out someone's house, instead of standing by the fence in their respective front yards on a sunny spring afternoon. They were watching several large moving men unload a leather couch from a truck into the right side of Lily's Victorian "twin house," the nineteenth century's version of a duplex.

From inside her half, Lily's French bulldog, Doug, could be heard barking as if the four horsemen of the apocalypse were galloping up the driveway. Through the closed window he sounded like a cartoon character underwater. *Bwoop-bwoop. Bwoop-bwoop.*

"My father's really happy with this tenant," Lily said, watching two of the movers bend an enormous mattress through the front door. It looked even bigger than a king size. Who in the world needed such a big bed? "That's why he wanted me to be here when the guy moved in, in case he had any questions. The guy's being bankrolled by a billionaire, as my father put it, so he won't be a deadbeat like Hugh was."

"It's a guy?" Nathan asked sharply.

Lily nodded. "Don't worry," she added. "I'm sure my father read this one the riot act about loud parties and beer cans in the backyard. You and your mother can rest easy. Besides, this guy works. He's not in college like Hugh was."

"What does he do?"

"He's a pilot. He'll be flying Sutter Foley's private jet. Apparently it's a full-time job." Despite herself, she was impressed with this. A pilot. It seemed so . . . adventurous.

Nathan nodded. "Nice, working for a billionaire. So I guess your friend Megan knows him. I mean since she lives with Foley and all. Did she say what he was like? Is he, like, old or anything?"

"I'm not sure she does know him." Lily leaned slightly sideways as the movers manipulated the long leather couch first one way, then the other, in an attempt to get it through the door. "She isn't very involved in Sutter's business stuff." She gazed down the street again, expecting that any minute a car would pull into the driveway. "Where *is* he, anyway? I don't have all day. You'd think the new guy would be here, directing the movers, so they know where to put stuff. Doesn't seem very responsible."

"Maybe he's on a flight," Nathan said. "Maybe he's gone a lot. Could be he'll *never* be around."

Lily glanced at him. "That would be great."

Even as she said the words, a motorcycle roared up the street, rattling the windows on nearby houses, then slowed to a crawl and pulled into the driveway. It didn't stop there, however. With a twitch of the driver's wrist the cycle gave a gratuitous growl and pulled right up alongside the moving truck, partially on the lawn, over the front walk to a patch of grass next to the flower bed lining the right side of the porch.

It was out of the way of the movers, she gave him that. But it stood in the front of the house like the prized possession of a redneck in a trailer park.

The motorcycle's rider wore a brown bomber jacket, faded and frayed jeans, a sweatshirt that seemed to fit snugly across a wide chest and drape loosely over a trim middle. He pulled off his helmet to reveal straight brown hair with a side part and dark sunglasses over a lean face.

He straightened his legs, swung one easily over

the saddle, and settled the helmet on the seat of the black-and-chrome beast.

"A bomber jacket on a pilot," Nathan said sourly. "What a cliché."

Lily laughed, but could not take her eyes from the pilot. "At least the sunglasses aren't mirrored."

He looked like trouble, she thought. Had her father actually met this guy in person? There was no way he'd be less difficult than Hugh had been, she could tell just by looking at him. Hugh at least had been nineteen and intimidatable. This guy was an adult who worked for a billionaire, and it was obvious simply from the way he moved that he had confidence enough for several normal men. Besides, he was a pilot. Didn't everyone know about pilots? They were all cocksure and obnoxious. She knew. She'd seen *Top Gun*.

In addition to everything else, he was good-looking. That was immediately obvious. In her experience, that meant a parade of bimbos through the house, not to mention parties and drunken revelry on a regular basis. Then there was that motorcycle. He might as well have been landing the jet in the backyard for all the noise that the bike made.

"Oh Daddy." She sighed, shaking her head. Why didn't he let her rent the place out? She'd offered, more than once. He always told her not to worry about it, that he'd take care of it, that she should just concentrate on grading papers or whatever the hell it was she did at that college.

The new tenant chatted with one of the movers a minute, gestured toward the house with broad, casual sweeps, laughed, then turned and headed for Lily and Nathan.

"One of you Lillian Tyler?" he asked, nearing them with a loose-legged stride. He removed his sunglasses in a smooth, practiced move.

His smile was pleasant, she had to admit. And he had hazel eyes that crinkled appealingly. A man who went into every situation knowing he'd be liked.

"That would be me." She raised her hand. "Most people call me Lily."

He reached out to shake. "Brady Cole. Nice to meet you."

She took his hand, and their palms met, his was warm and dry, hers cool in his grip. The guy exuded confidence even through his skin, she thought.

"And this is Nathan Williams." She gestured toward Nathan. "He lives next door with his mother, Edic."

She watched as Brady Cole shifted his gaze to Nathan, smiled easily, and moved his hand from hers to Nathan's. "Good to meet you, Nathan."

Nathan nodded once and shook the offered hand. Lily noted the flush in his cheeks and knew he hated meeting new people. It wasn't that he was shy, exactly. He just wasn't good with change.

"Glad I got to meet you so soon. Your dad said

you'd be keeping an eye on me, so I just want to say I'll be on my best behavior." Brady Cole grinned at her, his eyes direct.

So her father *had* read him the riot act, she thought. That was good. But this guy was going to have to do more than talk about good behavior. He reminded her of one of her good-looking students who thought he could charm her into a better grade than the work merited.

"Then we'll get along just fine." She let a pert smile tilt her lips.

His grin grew devilish. "He also said I should keep an eye on you. Apparently he doesn't think you're safe down here all by yourself. I get the impression he's a little protective."

"Is that so?" She wondered once again why her father felt the need to impress on everyone how incompetent she was to be on her own. "All he said about you was that you probably wouldn't be a deadbeat." She let her eyes graze him and smiled. "But the jury's still out on that."

Brady laughed. The sound traveled up her core to tingle at the base of her skull. She'd insulted him, and he laughed. She didn't trust people who did that. It wasn't sincere.

"She's tough," Brady said to Nathan, who startled and froze like a deer in the road. "I might have known, having met her father. Is she always like this?"

"No," Nathan said firmly, glaring at him.

"That's good." Brady ignored Nathan's curtness as if he hadn't noticed and turned candid eyes back to her. "I don't think I could keep up if it went on all the time. What *is* that noise?"

Lily glanced toward the house, saw Doug's white-and-black body bobbing up and down on the back of the couch like a piston, his enormous ears pointed straight up like a couple of satellite dishes.

"That's my dog," she said, and bit her bottom lip. She'd tried everything to shut him up when he got like this, but if there were men in the vicinity, he went nuts. Doug hated men.

"Your dad didn't mention a dog." Brady frowned, his tone cautious.

Lily's eyes narrowed. He could just turn those movers around if Doug was going to be a problem. Brady Cole would be gone long before Doug would be. "Maybe because the dog has nothing to do with you."

Brady shifted his gaze to her, his smile milder now. "Does he bark like that all the time?"

Lily took a deep breath, and said decidedly, "No."

No matter that Doug barked whenever he spotted a man, which would, in Brady's case, be all the time. The fact was she intended to fix the problem. Maybe she'd finally have to try that citronella collar the animal behaviorist had been advocating for so long, she thought, even though she hated inflicting any kind of discomfort on Doug.

"So, Brady," she continued brightly, "I wanted to be here to welcome you to the neighborhood and let you know that if there's anything you need, don't hesitate to call or knock on my door. I'm a lot easier to get hold of than my father, and I can help if something goes wrong."

He smiled at her with warm eyes. "Great. How . . . neighborly."

"I also know all the good restaurants, places to shop, library, city hall, whatever you need. And I'm happy to help." She nodded once, with a smile, punctuating the conclusion of her duty for the day. Now she could get back to grading papers with a clear conscience. She'd done what her father had asked.

He tilted his head. "You know, I lived eight years in a condo in DC and never even met the people who lived next door to me there."

"Things work a little differently down here—" she began, but was interrupted by one of the movers.

"Hey, Mr. Cole!" The mover took a few steps in their direction, holding what looked like a wrought-iron sculpture in one meaty fist. "Where you want this?"

Brady turned to the mover, then back to them. "Hang on a sec. I'll be right back." With a flash of a smile, he sauntered across the front lawn.

"I don't think he's going to like Doug," Nathan offered.

"He hasn't even met him yet," Lily protested, watching the pilot move across the grass. He took the front steps in two long strides behind movers who muscled a black-lacquered chest of drawers inside.

"You think that'll help?" Nathan asked.

Lily turned a glare on him, then, chagrined, looked back at the house and scowled. "No. Of course not."

It would only make things worse. Doug had a way of making his feelings known to whomever he took a dislike. And it usually wasn't pretty.

A second later Brady reemerged from the front door, leapt down the stoop in a single bound, and headed back toward them.

At the same time, a blue BMW convertible crept up Prince Edward Street and paused in front of the house.

Brady's stride slowed as he reached Lily and Nathan, and he glanced over his shoulder to see what they were looking at.

"Oh no." The words were muttered under his breath, but the dread in them resonated clearly.

Lily looked at him. His eyes were trained on the car, his mouth turned downward. He shoved his hands in his pockets and hunched his shoulders as if his mother were about to scold him for stealing the cookies.

"Someone you know?" Lily asked.

The question was answered a moment later, not by Brady Cole but by a long-legged blonde who rose out of the driver's seat like a monolith. She stood dramatically by the car, giving Brady a hard look, then slammed the door and marched resolutely across the lawn toward them.

"You two-faced, arrogant, lying son of a bitch," were the first words out of her mouth.

Lily caught her breath. She'd never seen vitriol so thoroughly embodied at such close range. The woman was a seething missile of rage.

"Tricia!" Brady's tone was so futilely welcoming that Lily nearly laughed. "How did you find me?"

"You *moved*? You just packed up and left without a word? Were you ever going to *tell* me? Or did you hope you could just disappear and never have to speak to me again?" She planted herself in front of him, hands on her impossibly tiny jeans-clad hips, and gave him a look that expressed loathing on a biblical scale.

On her feet were high spiked heels. Lily wondered if they were sinking into the soft spring lawn. She could never walk on grass in heels, let alone march with the propulsive force Tricia achieved.

"Now, Tricia, I told you I was taking a new job," Brady hedged.

Both Lily and the blonde issued a disbelieving scoff.

Brady glanced at Lily. She shrugged and mouthed *sorry*, with an unapologetic smile.

"Oh, *please*," Tricia sneered, throwing a hand out toward the moving truck. "A new job is one thing. But what about *this*? You never mentioned moving. You never mentioned a whole new town. What did you think, Brady, that I'd just forget all about you? About what we had? Huh?"

"What we had, Tricia, was—"

"Don't give me any more of your bullshit, you sadistic, misogynistic sack of shit," she growled.

Lily raised her brows. This woman could curse like it was a foreign language. It was impressive, if a little weird.

"I didn't want to fall in love with you, you know. But did I listen to my instincts? No! And do you know why? Because you turned on the charm. You couldn't even help it. You're such a goddamn *talker*, Brady. I fell in love with you— you *made me* fall in love with you—then you used me, goddamn it. Used me for sex, and now you've just up and *moved*? Is this how you break up with a woman?"

"Tricia, please," Brady said, his voice smooth as honey. "We did not break up. We couldn't break up because we—"

"Just stop! Do you think I'm some kind of idiot? Some kind of weak, gullible, desperate *idiot*? I'll tell you who's the idiot, Brady. *You* are, you cheap, dollar-store playboy." Tricia was so incensed that her long straight hair fell into her eyes. She swept it back with a manicured hand. It rippled like a yard of silk.

Lily could swear there was a sheen of sweat on her upper lip. This was no act the woman was putting on, she meant every word.

"You talk a good game, but you are *not* the guy you pretend to be," Tricia continued. "Is this the new one?" Glacial blue eyes shifted disdainfully to Lily. "You left me and came to this godforsaken outback for her? Well let me tell you, honey"—she jabbed a finger in the air toward Lily—"don't you trust this man as far as you can throw him. Don't get into his bed. All he wants is sex. Sex, sex, and more sex."

"Hey, I'm not getting in his bed." Lily raised her hands up and away from the offending party.

"Tricia," Brady said, his voice calm and patient, like he was talking to a six-year-old, "you know as well as I do that you and I did not have a—"

Tricia's hand flashed like mercury. The crack of her palm on Brady's cheek seemed to bounce off the houses around them. Lily and Nathan both jumped.

Brady moved not a muscle.

"Tricia," he said finally, in a voice that held a surprising note of kindness, "would you like me to call Silverman? Your parents gave me the number, you know. I'll call him right now if you want."

"Don't patronize me, you bastard," Tricia said, tears clogging her voice. "I just came here to tell you I'm through with you. I can do better. You've seen the last of *this* body," she said, with a sweep of her hand down her perfect torso. "And I defy you to find a better one. You didn't deserve me to begin with, and now you'll have to do without."

With that she spun on one slim heel—Lily was gratified to see that she did have to yank it out of the soil—and headed back to the car. The three of them watched as she revved the engine to life, slammed it in gear, and peeled off up the street, leaving a dark patch of rubber residue on the pavement in front of the house.

For a long moment the three of them stood silent in the echoing aftermath of Tricia's rage. Brady looked off down the street, his mouth a grim line. On his cheek was a vivid red mark in the shape of an outraged blonde's palm.

After a minute, Lily could stand it no longer.

"So," she said slowly, "she seems nice."

"Ooh, a *pilot*," Lily's friend Penelope said the following morning in the dog park.

Fredericksburg, Virginia, where Lily lived, had moved the city dog park over the summer when Lily had been on sabbatical in Boston, from the busy intersection of Kenmore and William Streets, to a sleepier area near the tennis courts and Memorial Park. It was a fine location, the dogs certainly liked it, but it was not nearly so centrally located as the last one. Which was a shame. Lily had liked seeing who drove by, liked waving to students who honked as they passed, and walking from there to Hyperion Espresso just up the street a few blocks.

But so be it. At least this one had a fence that Doug couldn't wriggle through. Lily watched as the dog concentrated with otherworldly intensity on a family of ducks that swam in the reservoir just next to the park.

"Is he nice-looking?" Penelope asked.

Lily looked at her friend and smiled ruefully. "Yes, in a very, very bad way."

"What do you mean?"

Georgia, another friend, who lounged on a folding canvas chair she had brought herself, snorted, and said, "I know what she means. So when are you havin' us over to meet this bad boy, hm? Some of us are not put off by trouble."

She rested a beringed hand on her huge, steel blue Great Dane, Sage, who sat beside her chair like one of those cement statues people bought for their gardens.

Penelope frowned at Georgia. "Yes, I know," she said. "Some of us are actually attracted to it, Ms. I-Brought-Down-The-Mayor."

"Oh please, I didn't bring down the mayor," Georgia said, with a wave of her hand. She looked pleased nonetheless. "He wasn't just sleepin' with me, you know. His wife would have found out he was cheatin' on her one way or another."

"Yes," Penelope said archly, "but without you she wouldn't have found out about it in her own driveway."

Lily laughed. "That's true. I have half a mind to set you up with this guy, Georgia. In fact, maybe you'll meet him at Megan's party."

"But that's *weeks* away," Georgia complained.

"Ooh, yes. He works for Sutter, doesn't he? I bet he will be there," Penelope mused. "And I've got a new dress . . ."

"I don't know, Pen. I don't think he's right for you. In fact, if I had to pick I have to say I think this guy needs a good dose of 'bringing down,' *Georgia* style," Lily said. "You should have been there for the scene that played out in front of Nathan and me yesterday." She proceeded to tell the story of the irate blonde.

"Oh, poor Nathan," Georgia mused when she was finished.

"Poor Nathan?" Lily echoed. "Don't you mean poor Brady? Or, more accurately, poor Tricia?"

"No, I mean Nathan." Georgia shook her curly blond hair. "The poor thing has been in love with you for years, and now he has to contend with a macho pilot next door? This'll probably kill him."

"Nathan is not in love with me." Lily put a hand on her hip. "He's just . . . a good friend."

This time both Georgia and Penelope snorted.

"*Really.*" Lily sighed. "I mean, I know he likes me. But he is not in love with me. He knows we're just friends."

"Honey"—Georgia laughed—"he'd be sleepin' on your welcome mat if it weren't for fear of being castrated by Doug when you came out for your mornin' paper."

"I do have to say," Penelope said, nodding, "I think Doug is the only reason Nathan isn't over at your house every night offering to fix your screen door or your leaky faucet or hammer nails for you."

"Or hammer you." Georgia cackled. "If it weren't for Doug, he'd have invited himself into your bed years ago."

"Come on," Lily protested. "Nathan's a nice guy. Why do you have to be so mean about him?"

"We're not being mean," Penelope said. "It's just that he's in love with you, and you should be aware of it."

"Especially now that a stud muffin has moved in next door." Georgia picked at a chip in one of her polished nails. "Nathan's pecker is probably goin' to shrivel like a petunia under a pine tree unless he gets somethin' from you soon."

Lily turned on Georgia, half-laughing, her hands on her hips. "What are you saying? You think I should sleep with Nathan to make him feel better about Brady?"

"It's the only nice thing to do," Georgia said

primly, brushing nail polish chips off her lap. "Otherwise, he's goin' to lose what little self-esteem he has left. You don't want to be responsible for that, do you?"

"I am not responsible for Nathan's self-esteem, good or bad. And I am not a public service—sexpert," Lily declared, then laughed.

Georgia and Penelope joined her. "Oh, honey," Georgia said, "that's classic. I'm goin' to have to remember that one. A sexpert."

"Besides, what would Gerald say if I had sex with Nathan?" Lily imagined Gerald's gray eyes hardening to flint, his dark hair dipping over his brows as he shook her, à la Heathcliff with Catherine, saying, *If he loved you with all the power of his soul for a whole lifetime, he couldn't love you as much as I do in a single day.*

Lily sighed. Sure, she was a literature professor, but she loved the movie version of *Wuthering Heights.* Nobody could deliver a line like that like Olivier. Except, of course, her mental Gerald.

"Ah yes. Gerald the magnificent," Georgia said, laying her head back and holding her arms out expansively. She raised a brow and eyed Lily askance. "I imagine he would be upset if he thought your infatuation with him was wanin'. So when is your next date with Mr. Elusive?"

"It is not infatuation. And he is not elusive. He's asked me out, hasn't he? *Four times,* now."

"Finally," Georgia said, eyelids heavy with

disapproval. "He's known you've been interested in him forever, and he's strung you along like his own personal puppy dog."

"He hasn't strung me along. I strung myself," Lily said, "because of who he is. And I've respected the fact that Gerald wanted to make partner on his own merits, not because he's dating the boss's daughter."

"So he's made partner?" Georgia asked dubiously.

"Any minute now," she said decisively. "And besides," she added, turning to search for Doug, "Doug actually seems to like him. Can you imagine? He's the only man on the planet to whom Doug hasn't done something awful, like chew up his shoes, or rip his pant leg."

She found the dog intently sniffing the ground near the picnic table, ready, Lily was sure, to roll in a family of grubs or some other disgusting item. Doug loved to adorn himself with dead things.

"That is something," Penelope said. "Though you do have to wonder if he's planning something bigger for later."

Lily laughed. "Planning something bigger," she scoffed. "Listen to you. As if Doug thinks of anything beyond the moment he's in. No, I think it's a sign. Gerald couldn't wait any longer to ask me out, and Doug doesn't hate him—there are good signs everywhere."

"Except that he abandoned his resolve to wait until he made partner," Georgia said.

Penelope frowned. "I thought it was a little strange that he actually *told* you he didn't want to date you until he made partner."

"Why?" Lily protested. "I thought it was admirable that he didn't want to get ahead by dating the boss's daughter."

Penelope's dog—a big black Labrador retriever—ran over to her with a saliva-drenched stick. She took it from him and tossed it, sending him tearing across the park. "It seemed a little . . . over-confident," she said.

"Girls, we're ignoring the central issue," Georgia said. "If he hasn't made partner yet, why did he ask you out now?"

"I told you," Lily said, feeling her face heat with defensiveness. "He decided he couldn't wait any longer."

"But—I'm so sorry to be negative, Lil, but I think it's important," Penelope said, "has he kissed you good night yet? If his passion made him abandon his resolve to wait, where is it when he's with you?"

"Hammer?" Georgia quipped. "Meet nail."

"He kisses me good night every time," Lily said, though admittedly her tone was weak.

"*You* know," Penelope said, "a *real* kiss. You're the one who said it was just a lukewarm peck on the cheek."

"Okay, no, he hasn't. But he's a gentleman," Lily said, throwing her hands out to the sides. "I know it's weird, but it's not the end of the world that he's a little slower than we expect, is it? Maybe that's even a good thing. Would we be less worried if he were jumping my bones?"

Penelope appeared to consider.

Georgia threw her head back. "Hell, yeah!"

"Look," Lily said firmly, "all I know is, the guy is finally asking me out. You guys should be happy for me."

"Honey, I would be," Georgia said, sobering. "If not for the fact that for the last two years the only thing he's condescended to do with you is go out for coffee. No drinks, no dinner, and—"

"And no play tickets," Penelope added. "Don't forget those incredibly expensive seats to *Phantom of the Opera* you sprang for."

"How could he put you off for so long?" Georgia said. "What's different now? He still hasn't made partner."

Lily shifted her weight on her feet and crossed her arms over her chest. "He got tired of waiting," she said again, clinging to the idea. "Like me."

"I'm sure he did," Georgia said. "The question is, was he tired of waitin' for you or for that partnership?"

Lily turned on Georgia. "That is so insulting, Georgia. How can you call yourself my friend and say something like that? Is it so inconceivable to you that he might actually *like* me, the way I like him?"

Georgia leaned forward and grabbed Lily's forearm. Her expression changed from droll to determined. "Lily, I *am* your friend. That's precisely *why* I'm sayin' these things. I don't want you to get hurt, and I'm afraid this guy is—or, all right, *could be*—usin' you."

"That's only because you don't understand the finer points of chivalrous behavior or respectable relationships," Lily said, extricating her arm from Georgia's grip.

"Oh no, not another lecture on nineteenth-century literature," Georgia moaned, leaning back in her chair. "You talk like you're a born-again virgin. Since when did you become Elizabeth Bennett?"

"No, that's *Pride and Prejudice*. It's Emma Woodhouse," Penelope corrected, "to Gerald's Mr. Knightley. From Jane Austen's *Emma*. I'm reading it now, and it's wonderful!"

"Stick a star on her forehead," Georgia muttered.

"And it really is true," Penelope continued enthusiastically. "Gerald is just like Mr. Knightley, the hero in *Emma*. Knightley was the old friend of the family, close to Emma and her father for years. And Gerald is close to Lily and *her* father, and has been for years. Knightley was known for being the perfect gentleman, and clearly so is Gerald.

Knightley and Emma took forever to get together, but when they did it was perfect. And you said yourself your father loves Gerald, right?"

"Yes, he does. And I admit to having said a time or two that Gerald feels like my Mr. Knightley." Lily blushed. "But I'm not hung up on that. Really, I'm not that naïve. It was just something I thought about, you know, the way you do when you like someone. The main thing is that I believe romance, *true romance*, isn't dead until we kill it with our tacky twenty-first-century mores. Gerald has a sense of propriety and restraint that I admire, and find attractive."

Georgia rolled her eyes. "Careful, Lil. It's easy to put a fantasy into a void. Gerald may seem like the perfect gentleman, but you never know. It could just be impotence."

Two

Brady sat on the front porch with a beer, listening to the sounds of female laughter emanating from Lily's side of the house. She had company, and while he couldn't hear what they said, they certainly seemed to be having fun.

It had grown chilly again, and a light drizzle fell outside the protection of the porch roof. The air smelled like soil, rich and loamy, and the sounds of raindrops on the newly minted leaves made him think of childhood. He had lived a long time in a high-rise, surrounded by other high-rises, in the cement environment of a city. He'd forgotten how peaceful a neighborhood could be.

Granted, he was still technically in "the

city"—Fredericksburg city—walking distance from its shops and restaurants, but this little town was quiet and quaint, not a hot, heaving monster like DC.

When the Realtor had first told him she'd found a "duplex," he'd pictured some ugly, boxy thing circa 1960; but this house—a "twin house," he'd been told—was a tall old Victorian with elaborate detailing and huge, high-ceilinged rooms. The two front doors and long porch with a rail separating the two sides were the only indications that it held two separate living spaces.

Across the street were a row of houses of probably the same vintage as this one—built in the nineteenth century—with one or two eighteenth-century models thrown in. The trees were huge, the sidewalks cracked with age, and aside from the parked cars he could easily picture the street as it might have been a century and a half earlier. The whole place oozed history.

He liked it. It would make a nice change. Not to mention that there might be more pissed-off women than just Tricia he should get away from.

He took a pull off his beer and looked up at the cloud-covered sky. He'd screwed up, badly. That was what came of getting bored and feeling invulnerable. You took advantage of people without even realizing it.

He was not proud of himself.

"You can change," his brother Keenan had said,

after telling him that where women were concerned he had "overgrazed" and that it was probably time to leave the city. "Look at this as a fresh start. A new life. Take a break from dating and decide you're not going to take what's handed out to you anymore. Think of it as being on a diet at a cocktail party. Take nothing that's offered. Save your appetite for the big meal."

Brady chuckled, picturing an hors d'oeuvres platter covered with small, pretty women. And in the middle, sitting up, was Lily Tyler, giving him that sweet but audacious smile and looking for all the world like a challenge worth taking.

He took a deep breath, let it out slowly. He was on a diet. A date diet. Keenan was right. He needed a break.

He'd tried to be a good guy, had always been up front with women he'd dated about taking things casually, not wanting commitment, but Tricia had taught him that no matter what you said, some women were going to hear only what they wanted to hear.

Granted, Tricia was certifiably nuts. But still. He hadn't seen it in her, not until it was too late. And he'd even seen *Fatal Attraction*.

No, he needed to get out of the game for a while, maybe learn how to get to know a woman, make friends with her, before diving into the unknown. According to Keenan, there was no halfway in relationships. Just happy people and unhappy people.

Brady guessed he'd made a lot of people un-happy.

It was a shock, he thought, taking another long draw off his beer, realizing what an asshole you'd been when you'd had no idea at all.

The door of Lily's house opened, letting a stream of light and warmth out onto the front porch and steps. Brady turned his head, leaned back on the porch column, and hoped the night shrouded his side. Music tinkled low in the background—Al Green, singing "I'm So Tired of Being Alone." He smiled at the irony.

A second later, Lily's porch light came on and a woman with a wide mass of curly blond hair came out the door, zipping up a raincoat.

"Well, shit and goddamn," the woman said in a strong North Carolina accent. "It's still rainin'."

Brady raised his brows. A woman who spoke her mind.

Lily stood in the doorway, her hair as dark as melted chocolate, accentuating that peaches-and-cream complexion. It figured, he thought, that on his new diet he'd end up next door to a world-class ten-thousand-calorie dessert. In her arms she held the ugliest dog Brady had ever seen. It was white with black blotches, small, but square, with a smashed face and enormous bat ears. On its face was a wide doggy grin that, if worn by a human, would mark a man not to be trusted.

"Why don't you take my umbrella?" Lily said.

"No, no. Give it to Penelope, she melts in the rain. I'll be fine. I have a hood." She pulled said hood up over her head and tucked in the curls around her face. "Besides, there's nobody I have to look good for at home, anyway, thank the good Lord."

She leaned over, and the two women kissed cheeks.

"Good night, honey." She patted the dog on the head.

"Careful driving," Lily said, closing the door as the blonde turned away.

Al Green and Lily disappeared.

The woman took a moment on the front stoop, looking out into the rain as if bracing herself for it. Brady took another sip of beer, and the movement must have caught her eye. She turned toward him. Her face was pale and round under the hood, and she cocked her head.

"Well, well," she drawled. He could hear the smile in her voice. It was a tone he recognized well. "You must be the new kid on the block."

She sauntered over to the railing that split Lily's porch from Brady's and put one hand on a column. With Lily's porch light on he could clearly see the woman's long, red fingernails and a couple of gold rings on each hand. With her other hand, she pushed the hood back off her head to reveal those curls and a hard, pretty face that showed an unnerving shrewdness.

The woman, he concluded immediately, was a man-eater.

Or was he just getting paranoid?

"Brady Cole," he said, straightening. He held out one hand, businesslike, and leaned toward her.

She stretched a languorous hand out to take it. Her grip was soft and hot.

"Georgia Darling." She didn't shake, she just held his hand a long moment. "Yes, indeed. Lily had it right. You are trouble." Her lips curved as if trouble were exactly what she was looking for.

Brady took a moment answering, holding her gaze. "I guess I can understand why she said that. We had a kind of . . . scene the day I moved in. But that's over."

"So I heard." She dropped his hand and leaned forward, both hands on the railing in front of her. "So, looking for a replacement? Something to, ah, *do* here in the Burg?"

Her lips curled and her eyelids drooped and he honest-to-God felt like an injured bird being studied by a cat. There wasn't much of a chance that he'd ever have taken this she-wolf up on her offer, even though it was obvious there'd be no strings attached, but on the heels of recent events there was even less possibility. He was a new man, and even if he hadn't turned over that new leaf, there was Lily. Virtually his landlord and already unimpressed with him. He'd rather not start off what should be a friendly relationship between very close neighbors with the tension of doing something stupid with her friend.

His eyes must have strayed to Lily's door because Georgia laughed, a low, sultry sound that was, in its way, mocking.

"It's like that, is it?" she purred.

"I got off to a bad start with my landlord's daughter," he said. "I'd rather not screw it up any further. At least not until she gets to know me better."

"I can be very discreet. Just ask the mayor," she said, then laughed in a way that made him think of a witch over a cauldron. She stepped back from the railing and lifted her hood over her curls again. "You think about it, Brady Cole, and let me know if you change your mind."

She stepped off the porch and started down the front walk. Halfway to the curb, she turned back.

"And if you're thinking of anyone else"—she tipped her head in the direction of Lily's door— "all I can say is, beware of Doug."

With that, and another wicked cackle, she continued down the walk to a large black SUV on the street.

A moment later she was gone.

The following day was Saturday, and a blustery one it was. Gone was the warmth of Thursday and the gentle spring rain of last night. Today was a screeching moody bitch of a day, despite the

dainty accessories of budding trees and brave cro-
cuses.

Brady closed the door of his house behind him,
headed down the stoop into the wind, and started
to turn up Lily's stoop to her door when he saw
the neighbor—what was his name? Stephen? no,
something formal—come out his front door.

The neighbor stopped when he saw Brady, so
Brady raised a hand to him. After a second, the
guy returned a wave and started down his front
walk.

After a second's thought, Brady changed course,
heading across the lawn toward the neighbor. The
wet earth sank under his weight and sucked at
his shoes, but he continued on. Might as well
cover all his bases while the opportunity was in
front of him.

The guy wore all black, from his tee shirt to his
jeans to his Converse hightops. He looked like he
wanted to be a rock star instead of a guy who
lived on a quiet street in a small town with his
mother. Even his house didn't seem to go with the
rest of the houses on the street. It was a one-story
brick affair that looked closer to 1960 than 1860,
and had a chain-link fence around the backyard
instead of the picket or wrought-iron that most of
the others sported.

Brady remembered the look on his—damn,
Ethan? maybe—the guy's face when he'd introduced himself on Thursday, and then again after

Tricia had gone. Or rather, vaporized in a scalding cloud of steam. The guy had without question decided he did not like Brady.

Brady hated being disliked.

He turned from Lily's walkway and headed for—he could call him "buddy." That's what he did with most guys. But he lived two doors down, how long could that go on?

Brady strolled down the sidewalk, taking his time, thinking, moving toward—Nathan! *Yes!* Jesus, no wonder the guy didn't like him. He could tell Brady was the kind of person who forgot men's names and needed to go on a date diet.

"Hey, Nathan, how are you doing today?" Brady smiled and held out a friendly hand.

For a second he thought he'd gotten the name wrong, because Nathan just looked at his hand as if hoping he wasn't expected to do anything with it. Then he gave a smile that wasn't happy and shook it.

"Not bad." Nathan gave him a hard look, as if Brady might be trying to pull something over on him. He jerked his chin in the direction of Lily's house. "Going to see Lily?"

The only thing to do was ignore it, Brady knew, but the guy clearly didn't like him. Was determined *not* to, in fact. He wondered if it had anything to do with Lily.

Lily, the delicate beauty with the devil in her eye. He'd bet anything old Nate had a crush on her. He was posturing like the lone stallion in a herd of mares.

Brady pushed a hand through his short, thick hair, and the wind pushed back. "Yeah, I thought I'd explain to her about the other day. I should probably explain to you, too."

Nathan shook his head. "No need."

"Actually, there is a need. That woman, Tricia, she's . . . uh . . ."

He really ought to be better at explaining this, he thought. He'd had to do it so many times.

He took a fortifying breath. "Well, she's ill. Under a doctor's care, actually. For, ah, obsessive behavior. About me, for some reason. She follows me, see, and usually makes a scene and conjures up all kinds of accusations that aren't true."

Well, mostly not true. They'd had one evening of inadvisable sex, and he'd paid for it for months. Fortunately, the relevant people knew what was really happening, understood that she had latched on to him and created a whole scenario that was vastly different than the one that was real. Her parents, her doctor, his family, the people she'd regularly harassed, all knew that she'd spent time in Chestnut Lodge and that her parents were eager to keep her from having to go back.

And hell, he was fine with helping them help her. He really was. He didn't need to see her locked up. It was just that she'd made his life a lot more complicated. Dating alone had become something he didn't want to risk. The one time he'd brought someone home after the incident with Tricia, she'd been treated to a tirade similar to the one Nathan and Lily had witnessed the other day.

It had been a startling lesson for Brady. A visitation from God, Keenan had said, in the form of an insane woman. Clean up your act, was what He was saying.

Brady figured He could have said it in a more subtle way, but that was just him.

"You have a *stalker*?" Nathan asked, and Brady'd be damned if it didn't look like the guy was happy about it.

"I guess you could call her that." He pushed his hands in his pockets and plowed on. "The thing is, when she gets like that—actually she can get worse—I need to call her doctor or her parents. I'd have done that the other day if she hadn't left so quickly. The reason I need to tell you all this, though, is because she can be very persuasive, so you have to watch out. She talked her way into my condo up in Arlington once, got my emergency key from the front desk, and went in and trashed the place. Looking for evidence I'd been cheating on her, she said. But, and this I swear, we've never had a relationship. Never even been on a date, really."

At this point, Nathan did chuckle. "Oh man."

Brady forced himself to smile. The wind blew hard against his back but was unable to penetrate his leather jacket. "Yeah, it's funny. But not really. So listen, if she comes back again and talks to you, just tell her you don't know me, don't know where I am, I'm just the new neighbor. You know, that kind of thing."

"No problem. I *don't* know you," Nathan said, looking happy about the fact. The wind rippled his black tee shirt like a sail in a nor'easter. The guy was impossibly skinny.

Brady paused. "Right. Okay. Well, thanks. Just wanted to let you know."

"Yeah, thanks. Good to know." Nathan smiled cheerily.

"All right, then. Guess I'll see you later." Brady turned and walked back toward Lily's door, thinking if there was one person on the street he wasn't going to give his emergency key to it was Nathan. Something told him the guy'd have Tricia in there in no time.

He should have called him "buddy."

"Oh, and, uh, Brady?" Nathan called.

Brady turned back. "Yeah?"

Nathan jutted his chin out toward Lily's house again, and his grin was positively confident. "Beware of Doug!" He turned and headed in the opposite direction down the sidewalk, his jaunty gait looking altogether too perky for his rock star outfit.

Who the hell was Doug? Brady thought. That was the second time someone had warned him about the guy.

"Hey, Nate!" he called. "Who's Doug?"

But Nathan didn't hear him. Or pretended not to. Those black sneakers just kept plugging away up the street.

Maybe Doug was Lily's boyfriend. Some jealous type. Maybe he shouldn't knock on her door right now, in case Doug was there. He scowled. Was he going to have to deal with an insane Tricia and a jealous Doug next door? Maybe he could get Tricia and Doug together. Get rid of all the problems at once.

Oh the hell with it, he thought. He wasn't going to tiptoe around Tricia, and he wasn't going to tiptoe around some guy named Doug, who obviously had problems unrelated to Brady, since everyone was warning him about the guy when they hadn't even met yet.

He walked resolutely to Lily's door.

As it turned out, Lily wasn't home that morning. But the bell had rung and someone had knocked and Doug had pressed his dense doggy body to the front door and done all he could to sniff through the crack to figure out who it was. He pressed his pug nose against the threshold, stood on his sturdy back legs to go as far toward the doorknob as he could, but it was through the mail slot that he caught the scent.

It was the new guy. When Doug discovered that, he barked a few times and pawed at the door, claws out so it would make a lot of noise. He wasn't a fool, he knew he couldn't open it. But the new guy needed to know there was someone here protecting Lily's territory even if she wasn't.

It took a while for the new guy to leave, which bothered Doug. Surely he'd heard Doug on the other side of the door. Still, he'd stood there. As if he could take Doug on. As if he didn't take Doug seriously. Easy to think from the other side of the door.

Doug grinned, panting, and stared at his side of the entry.

Then, with an idea in his head, he trotted to the back of the house.

Lily usually locked the dog door when she went out, but the weather had been so nice, and she'd left rather on the spur of the moment, she had forgotten.

Doug pushed his head out, then his two front feet, and looked around the yard. He took a good long sniff at the air—delicious swirling wet, muddy scents!—and popped out the door. Leaves and blossoms and twigs and all sorts of glorious playthings skipped around the grass, tempting him away from his duty. But Doug knew what he had to do first. He knew about the order of things. He and Lily had taken an agility course once. First the A frame, then the tunnel, then the seesaw . . . yes, there was an order to things.

The backyard was fenced, but Doug knew the

way out. He didn't use it often—why leave Lily?—but today he headed straight for the dip in the ground. The one at the back of the shed by the picket fence where, with some effort, he could wriggle under and out the other side. This he did in more time than he might have a few months ago. Winter was tough on a pup, less exercise and the same amount of kibble made for a figure that needed toning before the hot summer season of dog park days.

He trotted through the grassy alley between his house and the one next door—where that other irritating guy lived—then confidently up the steps of the porch next to his.

It smelled of New Guy, that much was certain. It was, however, better than Last Guy. A dog could only lap up so much stale beer before getting sick of it, though he did miss the occasional barbecued rib or piece of chicken that ended up in the grass when Last Guy cooked out with his pack.

Doug could feel the urge coming just as he made it to the front door. This had been a brilliant idea.

As he reached the front mat—which did not say "Welcome," though he did not know that—he turned his back on the door and squatted.

Lily picked up the big makeup brush for the finishing touch, swirled it in powder, and ran the soft bristles swiftly around her face. She opened her eyes, examined her face, rearranged a dark curl, then went back in the bedroom to dress.

Doug lay on the bed, grinning at her with that mischievous look she loved so much, big ears up, eyes twinkling.

"What are you thinking, devil dog?" she asked him, cupping his face in her hands for a second and scratching his neck with her fingers. She straightened and moved to the mirror.

Doug gave a happy snort and resumed grinning.

The doorbell rang. Doug sprang up on all fours, looking from Lily to the hall and back again.

Lily swung toward the clock.

"He's early!" she said, and grabbed up her dress. "Must have been good traffic on 95." She smiled at Doug as she unzipped the dress from the hanger. "Do you think he brought flowers again? I love a man who brings flowers."

She also loved a man who knew how to make her feel desirable, and so far Gerald had done anything but. She studied herself in the mirror as she wiggled into the dress.

Doug glanced from the hallway to her again, waiting for the word to go downstairs.

Lily stepped into her shoes and wondered if she would freeze tonight. Though the wind had died down some, it was still chilly. She just couldn't resist wearing the new garment—a short, pink sundress that hugged her curves and flattered her legs with a swingy flared skirt. She was going to save it for Megan's party, but since it was Gerald she'd had in mind when she bought it, she knew she couldn't save it. Fortunately she had a medium-weight shawl that would go perfectly with it. And the restaurant was always hot anyway.

"Now Doug, you've been very nice to Gerald so far," she said, turning as far as she could to see in the mirror how she looked from the back. "Keep it up. He's driven a long way to see us. All the way from DC. That's over fifty miles. And we want him to like you."

She sighed, a smile on her lips. It *had* to be a sign that Doug had been nice to Gerald so far. It was the first time ever he hadn't tormented a man who was Lily's date. Or any man, for that matter. The last date she'd invited in—unfortunately quite some time ago—had left with laceless shoes, thanks to Doug's ministrations. Another time Doug had actually peed on her date's jacket, which had fallen off the arm of a chair and onto the floor. (She'd gotten a coatrack after that.) And the last time a guy had actually stayed the night, Doug had drunk all the water from a glass in which he'd put his contacts, swallowing lenses and all.

She snapped up the shawl and headed for the hallway. Behind her she heard Doug's twenty-five pounds of muscular body hit the floor before he scooted out in front of her and down the stairs, his jaunty posture, oversized ears, and giant-sized air of confidence making her laugh, as they always did.

She opened the door, unable to repress the smile on her face.

Gerald stood before her, resplendent in a light spring suit with—how perfect was this?—a *pink tie*, holding an enormous bouquet of lilies. His nearly black hair was combed back in the precise, gelled style he favored, and his chiseled face looked freshly shaved. He smelled subtly of cologne.

"Darling," he said, showing pearly white teeth and looking her over with evident delight. "You look lovely."

"As do you," she agreed, thinking Georgia had been right when, after seeing a picture, she'd said he looked like Rupert Everett. Without the gayness, of course. "We even match!" She indicated his tie and her dress and smiled up at him.

"We are a perfect match," he said smoothly, stepping over the threshold.

His words sent her heart skittering. He bent to give her a kiss on the cheek, light but firm, and long enough for her to be momentarily enveloped in his cologne. It was a light floral scent that Lily loved.

At their feet, Doug snuffled around Gerald's ankles but did little more; he didn't even issue his trademark frustrated growl. Lily pushed him away from the door with one foot. He sat at the base of the stairs, giving Gerald an inquisitive look.

"Shit!"

The curse came from outside. Gerald and Lily looked at each other a minute, then Gerald stepped back out, and Lily peered around the door frame.

Brady Cole stood on his front porch, looking down at his shoes.

"Oh, Brady," Lily said, dismayed that he'd chosen that moment to come outside and be vulgar. She looked at Gerald. "Brady is Daddy's new tenant. Brady Cole, this is Gerald Lawson. Gerald, Brady."

"Hey," Brady said, with barely a glance. He wore a sour expression on his face and was scraping something off his shoe onto the edge of the first step. "Good to meet you, Gerald."

That was rude, Lily thought. He could at least have looked at them.

"Brady. How do you do?" Gerald said in the cultured tones she loved so much.

So much different than Brady Cole's husky voice and brazen grins.

"Well, have a nice evening," she called to Brady, stepping back inside. For once, Doug was simply sitting in the hallway, wearing his doggy grin, not barking at the new tenant or trying to get out.

Behind her, Gerald lingered on the porch, studying Brady across the rail. Then he turned toward her.

Before entering the house, however, he glanced across the porches again. "Brady?"

"Yeah?" came the curt reply.

"Word of advice." Gerald smiled chummily. "Beware of Doug."

Three

They had dined at Bistro Bethem and walked down the street to Hyperion Espresso on the corner for a late-night decaf. Lily felt like spinning around and singing "I Feel Pretty," strolling in her sundress with her tall, handsome man by her side.

Gerald had been lovely over dinner, as usual, keeping the conversation lively and chatting amiably with the waitstaff. Not only did he look good—she loved the way he was just old enough to have crow's-feet next to his eyes when he smiled, and one deep dimple on the right when he smiled—but he'd chosen the wine like an expert, ordered the most gourmet items on the menu, and even encouraged her to try the oyster appetizer—which she found she almost liked. She also thought it must be a good sign of things to come. Did a man order oysters and encourage his date to try one if he didn't have aphrodisiacs and their effects on his mind?

At Hyperion they both ordered decaf lattes and went outside to sit at one of the sidewalk tables.

"Lily, I have never enjoyed a date so much," Gerald said, holding out her chair for her while she sat. He moved around the table and folded his tall frame into the one across from her. His suit, she noted, was still neatly pressed, despite the fact that they'd sat for over two hours in the restaurant. "I keep thinking we won't be able to top the last date, and yet we always do. There's something about you that makes me feel . . . comfortable."

Lily beamed over her coffee cup, holding it in both hands after blowing across the steaming top. "I feel the same way. I can't tell you how happy I am that you transferred from the West Coast office."

"Well, that was, as they say, a no-brainer." He chuckled at the silly vernacular. "I had had enough of the West. I'm an East Coaster through and through."

"That surprises me," she said. "It's so beautiful out there. What didn't you like about California?"

"Oh, California is beautiful, I'll grant you that. It's just that everyone is so casual. I'm afraid I prefer a bit more decorum in my professional life. As well as in many aspects of my personal life." He chuckled again, wryly. "Which no doubt makes me sound like a pompous jerk."

She shook her head, smiling. "Not at all."

In fact, it only confirmed her impression that he was the incarnation of her beloved Mr. Knightley.

Lily put her cup back in the saucer and took a deep breath. "Gerald, there's something I've been wanting to tell you, but I'm a little nervous about it."

Gerald looked concerned and leaned slightly toward her. "Nervous? Lily, you know you can tell me anything."

She smiled grimly and looked down at her coffee. "I know. It's just, this is kind of personal, and you never know how people are going to react to these things."

He reached out and took her hand, pulling it up from her lap and onto the narrow bistro table. "Then let's hold hands while you tell me. That way you'll know we're in it together, whatever it is."

She looked up at him, tears unexpectedly stinging the backs of her eyes. She blinked them away. He was absolutely the sweetest man she'd ever known.

"It's nothing horrible," she hedged, knowing she should just spit it out before he began to think she had some kind of venereal disease. "It's just . . . I was married. Before. A long time ago."

"Yes?" He nodded, encouraging.

A little bubble of laughter escaped her. "That's really it. I guess I thought the fact might be more . . . unexpected. It is to me sometimes; it was so long ago. You see, I was a junior in college, and I suppose I was going through some kind of rebellion against my father."

Gerald tilted his head, his eyes twinkling. "That's certainly understandable. I can't imagine growing up with the imposing Jordan Tyler for a father. He must have ruled the house with an iron fist, as they say."

She smiled, feeling more relaxed by the minute. "That he did. And I was desperate to get out from under it. So I went off and married my high-school boyfriend. He was—is still, I believe—a"—she cleared her throat and looked at the table; Gerald's fingers squeezed hers—"a plumber. A plumber's assistant, really. Daddy was shocked. Appalled. And he stopped speaking to me."

Gerald continued to nod, looking concerned for her but not the least bit upset. "That was quite clever really," he said, when she paused. "Plumbers are handy fellows to have around."

She laughed, relieved that he was so unaffected he could lighten the mood for her.

"We only stayed together about a year," she continued. "It was never meant to be, of course. We were divorced eighteen months after the wedding—which was just a quick civil ceremony at the city hall—and I honestly don't ever think about it anymore. In fact, it hardly qualifies as a marriage in my mind. Just a youthful relationship that went bad, as most of them did."

"How long was it before your father started speaking to you again?" Gerald asked.

"Oh, God . . ." She raised her eyes to the tree branches overhead and calculated. "About a year after the divorce, I guess. It was almost three years altogether that he didn't speak to me."

"How did it come about? Did he apologize for abandoning you?" Gerald lifted her hand to his mouth and brushed her fingers along his lips as he waited for her answer.

Lily's heart pounded hard, every nerve alive with the intimate touch. She loved that he called her father's actions "abandonment."

"I contacted him," she said. "I told him I wanted to go to graduate school to become a teacher, and I'd appreciate his cosigning the loan. I knew he would approve and think I was back on the straight and narrow, and he did."

"Had you told him you'd divorced the plumber— what was his name?" Gerald's eyes were calm, kind, and interested.

"Duane. Duane McCall. I'm not sure my father ever even knew his name. He just always called him the Plumber, as if that said it all about how mistaken the marriage was." She laughed. "It certainly said everything about why Daddy disapproved."

Gerald smiled and shook his head, his eyes warm on hers. "You know, Lily," he said after a minute, "I truly admire you."

Lily's heart caught in her throat. "You do?"

"Yes," he said, squeezing her hand again. "That took a lot of courage, to do what you did."

"What, the marriage or the divorce?"

"Both. The whole episode. It took quite a bit of bravery to disobey your father like that. And a bit more to make up with him."

"It might have taken some nerve," she said doubtfully, "but not much intelligence."

"No, it was courage. You made some tough decisions and did what you had to do. I admire that kind of strength."

Lily looked at their clasped hands. "Well, thank you. I can't tell you how relieved I am that you're not upset."

Gerald leaned back, the look on his face scandalized. "Upset? Why in the world would I be upset? You've had some life experience. I like that in a woman. I *want* that in a woman," he added significantly. "You have nothing to be ashamed of."

She blushed. Her father never made her feel anything *but* ashamed when the subject of her first marriage came up. It was no coincidence that it only came up when he was displeased with her about something and *wanted* her to feel ashamed. Not to mention incompetent and foolish and unable to take care of herself.

Gerald leaned forward again and stroked the back of her hand, where it rested next to her coffee cup. "Thank you, Lily. Thank you for trusting me with this story."

Lily was so happy after that she fairly floated home on clouds of joy and relief. Between Gerald's heroic understanding, his intimate caresses at the coffee shop, and his ordering the oysters at the restaurant, she was convinced that tonight was the night he was going to make his move. No more chaste kisses at the door, she was sure. Her heart fluttered in anticipation.

He would be a fabulous kisser, she knew. He had that lovely mouth, those nicely defined lips, that white smile.

She couldn't wait.

What was *wrong* with her?

Lily looked down at her naked body as she lay in the tub on Sunday night. Her date with Gerald the night before had ended disastrously, and she'd been ruminating all day about it, driving herself crazy with worry and shame and, more than anything, frustration.

Finally she decided to light some candles, get out the bath oil, and soak herself until she relaxed.

Was it really something wrong with her? she thought again. She had a nice figure. Then again, the bathroom was lit only by candles. And everyone looked good in candlelight. Especially single, thirty-two-year-old women who are wondering if they're destined to be abducted by a terrorist since they haven't gotten married yet.

Still, she knew she wasn't ugly. And he clearly liked her. If he didn't, why would he continue to ask her out? Bring her flowers? Take her to dinner? Be so wonderfully understanding about her checkered past? And he was always so complimentary.

Yet he treated her as chastely as if she were his sister.

Lily blushed hot all over again as she recalled the night before. Oh God, what had she been thinking? She soaped up the washcloth and rubbed it hard over the back of her neck.

She and Gerald had gotten home and she'd invited him in. All she'd wanted was a kiss, a proper kiss. A *passionate* kiss. The kind she'd imagined having with Gerald ever since she'd met him at her father's office, two years ago. The kind of kiss where you needed to hang on to the man with all your might or the passion might blow you both to bits. Not that she'd ever had this sort of kiss before, but she was sure Gerald was capable of it. How could you have those movie star looks and not be capable of a passionate kiss? He was Olivier, Knightley, Rudolph Valentino, all rolled into one. He had to have it in him.

So she'd decided to let him know she was . . .

open to it. Ready for it. And after five whole dates, it was time.

She'd sat close on the couch, let her wrap drop low, leaned toward him so the dress revealed some cleavage, and put her hand on his arm *a lot*. She'd laughed at his witticisms and flipped her hair around. Around and around. Didn't they say that was body language men understood?

He'd been responding, too, she thought. Laughing with her, touching her arm, smiling.

Then she'd slid in for the kiss.

And he'd looked at her like he'd caught her picking his pocket. Shocked. Taken aback. Confused.

Had it really been that unexpected?

Maybe he *was* impotent, she thought, like Georgia had said. Or maybe he was afraid of her.

Or maybe she was a shameless hussy who'd ruined her chances with a very proper gentleman. It wasn't as if they'd been going out for months and months, after all. Surely she could have waited for him to get around to it on his own.

But no. She hadn't. This was what came of dating so infrequently, she thought. Her physical desires had gotten totally out of control. She just hoped she hadn't put Gerald off forever. He'd left shortly after her attempt.

The warm tub water lapped against her breasts as she soaked the washcloth again. Even that caress sent her into a state of frustration. How long had it been since she'd been touched? Since she'd been naked with anyone other than Doug in the house?

Speaking of Doug, Lily heard his raspy breath outside the bathroom door, heard his snort as he found the crack where it had drifted closed, the slant of the older house ensuring the door never stood open but never completely closed. He pushed it with his nose and it slowly widened. She was about to imagine it was Gerald, coming to pull her from the oil-scented water to carry her into the bedroom and ravish her, but the moment she saw Doug all thoughts of Gerald fled her mind.

The dog trembled visibly all over, his back hunched and the whites of his eyes showed as he looked from her to the door behind him. If he'd had a long enough tail, it would have been between his legs. His whole posture screamed fear.

She sat up, water sloshing out of the tub onto the tile floor. "What is it, Doug? Come here," she cooed, holding out a dripping hand.

But Doug stood trembling and wheezing with anxiety on the bathroom rug.

This was bad. Something was wrong.

Lily stood and grabbed her robe. It had to be the wind, she thought, listening to it howl around the eaves of the old house. Sometimes, when the wind got really strong, she almost felt as if the whole house moved with it, but tonight she'd been so caught up in her thoughts of Gerald she hadn't even noticed it. Hard to believe since it blew like a cyclone, thrashing the trees, rattling the window-panes, and whistling through the railing on the front porch.

"Come on, Doug, you know it's just the wind." She bent down to him and stroked his quivering back. "You love wind."

And he did. It was one of his favorite things. There was nothing Doug loved better than to chase a piece of paper, or a plastic cup, or pretty much anything the wind whipped erratically around the yard. He even seemed to love the feel of it on his body, sometimes standing stock-still, nose high, and face into the gusts as they brought caresses and messages from God knew where.

She tried to remember the last time she saw him like this—anxious and timid—and couldn't. He was normally so bold, so brave, almost stupidly so. One time he'd even charged a police horse that had been pawing the ground and making aggressive noises, as if the thing couldn't plant one hoof on Doug's back and kill him. The only things that ever scared him were, ironically, cats—and by lucky chance there were none of those in this neighborhood. Certainly none in the house.

She moved into the bedroom, Doug hard on her heels, and scrubbed herself dry. Then she redonned her thick pink robe.

"Come on, Doug, let's go see what has you so spooked."

She left the bedroom and marched down the hall to the top of the stairs. Doug stayed trembling in her doorway.

Despite herself, Lily felt a shiver of fear race up her spine to pause, tingling, at the base of her neck.

She was reminded of that moment in every horror movie where the girl stupidly ignores all the signs and goes searching through the house for the source of some ominous sound, only to be killed by a creepy, hooded bad guy.

"Doug, come," she said firmly, patting her thigh.

Doug took one step forward, looked at her with white-rimmed eyes, and whined.

Lily looked down the stairs. She'd left no lights on, so the bottom of the stairwell was immersed in a black pool of scary possibilities. She swallowed. This was silly. She was never afraid in her own house. This was one of the safest neighborhoods in town—and they were all pretty safe.

She clutched her robe more tightly around her and descended the stairs. When she reached the bottom she flipped on the hall overhead. Light swept through the space like a flash flood, but though it spread some brightness to the living room, it deepened the shadows behind the chairs and couch, and turned the windows into fathomless inky holes in the walls.

She moved swiftly into the living room and

turned on the floor lamp, then the table lamp, then moved through there to the dining room and turned on the chandelier, stopping only after the rooms were lit up like a children's birthday party.

She took a deep breath. This was better. Still, the windows gaped like the eyes of a madman. She was in a fishbowl. Anybody outside could see right in if they wanted. If Doug was nervous because someone was breaking in—or worse, *already* in . . .

But that was ridiculous. If someone had broken in, Doug would be a tornado of barks and growls and bodily action. He wouldn't be trembling upstairs in the hallway. The only answer was to get him down here and see what he was reacting to.

She moved back through the living room and, after closing the plantation shutters on the front windows, went to the base of the stairs.

"Doug, come!" She looked up the steps. Doug stood at the top, head cocked. "Come on, Doug. It's all right. Want a cookie?" She raised her brows and put on her ecstatic look.

Doug's stubby tail began to wag. She could tell because his body twisted with the motion, and his smile came back, albeit tentatively and interspersed with some anxious, tongue-curling panting.

But something sharp hit a window. Doug fled and Lily jumped, a yelp of fright popping from her throat. She whirled and looked into the living room.

Nothing moved. The windows looked fine,

uncracked, and nothing she could see moved beyond their panes. Except she couldn't see the front ones now that she'd closed the shutters.

That was silly, though. If someone were breaking in, they wouldn't do it in *front* of the house. Especially not with the whole place lit up like a Christmas tree.

Then she heard something at the back of the house. Like a skeletal hand scratching at the back door. It wasn't a knock, it was a pitiful, otherworldly-type of cry for entry.

She was reminded of the scene in *Wuthering Heights* when the traveler staying the night was awakened by the ghost of Cathy, scratching at his window with a clawlike hand.

Goose bumps stole up Lily's arms, and she clutched them to her stomach, squeezing fistfuls of robe in her fingers.

She turned from the stairs and walked through the living room, turning on every light, then moved to the dining room, kitchen, office, and even the basement (which she could thankfully do from the top of the stairs) and did the same. The house was a stadium of illumination, not a shadow could survive. At least not one that could hold a person.

A *spirit*, on the other hand . . .

She shivered, and wondered briefly about the history of this house. Her grandmother Bernice had owned it initially, and she'd lived there with her good friend in the other half, a woman whom everyone had called Aunt Vivien. Her father had inherited the whole thing after the two had died, and rented one side to Lily and the other to whomever he could get.

As far as Lily knew, however, no one had died in this place or the other.

Just as she was chiding herself that suddenly worrying about spirit manifestations in a house she'd lived in for seven years was the ultimate in gullibility, the scratching started up on the back door again.

She jumped and pressed herself against the basement door. If it was a person, they'd be able to see her through the kitchen window. They'd see her frightened and alone, vulnerable in her robe.

If it was a person, they would knock.

Unless they meant to do her harm.

Maybe it was something caught against the door by the wind.

She took a step away from the basement door, then paused. She should just turn off the lights and head upstairs to bed. Whatever it was would be gone in the morning, and she could investigate in the full light of day.

She glanced at the microwave clock. It was only eight o'clock.

So what. She could read. She reached for the kitchen light switch, then changed her mind. It was her house, she could go to sleep with all the lights on if she wanted.

She passed through the kitchen, her stride quickening past the back door. The hairs on the nape of her neck prickled as she imagined someone watching her through the kitchen window, so she picked up her pace through the dining and living rooms to the base of the stairs. Once there, she looked up. Doug was nowhere to be seen. What if someone had taken him? What if the killer had gone upstairs when she'd been in the office and slit his throat? There was no other reason the dog would be so quiet.

She looked up the stairs, trepidation pounding a swift tattoo in her chest.

Then a sudden, sharp knock sounded on the front door just behind her.

Lily shrieked and spun toward the door, hands to her chest.

It would be just like a clever killer to come on a night like this, knock on the door, and have her open it. *No sign of forced entry* . . . she could hear the policemen say.

It was a dark and stormy night . . .

For the first time she cursed the pretty frosted oval in her wooden front door. Whoever was out there would see her moving in the light from the hall. Not to mention the lights from the living room, dining room, and kitchen. There was no place she could go that she would not be the one in the spotlight.

Tomorrow, she vowed, she'd put a curtain on the oval.

The knock sounded again and, despite expecting it, she jumped again.

Why didn't whoever it was use the doorbell? she wondered.

Why wasn't Doug down here barking his head off? The image of the knife-wielding killer upstairs warred with the image of the killer knocking on the door.

"Lily?" a male voice called. "It's Brady, from next door."

She wilted in relief. Her heart seemed to expand in her chest, taking deep, thumping beats to slow the racing of her blood. With a huge breath she reached for the door and swung it wide.

Wind and leaves and dirt blew in on the gale from outside. Her hair blew partly out of its clip and gently buffeted her face.

Brady Cole, big and broad and blessedly real, stood on her welcome mat with his hands in the pockets of his bomber jacket. She wanted to reach out and grasp the reality of that cracked leather coat, to put her hands on the warmth of his body through the fabric, to usher him in and curl into his strength and normality.

He wasn't a spirit, he wasn't a killer, he was just the next-door neighbor.

"Brady!" She beamed at him. "Come on in."

He smiled—surprised, she thought.

"Thanks," he said, his slightly husky voice real and strong and warm. "I hope it's not too late to drop by, but I saw the lights on . . ."

His eyes trailed from her face to the hall behind her, to the living room and beyond that the dining room.

"*All* the lights are on," he added.

"No, no, not too late at all!" she enthused, taking another deeply relieved breath.

His mouth quirked in a half smile, and those hazel eyes looked down at her, their expression kind. He really was a good-looking guy, she noted. And not just because he wasn't a murderer.

He didn't have the look of a Valentino, say, like Gerald did. He was more like an explorer out of *National Geographic.* The kind of guy, she concluded, who could banish scary presences from an old house.

"Were you . . ." He hesitated, then said gently, "Were you afraid of something, Lily?"

"What?" she protested, a note of hysteria in her voice that she hoped was detectable only to herself. "Afraid? Of what?"

She didn't care if she appeared slightly deranged, she told herself. She didn't care, didn't care, didn't care. Because Brady was here—friendly and real, not an evil spirit or a murderer—and that was what mattered.

Still, it was strange and worrisome that Doug

was not down here, doing his insane intimidation thing.

"I don't know," Brady said. "The only time I've seen a house lit up like this was when our old baby-sitter used to get spooked. Then we'd all go around the house and turn on every light we could find."

She laughed, a high-pitched, unnatural sound. "I used to do that, too. Come on in, Brady. Can I get you something to drink?"

He stepped in, let her close the door behind him, and watched her with compassionate eyes. "Are you sure you're all right? You seem a little . . . nervous."

She glanced up the stairs, hoping to see Doug on the landing, but he wasn't there. She swallowed over a lump of fear in her throat.

Looking back into Brady's eyes, she sobered. "Okay, here's the thing. Doug was acting really weird, like he was afraid of something, and it's kind of freaking me out. You see, it's really odd for him to do that. And then I started hearing noises, weird noises, and I came down to investigate, and . . ." She held her hands out to the sides, helpless, hoping he understood.

His brow furrowed. "Why didn't you send Doug down to investigate?" His eyes strayed up the stairs.

"I tried," she said. "But he wouldn't come down the steps. I could barely get him to come out of the bedroom."

"You're kidding."

"No! I know." She shook her head. "It's the weirdest thing. He's usually so brave. But something spooked him. That's what got me. So I . . ." She indicated the house with her outstretched hands. "I did what your babysitter used to do. And turned on every light in the house." She laughed slightly, but at least it sounded normal this time. "Even the basement."

"Well," Brady looked confused, sounded a little incensed, "where is Doug now? Upstairs cowering under the covers?"

She shook her head. "Oh no. He's probably in the bathroom. In the tub, most likely. That's where he goes in the few situations when he gets scared. But that's usually during fireworks or something out of the ordinary like that."

"He's afraid of fireworks," Brady repeated, like he was trying to get the facts straight.

"Yes. That might be the only thing he's afraid of." She shrugged. "And whatever scared him tonight."

"And he hides in the *tub*?" His voice was incredulous.

She nodded. "I know that sounds strange, but it's not actually that unusual. The thing is, he couldn't tonight, because I was in it, taking a bath. That's where I was when he came in, trembling and whining like something was really wrong."

"Trembling and whining . . . And he didn't *tell* you what was wrong?" Brady asked.

She smiled slightly, gazed at him as if she'd misjudged him. Maybe he was a dog person, she thought. Who else would ask a question like that? Who else would know that a devoted owner understood her dog as if he actually spoke to her?

"He told me as much as he was able to." Then she gasped, looked at Brady in alarm. "The tub! I'm not sure I emptied the water. What if he got in and—and—and that's why he's not down here now? He's *always* here when someone comes to the door. What if he *drowned*!"

Less afraid of the killer now that Brady was here, she grabbed his arm and bolted up the stairs. Doug, drowned, clawing futilely at the enamel sides of the tub, trying to get out, trying to let her know while she obliviously obsessed over the scratching at the back door. Oh, she'd never forgive herself if something had happened to Doug.

Brady stumbled after her.

"Lily wait, I don't think—"

"I just want to find Doug, make sure . . ." She couldn't tell him about the killer up there, slitting Doug's throat, not while Doug might be drowning in the bathwater.

"I really think you should check this out—" He pulled back firmly from her grasp when they reached the top of the stairs. *"Alone."*

She turned on him. *"What?"*

He gestured in the direction of her bedroom. "I don't think I should go in there."

Lily put her hands on her hips and eyed him with furious disappointment. "Brady Cole. Don't tell me you're *afraid* to go in there!"

He gave her a dry look. "I've never been afraid to enter a woman's bedroom in my life."

Four

"What I am afraid of," Brady said, "is catching your boyfriend in the tub."

"My boyfriend?" Now she looked confused.

"Okay, maybe he's not your boyfriend. Whatever, that's your business. But I'm not charging into your bedroom to make sure some guy who's too scared to investigate a noise in the house didn't drown in your bathtub."

Brady ran a hand through his hair and looked beyond her to the bedroom. Surely the guy heard them talking. Was he still too scared—or too embarrassed—to come out now?

"Not that I wouldn't like to kick his ass at some point," he added.

Slowly, Lily's eyes widened. "You thought . . . Doug? But Doug is . . ."

To his amazement she started to laugh.

"Oh my God," she wheezed, laughing, eyes tearing. "Come with me."

She grabbed his wrist.

"What are you doing?" he protested. "Lily . . ."

Her fingers were delicate but strong, and as she led him into her bedroom, he was suddenly convinced it was the last place he should be within ten feet of.

Then he heard snoring.

"Oh thank God," Lily breathed. She dropped his wrist and ran for the bathroom door.

She pushed it open and Brady saw that there, curled up next to the toilet, was the ugly dog he had seen in Lily's arms the other night.

Slowly, she backed out of the bathroom and closed the door as gently as if a newborn baby was asleep on the other side.

"*That's* Doug," she whispered.

Brady felt heat scald his face, then laughter bubbled up in his throat.

Doug was *the dog*. The friggin' *dog*.

"I—" he began, but Lily tugged his arm again, leading him from the room.

"Trust me, it would not be good if Doug woke up and found you here." She gave him a conspiratorial look as they headed for the stairs.

Brady rubbed a hand over his face. "Oh Jesus," he

said, moving the hand up and through his hair. "I thought—I thought Doug was—" He couldn't stop the laughter now.

He glanced at Lily as giggles burst from her. She covered her mouth, but her eyes teared again with mirth as she looked up at him.

"My—boyfriend!" she squeaked, bending at the waist and giggling harder, hand clasped firmly over her mouth. She straightened, attempting to sober. "Shhh, shhh."

She put her hand around his upper arm and directed him toward the stairs.

"I'm serious," she said. "Doug mustn't know you're here."

They moved down the stairs to the landing at the turn, several steps above the foyer, where Brady turned around.

He had time now, to notice that she wore only a robe, and that beneath the fluffy pink fabric was the creamy skin of her neck, leading down to her chest, and he knew what was below that. The sash was cinched tight and, with her hair up and her cheeks flushed, she looked soft, cozy, and delectable.

"Are you going to be okay now?" he asked.

She looked down on him from a higher step. If he moved forward half a foot he could bury his face in that creamy vee where her robe opened. He trained his eyes on hers, willing himself not to look down.

She descended a step so she stood on the landing with him. "Yes. I'm fine. Thank you so much, Brady. I'm sorry I behaved like such a ninny. I just—it's just so unusual for Doug to get spooked."

Despite himself, he started chuckling again, remembering his mental image of an adult man cowering in the tub while this petite beauty searched the house for an intruder.

"Don't worry about it," he said, "I understand. Sometimes it only takes a mood."

"Exactly." She gazed up at him with a smile. Her dark eyes were warm, with none of the mischievous merriment of their earlier meetings. This was friendly, not challenging, and he enjoyed the sensation of being in on the joke together.

They stood for a long moment, looking at each other, before Brady realized she was waiting for him to leave.

"Okay, I'll let you go," he said, taking the last two steps toward the front door, forgetting that he had come to see her for a reason, forgetting everything but that creamy vee of skin above her robe.

"Again, let me thank you." She started to follow him when a great burst of wind blew the front door open, and the lights went out.

Lily shrieked and stumbled on the steps. Before Brady could move, he felt her body hit his shoulder, soft as a stuffed animal in the robe, and he reacted. He grabbed her, one hand yanking the fabric as the other closed around her waist. He pulled her close, securing her against his body, as the wind whipped into the hallway.

It took only a second for him to realize the robe had come open and his left hand was around her bare waist. Skin—soft, hot, and beckoning—seemed to radiate under his palm, and he instinctively spread his fingers, tightening his grip. Her body pressed against his, and her hands clutched his coat. The top of her head brushed silken hair against his chin.

She smelled of flowers.

For a long moment he didn't move, just felt the hot bare skin on his hand, her body along his, and his heart thundered in his chest. His gut tightened, and with it everything in the vicinity. He moved his other hand from her shoulder to the back of her neck, where tendrils of hair caressed his knuckles. He gently held her head.

"Are you all right?" he asked quietly.

She took a quick breath, and the spell was broken. She backed up, away from him and in the ambient light from the street he saw her hair, nearly out of its clip, dancing in reckless curls around her face with the wind. He couldn't be sure, but he felt her eyes burn into him.

She swallowed. "Yes, uh, yes." She straightened her robe and cinched the sash tight again.

He moved to the door, grabbing it with one hand but not losing sight of Lily, and closed it against the heaving gale. The sudden silence in the hall nearly undid him. He wanted to hold her again, feel that hot velvet skin, peel off that robe and run his hands the length of her body. Something inside of him said if he did that right now, before the moment was totally lost, she would fall into him as willingly as he would her.

A sharp crack sounded against a living room window, and they both jumped, turning toward the sound. Clearly the wind had hurled something against the glass.

"Do you think someone's out there?" she asked, her voice barely above a whisper. "Did someone do this? Turn out the lights?"

The trembling in her voice had him aching to hold her again.

"I'm sure the whole street's out. A tree probably went down on a power line."

She sighed. "Of course. Of course you're right. I—I just feel so unsettled."

"It's all right, Lily. Don't worry," he said, his voice low, as if raising it would awaken them to the fact that she was nearly naked, and he was hard as a rock.

Silence descended again. Brady could not move his feet. It was as if his body knew there was a beautiful woman right next to him in the dark, and it was not going to cooperate with his brain until it got to touch her again.

A scratching sounded at the back of the house. Brady's eyes flashed toward the kitchen.

"Do you hear that?" she hissed.

A bad feeling grew in his stomach. "Yes."

If this wasn't because of the wind, if the houses next door had power . . . He couldn't help thinking of Tricia. Lily had been frightened when he'd arrived, and it would not be beyond Tricia either to mistake the side of the house he lived in, or to be trying to torture the woman she thought he'd moved here to be with.

"Listen," he said, "why don't I just take a look around outside. Make sure nobody's lurking in the shadows."

He saw Lily's body spin back toward him. "You think someone might be lurking in the shadows?"

He cursed himself. "No, I was making a joke. I thought maybe you were worried about that. Let me put it this way, if you want me to, I'll check around outside."

It wouldn't do him any harm either to get his inappropriate response to Lily Tyler out in the cold where it could . . . recede.

He backed toward the door. Lily's hand reached out and grabbed his sleeve.

"Brady, I—" she began, then stopped herself.

He took her hand and loosened her fingers. If he didn't get outside now, he was sure he would do something he'd regret. Or she'd regret it, then he'd have to.

He just couldn't let go of her fingers.

More importantly, though, it seemed she couldn't

let go of his. Was it fear? Or was this thing crackling between them desire? Brady knew what it was on his part.

He stood still, literally paralyzed with indecision. Stay or go? Let go of this warm, beautiful, scented woman in her puffy robe, or stay and peel back that thick, soft layer to her silken skin, her obvious passion?

Say no, he heard his brother saying, like the good angel on his shoulder. *Wait for the big meal, the main course.*

But God, Brady was starving now, and this woman was a feast fit for a king, nourishment he could not do without.

Brady didn't make the decision. At least he didn't think he did. Without feeling like he'd moved a muscle, she was in his arms. Someone had crossed that divide, those slim inches that had stood between them, and Brady responded with every instinct he had cheering him on.

His arm tightened around her waist, and his hand buried itself in her hair. Dimly he heard the clip she'd used hit the foyer floor, and her hair cascaded around his fingers, soft as a morning fog.

His lips found her mouth, and she opened beneath him like she was as hungry as he. Their tongues met, and Brady felt himself dive headlong into the dark, swirling whirlpool of her desires.

Her body pressed against his, and still he pulled

her to him. He leaned back on the door and gripped the robe, then moved his hand to find the opening, sliding bare hand onto bare skin. She gasped—a short little intake of breath that somehow conveyed intense arousal—and Brady groaned softly.

His hand found the small of her back and dipped just low enough to feel the rise of her hips, the impossibly tender skin of her backside. His fingers grazed the cleft, then slipped up her side, over the curve of her waist and higher, up her rib cage until his thumb felt the underside of her breast, round and firm.

She seemed to arch into his palms, throwing her head back so that his lips found her neck. He traced his tongue on the skin just below her ear. She sighed, a quiet, kitten sound so close to his ear that it tickled his eardrum.

Brady was suddenly acutely aware of where they stood, that the stairs were a foot away and Lily's bedroom just at the top of those. His body grew hotter at the thought of leading her up those stairs to her bed. He remembered the plush comforter and numerous pillows that graced it, inviting him to plunge into its depths and take his pleasure with its owner.

Blood thundered in his ears and pulsed in his groin with a staggering heat. He moved his other hand from her hair and pushed the opening of her robe wide, pulling her naked body against him with both hands around her waist. Twisting, he turned them both so that she was against the door and he pressed his hardness up against her, a primal instinct he could not refuse.

Her hands rose up to his face as their lips met again, and her hips answered his with equal force.

It's not too late to stop. She's your landlord's daughter, your neighbor, a virtual stranger. She's a woman you do not know.

But he was like a train barreling down the track at full speed. There was no stopping now. His body was on fire, his blood rushed with a momentum that would not be denied. Every ounce of desire he had, the accumulation of hungers he'd held in check for months, pounded through his veins and demanded he take what he was being offered.

Her fingers found the opening of his jacket and pushed it back. Their lips separated with a soft sound, and he dropped the leather coat on the floor. Her hands went for his shirt buttons, working the closures as he pulled the tails out of the waistband of his jeans.

His eyes were accustomed to the dark, and as he helped her with the bottom buttons of his shirt, his gaze raked her body. Framed by the robe, her skin glowed pale in the darkness, her breasts stood high and firm, and her hips curved with exquisite grace.

He took a deep breath. Then her hands found his bare skin. She pushed them into his open shirt and laid her lips against his chest just at the rise of one pectoral muscle.

He closed his eyes with the sensation. "Yes," he murmured.

"I want you," she said, low, her fingers tightening on his rib cage.

Her hair touched his chest, like a feather being traced along his skin, soft, tantalizing.

"I—I can't stop," she said between tiny sucking kisses on his chest. "I need you. I need . . . *this*."

Brady paused, recognizing where Lily's words came from, what they meant. He recognized that urgent, blinding, purely physical place that he also had been so many times. The place where he was consumed by his body's wants and ignored his head, his instincts, his *sense*.

The place he was right now, too. The place he swore he'd never be again.

"Jesus," he said on an expulsive breath. He pushed her gently against the door and moved his body back, away from the lure of her lips, the magnet of her body. He dipped his head, stared at the floor with wide, alert eyes.

I don't know this woman. I don't know her. I can't do this.

He stepped back, feeling as if he'd dipped his hand into a beehive and swirled it around. He was going to get stung no matter what he did. But he could stop the bigger mistake. He could avoid doing the one thing he'd sworn he wouldn't do again.

"Brady." Her voice was a whisper, his name a plea on a breath.

He lifted his head, looked at her, and felt regret sweep over his skin, pound in his veins, quiver in his gut.

She looked so beautiful, her eyes black in the darkness, her body like an alabaster goddess's come to molten hot life.

"I should check outside," he heard himself say, his voice strangled and deep.

What kind of gutless idiot had he become? he asked himself. Was he afraid? Had Tricia scarred him for life? Or was sleeping with Lily really the wrong thing to do?

He heard his brother's voice in his head again. *It's not worth it.*

It was just so hard to believe that, looking at Lily Tyler leaning against the door with her hair tumbled loose on her shoulders and her robe open to expose that perfect, receptive body.

"Lily, I . . ." He shook his head, his hands aching to grab her again, to sweep her upstairs and the devil take whatever happened next. "I can't."

She froze. He saw her body stiffen and knew he'd wounded her.

"You have a boyfriend," he said, pleading for understanding of something he couldn't even articulate. Or maybe it was that he couldn't quite believe it. "You'll regret it, trust me."

After an interminable moment, she said, "You're not stopping because I have a boyfriend."

He shook his head. *No.* The word sounded in his

head—he nearly said it—but he couldn't explain, not now. Maybe tomorrow. But not now, while his body was revved and his mind only barely holding on to the right thing to do.

"I'll be right back," he said, knowing with every word that he was nailing shut the possibility of friendship, of anything, with this woman. "I'll just check outside."

He reached for the doorknob next to her hip, and she stepped sideways, away from him.

He paused. It was not too late, he thought, there was still time to ease this desire with something other than a brisk north wind.

But he didn't. He couldn't. He made himself open the door and walk stiffly onto the porch.

The moment he was out he felt something soft hit him in the back. When he turned, he found his coat on the porch floor and the door slamming behind him.

Five

In the end he'd left her a note. Slipped it through the mail slot telling her everything was all right, that the whole street had lost power, that the wind was kicking up so much debris the odd noises around the house were normal.

Then he'd gone home and kicked himself for so easily forgetting his resolution. He'd gone over there to tell her about Tricia. Let her know that he was a normal guy who'd just happened to get mixed up with a psycho. And instead he'd done the *exact same thing* with her that he'd done with Tricia: jumped into the physical without any idea of who she actually was. What she actually was. What he might ultimately want.

Brady picked up the phone and dialed the New York number he'd memorized in the last few months. He and his brother—half brother, to be specific—had not been close growing up. In fact they'd fought constantly as little kids, then ignored each other through the teen years, and lived in separate states through their twenties.

It was only now, as they were entering their thirties, that they found having a brother was worth something.

Keenan was four years older and had a personality that could not have been more unlike Brady's. Where Brady was reckless and impulsive, Keenan was reasoned and methodical. Where Brady could be selfish and heartless, Keenan was invariably considerate and kind.

Take for example the fact that Keenan never accused him of being selfish or heartless, merely unthinking, he always said. But not deliberately unthinking, not in the inconsiderate sense, but because there were underlying *issues*. Keenan loved talking about people's *issues*. He had always been the psychologist/philosopher of the family, and lately had parlayed the skills into a fine living writing a television series about a psychologist who helped women with their relationships.

So it was only the last couple of years they'd gotten closer. Pretty much since their mother had gone into the nursing home.

"Kee," Brady said when his brother picked up the phone. "It's me. I think I need an intervention."

Keenan laughed. "Who is this?"

"I'm serious. Remember the date diet?" Brady stood in his kitchen and bounced the eraser end of a pencil against the counter. "I've already fucked up. And with the worst person I could have chosen. What is *wrong* with me?"

Keenan sighed. "Do you think you do these things because regret is easier than restraint?"

Brady paused. "Wow, good one. And right off the bat, too."

Keenan laughed. "I'm already warmed up. I just did a radio show."

Brady let that pass. His older brother's success was another one of his *issues,* though not one that he shared. "Hey, for the record I did show *some* restraint. I walked away before it went too far."

"I thought you said you'd fucked up."

"Yeah, but I didn't, you know, fuck. I just kissed the wrong girl. Repeatedly. I think I . . . might have . . . set up expectations." Brady walked around the counter to the stool on the other side and sat, his head in one hand.

"Ah—"

"And I like this girl. I really do. I don't want to piss her off or get on her bad side, either. I'd like to be friends. Not just because she's the landlord's daughter, but because she's, I don't know, interest—" think she is, anyway. She *seems* interesting."

The words came out in a rush, as if he were explaining it to himself. Some of what he said even came as a surprise to himself.

Not as much as it surprised Keenan, however.

"Your *landlord's daughter*?" he laughed incredulously. "How did you even find her? I mean, that must have taken some work."

"She lives next door," Brady said dourly. "We share a wall."

"A wall."

"Yeah. The twin house thing, I told you." He pulled the phone pad toward him and began doodling with the pencil. Hard, dark circles with spikes coming out of them—a series of black suns.

"Oh right. You're in a duplex." Keenan sighed. "So she lives next door, and there's no avoiding her."

"Right. So she's out there like some kind of delicious, unhealthy temptation sent to test me. And she's not like some Twinkie I can leave on the shelf in the food store and pick up broccoli instead. She's just there, waiting."

"Okay, I think we're taking this food metaphor a little far. I've got a weird picture of her in my head now."

Brady rolled his eyes. Sure, it was fine for Keenan to be amused. He hadn't been there when Tricia popped her clutch. *That* had been scary.

"The fact remains," Brady said, "she's over there all the time, and I'm here all the time, and I don't know how to avoid her. Although she's probably not speaking to me now."

"Don't either of you work?"

Brady sighed heavily, to be sure Keenan heard him. "You know what I do. I'm on call, twenty-four/ seven. Which means the rest of the time I'm ... around. She's a teacher. She's home a lot. It's a dangerous situation." The rays on the dark suns got longer, and wavy, like microwaves. Or super-sonic death rays. He drew a bad-guy, troglodyte-type creature below them.

"Didn't you know this when you got into the situation? Couldn't you have avoided it to begin with? You decided on this date diet thing before you even moved, remember. And you know what you're like."

"Of course I remember. And no, I couldn't have avoided it. I mean, Jordan Tyler said his daughter lived next door, so yeah, I technically knew she was there. But I didn't picture her as ... that is, I didn't imagine, you know, after Tricia—well for God's sake, Keenan I don't anticipate having sex with every woman I *hear* about."

"It just happens," Keenan said dryly.

"Look, I don't need a lecture. I just need to know what to do."

Keenan was silent a long moment. Then he said, "Tell her."

"Tell her *what*?" Brady dropped the pencil and

ripped the top sheet off the pad, wadding it in his hand and tossing it across the kitchen.

"Tell her about the date diet. Tell her you've given up women for Lent, or whatever."

"Lent's over," Brady said morosely. "Guess you'd already moved out when Mom went through her Catholic phase."

"Oh yeah. Well, tell her you're not dating. That it's nothing personal, but you'd appreciate it if she rebuffed you from now on. Be honest. Tell her what's going on."

"She'll think I'm some kind of sex addict," Brady protested, trying to imagine the conversation. *Hi, nothing personal, I just need to keep away from women for a while. I don't seem to have very good judgment, and I jump into bed with anyone who'll have me.* That ought to make her feel special.

"So?"

"*So?* So I'm not a sex addict, and I don't want her thinking I am. My God, she'll look at me like some kind of—of deviant."

"Well, you can tell her you're not a sex addict. Just a guy who needs to be on his own for a while. Tell her you've just gotten out of a bad relationship."

"I thought you said 'be honest.'" Brady liked laying this on Keenan. It was so rare that Brady got to be the right one.

"And you wouldn't call Tricia a bad relationship?"

Shit.

He thought a moment. "And Lily sort of met Tricia, actually."

"Uh-oh."

"Yeah." He recounted the scene for Keenan, who couldn't stifle his laughter long enough for Brady to get through the whole thing without seeing some humor as well.

"So it's perfect," Keenan said. "You tell her about Tricia, tell her you don't like your own actions, and see what she says. If she's a good candidate for a friend, she'll understand. If not, no problem. You said she's probably not speaking to you anyway, right?"

"Right," Brady said, thinking that wasn't exactly what he'd call an "upside."

Doug was in a stew. He'd hated waking up to find himself caught in the bathroom again, especially when he could hear voices downstairs. One of which was male.

He'd forgotten exactly why he'd gotten caught in the bathroom, remembered only that it had happened before, and the knee-jerk frustration of not being by Lily's side when a man was in the house bloomed inside of him.

It didn't help, of course, that when she did finally release him he could smell New Guy all over her and the rug in the hallway, not to mention the stairs, the front foyer and, well, all over the place.

The guy had gone everywhere. Like *he* was the protector.

No, it was unacceptable, and as Doug knew well, when training you had to be consistent. Never let them get away with anything. That's why the first day Lily left the doggy door unlatched he made his way out into the yard again and over to New Guy's place.

New Guy's vehicle—not a car like Lily's, but something louder and sparkly—was parked out back this time, making it easy for Doug to get to. As he considered his options, he peed on the back tire, an activity that relaxed him and generally aided his creativity.

There wasn't a lot there he could accomplish, most of the thing being metal, but the seat was soft and smelled of rawhides. With a little effort he could leap up there and get a grip, not to mention see how it tasted.

His first effort was a bust. He didn't get quite high enough—the seat was way higher than the couch at home—and his body hitting the machine merely made the thing shudder and clank. But that gave him an idea. Throwing his body at the bike a second time, he succeeded. Skittering back from the noise it made as it toppled over and hit the ground, Doug watched a couple of shiny parts break loose and roll away.

One caught the light more than the others so he chased it, nipped it up in his mouth, and tossed it in the air. Then he pounced on it again. It lay dormant and glistening under his paws. He jumped up, play-bowed to it, and hit it with a paw, which made it roll away again. Delighted, he bounded after it, taking it up in his mouth once more and biting down hard.

With a yelp, he spat the thing out and stared at it. When it became motionless again, Doug decided it really wasn't all that interesting. A moment more of study, and he became aware of the rawhide scent behind him.

He turned back to the machine, now on its side, and eyed the leather seat. He panted a moment in satisfaction, then set to work. A few licks confirmed his initial impression. It was soft and tasty. This would be enjoyable work.

And hey, a bonus, he could even lie down as he worked; the leather seat was now comfortably at snout level.

Lily stood in front of the class—ten women and one man, if you could call freshman college students women and men (some deserved it, some didn't, in her opinion)—and looked at each of them in turn.

"I'm sure at one point or another each of you has been in love with the wrong person," she said. "Can you give me examples of where this happens in the novel?"

As usual, the students were silent in the beginning, no one wanting to be the first to raise their hand and dare an opinion. For that reason, she preferred her upper-level courses. The older students were more confident in their convictions and voiced them freely. This group of freshmen, however, was still uncertain of their opinions, despite the fact that it was the second semester.

On the other hand, freshmen were more open to discovering new passions, which is why she chose to teach a class on nineteenth-century novels at this level.

"I assure you, there are many in the book. Austen could even be said to be making a point about the vagaries of love. Even about how we convince ourselves we have feelings for one person, when perhaps it's only because we think we should." She paused. For a moment, she thought of Brady Cole's hands on her skin, and how a few years ago she might have felt she had to convince herself she was in love with him, simply to justify the startling physical passion she'd indulged in with him.

That was one benefit to being in her thirties, she mused, looking at the students in front of her with something like pity. She didn't have to kid herself about the difference between love and lust. Love was Gerald Lawson; lust was Brady Cole. Simple and defined, if a little confusing on the mechanics of the situation.

For a second she amused herself with the idea of telling the students all about the situation, showing them how vividly Austen's work reflects even modern situations.

But of course she'd never do that. Her private life was sacrosanct; she never brought it up here, at the school. For that reason she even had a policy of not dating colleagues, despite having been asked out by more than one of her peers.

Several students were flipping through the pages of the book, looking for answers to pop out at them.

"Maybe it would be better if I asked you for examples from your own lives," Lily said. "I bet that would make for a much livelier conversation."

For a moment the students looked stricken. But when she smiled a chorus of nervous laughter ensued.

"Jennifer," Lily said. "Give me one example of someone falling for the wrong man in Jane Austen's *Emma*. I know you read the book. Your essay last month on the first half was very good."

Jennifer blushed and smiled, looked down at her book and offered, "Um, Harriet Smith?"

"Excellent! And whom did she fall in love with who was wrong for her?"

"Well, everyone," she said, with a tentative smile.

Lily laughed. "Exactly. Name one."

"Mr. Elton was the worst. And he was, like, so awful to her when he found out. He thought she wasn't good enough for him."

"And Mr. Churchill," Chuck, the only male in the class, offered. "She got a crush on him, too."

"No, that wasn't Harriet," Lily said. "Who mistakenly fell for Mr. Churchill?"

Silence greeted this question until Jennifer tentatively raised her hand.

"Um, Emma?" Jennifer said. "Or she thought she did."

"That's right," Lily said. "She *thought* she did. And why did she think that?"

Silence. Jennifer paged through her notes, several of the other students continued to turn listlessly through the pages of the book. An age-old ruse that Lily knew well.

"Kathy," Lily said. The girl in the back row visibly started. "Why do you think Emma would try to convince herself she was in love with Mr. Churchill?"

"Um . . ." Kathy stared intently at the book. Lily could tell from the front of the room, from the crack in the spine, that she was in the wrong place. "Haven't you ever tried to convince yourself you loved someone, maybe because it would make things easier?" she prompted.

Kathy blushed and glanced up, then back down at the book. "I—I guess Emma would do that because her, um, family expected it?"

Lily nodded slightly and turned to the blackboard, writing a "1" and "societal expectations."

She turned back around. "In a way, yes. Many of us have probably been in the position of wanting to fall for the right person because they're part of our social set, our families like them, our friends want us to, they fit in with some idea we have about how we want our life to be. Does Emma do this?"

Jennifer raised her hand. Lily nodded at her.

"Sure, because it would have been so perfect. Mr. Churchill was the son of her good friends, the Westons, and she knew they were hoping she and Mr. Churchill would get married. So she tried to convince herself she was falling for him."

"So why didn't she?" Lily asked. "Marry him, that is."

"Because he was an asshole," Chuck said. "I could tell the minute he showed up."

Despite herself, Lily laughed. "In what way?" Silence again. "He took advantage of her, right? He toyed with her affections, and was false with her. He acted like he wanted to court her and . . . ?"

"Like I said . . ." Chuck muttered, looking at his notebook. "An asshole."

"What was it he did? How could Emma tell he was not what he appeared to be?" The quiet lengthened.

"How can anyone tell?" Marianne ventured, from the front row, looking as morose as if she'd recently been deceived herself. "I mean, even in real life? If you're attracted to a guy, and he lies to you, how can you tell? How do you know who's the right one?"

"You feel it," Kathy said strenuously, from the back row. "You feel it even when you don't want to."

On the heels of this surprising answer—just as Lily was reluctantly associating Kathy's "feeling it without wanting to" with that unbelievable kiss with her new neighbor—the door to the classroom opened and there he stood, like an apparition: Brady Cole.

"Brady?" Lily took a step toward him.

Brady, apparently not expecting the full classroom, backed up a step. "Oh, sorry. They told me this was your room—I didn't know you had a"—he spread a hand in the direction of the students—"a class."

"What are you doing here? Is everything all right?" Her first thought was the house. A burglary. No, a fire.

His eyes swept the students. "Yeah, everything's fine. It's just Doug." He edged toward her half a step, and said quietly, "But it's not that big a deal. I can come back. It's just—I have a flight this afternoon, and I wanted to let you know—"

"Just Doug!" Little did he know he'd hit her panic button. She turned swiftly to the class. "Start work on the last study question for Emma. I'll be right back."

She grabbed Brady by the arm and drew him

out of the classroom, closing the door behind her. She spun on him. "What is it? What's happened? Is he all right?"

Her hand was still on his arm, gripping the leather coat as if the world were tipping, and she might topple off.

He gazed for a second at her hand, thinking, perhaps, about the night . . . *that* night . . . ? She dropped his arm.

"He's fine." Brady let out a breath. "He's at your vet, at your friend's, Megan's, and she said he's going to be fine."

"What *happened* to him?" her voice was dangerously high.

His face darkened, and he raised one eyebrow. "He ate the seat off my Harley. So he may be passing quite a bit of leather, and maybe a few rivets, over the next few days."

Lily put a hand over her mouth. "He ate your Harley?"

He smiled then, slightly. "Just the seat."

"How—when—?" She ran her fingers through her hair, searching the ground for the right questions, her mind spinning. "How—how did you know where to take him?"

"Nate, next door. Look," he said, glancing over her shoulder toward the classroom. "I gotta go. Doug's okay, he's at the animal hospital, and I'll be gone for a couple days. I just wanted to tell you before I left."

He started to turn, and she took his arm again. He stopped, looked back.

She felt an unexpected shiver run up her spine at the directness of his hazel eyes. "Thank you. Thanks for taking him to the vet. And I'm sorry about the seat. I'll—I'll pay you back."

He grinned then, and the shiver stole right back down her spine. "I know," he said. "You owe me two hundred eighty-four bucks. See you Thursday."

With that he turned and sauntered down the hall. Well, maybe sauntered wasn't the right word, but for some reason she found it impossible to take her eyes off him until he turned the corner to the exit.

She swallowed. Brady Cole had saved Doug. Doug had mauled his Harley and he hadn't killed him, he'd saved him. She tried to imagine the scene. How had Brady caught him? Had he picked him up? Had Doug *let him* pick him up? Had Doug been unconscious?

She had to call Megan.

She turned back to the classroom door, opened it, and was greeted by students scurrying back to their desks from, presumably, looking out the window in the door.

Monica was one of the last to make it to her seat. "Oh my God, Ms. Tyler, is that your *boyfriend*?" It was the most engaged Monica had ever appeared in class.

"What a hottie," Kathy said, shaking her head.

Even the studious Jennifer, in the front row, seemed to be looking at her with new respect.

She wondered what they'd have to say if they saw Gerald, but she knew that with his tailored suits and clean-cut looks he'd be just another corporate drone to these young women. Nothing like the dashing adventure hero Brady projected.

"No, he's not my boyfriend," Lily said, hating herself for not wanting to burst that bubble of theirs. What a traitor she was to Gerald, to her stalwart Mr. Knightley.

"Too bad," someone said low, and a few of the girls chuckled together.

"Is he a pilot?" Chuck asked. "He said something about a flight. I was thinking about going to flight school—think he'd talk to me about it?"

Lily shook her head, feeling flustered. "I don't know, Chuck. I mean, yes, he is a pilot. I'll ask if he'll talk to you."

"What's he fly?" Chuck continued. "DC-10s? 757s? I'm really into the big jets, but some of the small ones are cool, too."

"He—he's a private jet pilot. I don't know what he flies." She pushed her hair back from her face again and wondered why she felt so thrown. No doubt the collision of her two worlds—home and work. That had to be it.

Now where was she? What had they been talking about?

The bell rang, jerking her out of her confusion, and the students began to rise, slamming books and squeezing papers into backpacks.

"Okay." Lily cleared her throat. "Okay, we'll continue this next Tuesday. I want you all to finish that last study question on Emma. Then we'll start reviewing for the final, all right?"

Jennifer shot her a shy smile. "This was my favorite book so far this year, Ms. Tyler."

Lily smiled, back on track. "I'm so glad you liked it. Austen is my favorite author of all."

"So, do you think that guy is your Mr. Knightley?" Jennifer asked, then blushed. "He sure looks like a romantic hero."

Lily felt herself blush as well, and sat down behind her desk. "No, he's not. He's just a friend."

Not even that, really, just a neighbor. Heck, a tenant.

"Just thought I'd ask." Jennifer shrugged. "He was cute."

"I'll tell him you thought so," Lily said, stacking up her own books and papers.

With a giggle, Jennifer headed out. Once the girl passed through the door, the last one to leave, Lily muttered to herself, "He's *not* my boyfriend, and he's certainly not my Knightley. In fact," she added, feeling the revelation hit her, "he's my Mr. Churchill."

And don't you forget it, she told herself.

Six

Lily called Megan right away and was assured that Doug was fine. She had to stay for her last two classes, but immediately after the last one she raced over to Rose's Animal Hospital.

"He threw up most of it," Megan said, leading Lily to the back, where Doug lay curled like a black-and-white soccer ball in a metal crate. "And I did an x-ray to make sure there weren't any blockages, but it's still a little early for that. You should add a teaspoon of Metamucil to his food for the next couple of days, just to make sure everything moves along smoothly."

"Thank you so much, Megan," Lily said, bee-lining for Doug's crate and putting her fingers through the metal gate. "What in the world were you *thinking*?" she asked him. "And of all things to chew up!"

Doug lifted his head, and his whole body seemed to react to her presence. He surged to his feet and wriggled toward the mesh door, his stubby tail going a mile a minute and his body writhing with joy. His head was down and his ears back, but his mouth was grinning. He looked simultaneously embarrassed and elated, as he snorted his happiness at seeing her.

It was obvious he knew he'd done something wrong, even if he knew it only because he had a stomachache.

"Oh Lord, Doug, what am I going to do with you?" she asked, shaking her head.

"I guess he doesn't like your new neighbor, huh?" Megan said.

Lily turned back to her with a wry grin. "He's male, isn't he?"

"And how," Megan said. She reached back and redid her long, dark ponytail, raking her hair back into the elastic with her fingers.

Ever since she'd had a baby, Megan had let her hair grow long. Easier to keep it away from tiny grasping fingers, she'd said, and Lily remembered vividly how Penelope—poor, single Penelope, who had longed for a child of her own ever since Lily had known her—had fingered her own long hair when Megan had said that.

Did Lily get that same look on her face when people talked about their husbands, she wondered. Not that she was necessarily dying for a husband, just a successful relationship. How long had it been since she'd had one? And could it even be called "successful" if it ended in a breakup?

"Sutter had Brady over to the house for dinner the other night," Megan continued, "and I couldn't believe how good-looking he was."

Lily blushed and turned back to Doug. "Is he?" Then, realizing how disingenuous that sounded, she added, "I mean, sure, I guess he is. He's just not my type."

He was just the type to get her blood boiling with his good-looking hands, and her morals flying out the window with his good-looking lips, and her head spinning with his good-looking, muscled, athletic body . . .

Megan was quiet a long moment, so Lily turned back toward her, guiltily trying to come up with something that sounded more honest—Megan was just the type to see right through her protestations of disinterest—but Megan was simply writing on Doug's chart.

"So," Lily ventured, "was he mad? Brady, that is? Did he seem mad about . . ." She tossed a hand in Doug's direction. "About Doug ruining his Harley?"

Megan chuckled. "Well, I'm sure he wasn't happy, but honestly he seemed mostly worried that your dog was going to die. He kept saying, 'He's going to be all right, right? It didn't kill him, did it?' No matter how many times I told him Doug would be fine."

"Oh God." Lily put a hand over her face. "How did he get Doug in here? He wasn't *unconscious*, was he?"

"Hah! Far from it." Megan folded Doug's file shut and walked to the counter near Doug's crate. She picked up a piece of maroon fabric and held it out to Lily. "He brought him in this. Neither one of them seemed very happy about that."

Lily took the fabric and held it out in both hands. "A *pillowcase*?" Despite what she thought should be her indignation, she burst out laughing.

"It was the funniest thing I've ever seen," Megan said. "Honestly, for a second I thought he'd captured a leprechaun."

"Oh, I would have loved to see him getting Doug into this. I wonder how he did it."

"He said something about rolling one of the rearview mirrors into the bag. In fact . . ." She held up a finger and went back to the counter, pushing aside a stack of folders and a jar of cotton balls, then turning back with a cracked round mirror. She handed it to Lily.

Lily took it and sighed. "And Doug chased it right into the bag. Guess that utility training was good for something after all; he wasn't afraid of running into a tunnel." She fingered the mirror, looking at the back of it where the connection had obviously snapped. "I'll have to get him a new one of these, too. I can't believe he wasn't furious."

"He didn't seem like it. I think he's a pretty easygoing guy."

Lily thought back to that night that they'd kissed, to the raw passion that swept through them both. Brady was not easygoing then. He was alive with passion, wrestling as strenuously as she was with desire, raw and intense. Every muscle strained toward completion—she could still feel his tautness under her hands—to consummate that primal, irresistible union of man and woman.

That is until he decided not to.

Megan moved toward the crate that held Doug. "So how's Gerald?"

"He's fine," Lily said vaguely, automatically, stuck on the feel of Brady's hard body beneath her fingers, Brady's hot hands on her bare skin . . . *Gerald* . . . "Oh! Yes, *Gerald*. Gerald's fine. We have another date this weekend."

"Wow, that's a lot the last few weeks," Megan said, opening up the crate and lifting Doug down. She placed him on the metal exam table in the middle of the room and palpated his abdomen. "Things must be moving along well."

"Yes," Lily said, then added, "Yes!" trying to infuse her tone with more enthusiasm and failing. She scratched Doug's neck while Megan examined him. Doug effusively licked her hand.

Megan looked up.

Lily sighed. "It's just, he doesn't seem very passionate. He might be waiting on me, trying to take things slowly, be gentlemanly, you know, but . . . it's just not good. I need a little passion. All this waiting has me a little . . . crazy."

She remembered again the way she'd fallen into Brady's arms, almost without a second thought. What was that if not crazy?

It was Gerald's fault, she thought suddenly. She'd been all revved up over Gerald, and it was Brady who'd followed through. If she hadn't been thinking so much about Gerald that night in the tub, she never would have reacted the way she had to Brady.

"Oh God, Megan," she burst, "how did you finally get Sutter to, you know, *make his move?*"

Megan laughed. "Well it didn't take much, I'll tell you." She stopped examining Doug and looked abashed. "Sorry, that probably wasn't the right thing to say, was it?"

Lily shook her head miserably. "I'm dying to get on with things with Gerald, and it just seems to be moving too slowly. He gives me a peck on the cheek when he arrives, and one when he leaves, and that's *it*! Am I being impatient, or is there something wrong?"

Megan took a deep breath, and Lily felt immediately embarrassed. "I'm sorry, I know you're not a psychiatrist, I shouldn't burden you with this."

She grabbed her purse off her shoulder and unzipped it. "What do I owe you for Doug?"

Megan placed a hand on her arm and squeezed. "Lily, relax," she said and smiled. "I was just thinking about what to say. And I happen to have a free half hour right now, so why don't we go into the house and have some coffee?"

Lily sighed and briefly closed her eyes. "That would be great."

Megan put Doug back in the crate—despite his whining protest—let her receptionist know where she'd be, and they went through the clinic's back door. They crossed a short outdoor walkway and went into the house that was Megan's father's. Megan had lived there, too, when she'd taken over her father's veterinary practice, until she'd met Sutter, had his baby, and moved into his mansion on Washington Avenue.

Half a pot of coffee stood in the coffeemaker in the big country kitchen, and Megan pulled out a plate of cookies to go with it.

"Oreos okay?" she asked with a grin, placing them on the table between them.

"Too good," Lily said. She picked one up and twisted it apart.

Megan moved back to the refrigerator, took out a small carton of cream, and brought a sugar dispenser back to the table with her along with a couple of spoons.

"Look, Sutter and I jumped way too quickly into

the physical part of our relationship, and everything after that was catch-up," Megan said, stirring cream into her coffee. "So I'm thinking this slow pace probably isn't such a bad thing. You have a chance to really get to know Gerald before doing the one thing that distracts you most effectively from understanding his personality."

Lily looked up. "You don't think the physical part says something about their personality?"

Then again, what had she gleaned about Brady from that startling kiss the other night? Except that he was a fabulous kisser.

And an opportunist, Lily added to herself. He'd come over and was able to take advantage of her aroused state without a moment's hesitation.

Though he hadn't taken the advantage he could have, she remembered hotly. He'd left at the exact moment she'd been ready to haul him up to her bed.

Why had he come over in the first place? she suddenly wondered.

"Well, sure," Megan went on. "It says *something*. And God, for me it was like a long drink after a deep drought." She laughed. "But it was hard, after that, separating what was physical passion and what was love. We had to backtrack quite a bit."

Lily sighed. "I know all about confusing love and passion. I don't think I'm doing that here." She blushed, realizing Megan didn't know she was talking about Brady, and poured way too much sugar into her coffee. "But here's the thing, I've known Gerald for two years, since he joined Daddy's firm. And the lack of passion, well, it does make me wonder about the emotions he does or doesn't have."

Did that mean she thought Brady—with all *his* physical passion—had feelings for her? No, certainly not.

"But you haven't known him in this context," Megan countered. "Look, I know it's hard, but he keeps asking you out, right? So he's interested. Let him go at his pace and see what happens. That's my advice." She laughed. "Such as it is. I'm not sure you can call dating advice from the unwed mother of a one-year-old particularly sound."

Lily smiled. "You and Sutter were made for each other. Everyone can see it. I just wish it were as obvious for me."

"It's never obvious from the inside. And it definitely didn't feel obvious to me. Or him." Megan shrugged and blew on her coffee. "So when do we get to meet him, anyway? Why don't you invite him to my party? Georgia's bringing a date, you know."

Lily took a sip of her coffee and felt it scald the back of her throat. She coughed. "When does Georgia *not* have a date?"

Megan grinned. "Yeah, but this time she's *calling* the guy a date. Not just another bed buddy."

Lily laughed. Megan's party would be perfect to introduce Gerald, but . . . would Brady be there? How could she ask, without arousing suspicion?

"That's a good idea. I think I will invite Gerald," Lily said, imagining Brady and Gerald in the same room. She had to talk to Brady, that was all there was to it. Had to straighten this mess out before it got any more complicated. So they'd slipped up, shared a kiss. It wasn't too late to make clear that she was not interested in him in . . . *that way*. Although, what with the way he'd left with her still practically clinging to his chest the other night, *her* interest wasn't exactly the issue.

Still, she could make it the issue, and that would solve all her problems at once. Act like she was the one who wasn't interested—and she wasn't!— and Brady would understand that his decision to leave despite the heated circumstances was just what she had wanted, too.

Oh what the hell, she thought, *just ask. It isn't as if Megan can read my mind*.

"Is Brady going to be there?" she asked.

Megan looked up, eyes alight. "As a matter of fact, he is. Isn't that great?"

Lily swallowed over a lump of dread in her throat. Good God, had she tipped her hand without knowing it?

"And I know just what you're thinking," Megan said.

Lily's blood pressure leapt into the stratosphere and she gripped her coffee cup hard enough to scald her fingers through the ceramic. "You do?"

Megan nodded, smiling smugly.

Holy God, Lily thought, *maybe she* can *read minds.*

"Because I'm thinking the exact same thing," Megan said. "He's perfect for Penelope!"

Who cared? For God's sake, who in the world *cared* if Megan set Penelope up with Brady? Because there was *nothing* going on with her and Brady, Lily thought.

She walked in her front door with Doug in her arms and slammed it shut behind her.

Except that something *had* gone on, in a way. Which begged the question. Did she tell Penelope about the kiss, and if so, when? Before she got introduced to the pilot? After? Never?

Or maybe she should tell Megan. Megan could be discreet, Lily knew, and Megan would speak her mind, tell Lily if she thought it was something that should be disclosed. But then, if it *was* something to be disclosed, then by the time she told Penelope that would up the number of people who knew about the encounter to three. Well, four if you counted Brady. Which Lily was desperately trying not to do. In fact, somewhere in her heart of hearts she hoped he'd forgotten all about it. Though in her brain of brains she knew that was ridiculous.

She put Doug on the floor and watched him totter off on uncertain feet toward his water bowl. He was not feeling well, she could tell. But Megan had assured her he would be fine, so she was resolved not to worry. She was, however, going to get his crate out and settle him down for a while to digest and think about what he'd done.

After setting him up in what she thought of as his sickbed, she went back to the front hall and picked up the pillowcase she'd laid on the table with her purse.

She unfolded it and held it up in front of her. It was a nice print, if masculine, decent thread count. She laid a palm against it, thinking *this is his pillowcase, from his bed, where he sleeps . . .* It seemed a very intimate thing to have in her possession, considering how little she knew him. Their relationship, if it could be called that, was an odd mixture of unfamiliarity and intimacy. She had felt his body, touched his skin, been naked before him, and yet she knew him not at all, had never even seen the inside of his half of the house since he moved in.

She lifted the pillowcase to her nose and inhaled. Despite the fact that it had held an angry Doug, it still smelled like laundry soap. She tried to picture Brady doing laundry, folding this pillowcase. Then her thoughts strayed to Brady laying his head on it. He probably slept naked, she thought, he seemed like the type. She could picture his well-defined chest, his round muscular shoulder above the edge of a sheet like this, his straight brown hair mussed from sleeping, his—

A knock sounded on the door.

She dropped the pillowcase. She really needed to stop hanging out in this hallway. Bending down, she plucked the pillowcase off the floor, laid it on the table, and reached for the doorknob.

Brady Cole stood in the doorway, larger than life.

She also had to stop thinking about *him*. Every time she did he showed up.

"I thought you had a flight," she said, then grimaced at her own accusatory tone.

Other than his brief visit to her classroom that day, it was the first time she'd seen him since The Kiss. What with being here, right at the scene of the crime, she wasn't sure what or how to feel about seeing him now.

Brady looked taken aback. "I did. It was pushed back to tomorrow." He shrugged. "Life of an on-call pilot."

She shook her head, pushing one side of her hair away from her face. "I'm sorry. I didn't mean to snap at you. I just . . . well, with Doug and all . . . I guess I'm embarrassed about what he did."

Not to mention what she had done, with Brady, right here in this hallway.

Brady put a hand on the door frame and

leaned. "That's one reason I came by. How is he? I wanted to make sure Megan wasn't just trying to make me feel better. He's going to be okay, right?"

"He'll be *fine*. You should know that Megan is invariably honest. It's one of her most dependable qualities."

He exhaled. "Good. I was worried there for a while. He didn't look good when I found him."

"He looks okay now," she said. "I've put him in his crate for a while. To sleep it off." She laughed wryly. "But I hope your motorcycle will be okay. I can't tell you how sorry I am about that, and of course I'll reimburse you the cost of the seat. Doug, he's, well, temperamental about men. I probably should have warned you, but he's never been so destructive before. I promise you, it won't happen again."

"I hope not, for his sake," Brady said, with a lopsided smile.

A smile that for some reason turned Lily's heart upside down, it looked so boyish and sweet. Maybe he *would* be right for Penelope, she thought. *Dammit.*

"When I looked outside and saw him," Brady continued, "his belly was blown up like a beach ball. Then I saw the seat, and, well . . . I thought that was it. How does a little dog like that consume so much cowhide?"

"Apparently he doesn't do it very well," Lily

said. "But here I have you standing on the porch. Why don't you come in. Can I get you some iced tea or something?"

He hesitated, and she wished she hadn't said anything, though she was desperate to get them away from this spot, the very spot where . . .

"All right," he said, and stepped across the threshold. "Listen, I also wanted to talk about the other night. I hope you don't mind my bringing it up. I just thought we should clear the air."

Lily swallowed hard and turned, heading down the hall toward the kitchen. "The other night?" She squinched her eyes shut at how ridiculous that sounded, but kept her back to him. "You mean when you kissed me?"

Damn. That sounded accusatory again. But he had kissed her, hadn't he? It hadn't been the other way around, had it?

Her face burned. Maybe she had kissed him. How long could she keep her back to him? Long enough for this four-alarm blush to fade? And how long would that take—a week?

"Uh, yeah," Brady said. "The night I kissed you. And walked away from it."

Ah, so that was it. He thought she was upset he'd walked away. Well, she had been, at the moment. Then she'd been relieved. Hugely relieved.

"Have a seat." She motioned to the stools tucked against the center island and opened the refrigerator door. Maybe she could leave her head in there for a while, until it returned to its normal color. Unfortunately, the pitcher of tea was right in front.

She grabbed it, then turned to the cabinets for some glasses, hearing the stool scrape on the floor as Brady, presumably, sat down.

She turned back to the freezer for some ice cubes. This was working out well, maybe she'd never have to face him.

"Lily," Brady said.

His voice was low and sent a thrill up her spine. What was it about that slight huskiness that made it so sexy? It couldn't have been more different from Gerald's crisp tones, and yet it made her skin tingle whenever she heard it.

"Yes?" she replied, cracking the ice cubes out of the tray.

"This is awkward," he muttered.

She paused and stared at the ice cubes in front of her. Did he think he was having to break something to her gently? Was he afraid she'd fallen for him? Did he expect her to go postal like that Tricia woman? Is this what he had done to her?

"It doesn't have to be awkward," she said, her voice higher than usual. She turned and faced him, gripping the counter behind her with both hands. "I hope you don't think—that is, I really don't—Brady, that night was *a mistake*. I'm sorry to say it, but you caught me at a weak moment. I— I'm involved with somebody else already. And I don't know what came over me that night, I was just . . . it . . . The bottom line is, I'm sorry. I hope I didn't lead you on."

Brilliant, she thought, let him think *she* was the one worried about an undue attachment.

He let her stumble through that whole speech, looking at her all the while with those hazel eyes, and the expression in them was some-how . . . *kind.*

"No, Lily." He smiled, but to her it looked sad. Or was that pitying? "*I'm* sorry. I've been wanting to apologize for days, and just—haven't known how to do it." He shrugged and looked at her with his mouth quirked up on one side. "I'm a coward at heart. You should know that."

Lily slumped against the counter. "You're not a coward. I've been wanting to say something, too, and I haven't either. Though I guess that could mean we're both cowards."

He chuckled, and she smiled.

"Weird, though, huh?" she said. "That it hap-pened? I mean, something got into us both at the same time. I've never had anything like that hap-pen before."

The moment she said it she was sorry. It sounded as if she were asking if it had happened to him before, and the fact was she really, really didn't want to know if it had.

He looked down at the counter, and she could swear he looked ashamed.

She turned back to the ice-cube tray behind her. They sat in little pools of water in their squares. She plucked them out with her fingertips.

"Do you take sugar in your tea?" she asked. "Or lemon? Or both? Most people around here serve sweet tea, but that's a little too much sugar for some people. So I just make it unsweetened and let people put their own sugar in."

She was babbling, she knew, but it was better than letting that awkward silence reign.

"It doesn't matter," he said. "Lemon, I guess, if you've got it."

"Sure." She went to the refrigerator, glad to have something else to do. She pulled a lemon from the drawer and got out the cutting board. Sliding a knife from the block on the counter, she said, "So where are you flying?"

At the same time, however, Brady said, "There was one other thing I wanted to talk about."

Lily turned her head and glanced at him. Were his cheeks red? "Sure. Go ahead."

Please. Change the subject. She turned back to the lemon, slicing slowly and carefully.

"It's kind of related, actually. There was a reason I stopped by that night." He cleared his throat, and she pictured him looking at the counter again. "Though I never got around to it."

She squeezed lemon into the glasses, shooting one wedge across the counter to bounce off the wall and onto the floor. She closed her eyes, then opened them, picked up another wedge like that was just how you did it—one for the floor, one for the glass—poured the tea, and turned around, placing a glass in front of him.

She downed four big swallows of hers. For some reason her mouth was Sahara dry.

"I wanted to explain about Tricia," he said, looking back up at her, his eyes concerned. "But now I find it's even more awkward than usual. Because of . . . of what happened . . ."

"Brady, we've already sorted that out," she said, proud of herself for sounding firm. "Let's not give it another thought. *Really.*"

He took a deep breath, sent her a tentative smile, and said, "Okay, then. Here's the story with Tricia."

He proceeded to tell her about an indiscriminate past—though he glossed it over, she was sure it was a past filled with easy women, random liaisons, and generally unexamined indulgences—and how it finally caught up with him in the form of the mentally ill Tricia, a woman who had delusions about him, herself, and their relationship. Delusions to the point that her parents had actually committed her to an institution, albeit temporarily.

Throughout the story Lily began to feel strange. Though he implied that he'd been every bit as dissolute as she would have imagined, despite all his self-flagellation and embarrassment, or perhaps because of it, Lily began to see him in a new light. He was not squeaky clean and admirable—not ethically constant, as Gerald was—but he was someone who was aware of and struggled against his flaws. He was someone striving with all his might to do better, to do *good*. He was someone intent on not hurting anyone ever again.

Even though he'd screwed up pretty thoroughly with her the other night—just as she had with him, she reminded herself—he was obviously trying now to make it right. Though she didn't particularly like that his backsliding had involved *her*, she respected his resolve to become a better person, to not let the setback negate the whole plan.

And, as surprising as it seemed in the circumstances, she began to like him, very much.

Seven

"So now you know," Brady finished, exhaling. He rubbed his hands over his face and up through his hair. Then he rested his elbows on the counter and looked at her. "That's my history and that's why I've decided . . . well, this might sound ridiculous. I'm embarrassed to even say it, but the fact is I've decided that I can't—or I should say 'I don't want to,' my brother's always after me to *own* these things." He rolled his eyes. "That's why I don't want to get involved with anyone right now. No matter how attractive I find them." He shot her a conspiratorial smile. "It's kind of a . . . a date diet."

"A 'date diet'?" Lily's brows descended, and she

looked at him skeptically, unsure what to make of this finish. She'd been admiring his struggle, his desire to make things right, but this . . . this just didn't sound true. It sounded like an excuse you gave someone you didn't want to have to ask out just because you'd kissed them.

"I've made too many stupid decisions," he continued, "or nondecisions, based on nothing but knee-jerk physical reactions. And I can't do it anymore. I'm getting too old. I don't want to just play around."

"Okay." Lily nodded slowly. The last thing she would have pegged Brady for was a man in search of . . . psychological clarity. Although she'd seen Tricia, and she was pretty sure the woman was nuts. That might put the fear of God into someone who was not ordinarily afraid of anything.

She took a deep breath. "Well, that's good, Brady. Very mature."

Brady laughed. "I don't know about that. It's still about getting what I want. It's just that what I want has changed." He lifted his glass and drained it.

"So, what you want is . . . ?"

"Friendship. With a woman." He shrugged his eyebrows and gave a despairing little laugh. "A connection that isn't sexual."

Lily nodded, wondering how you undid a connection that was already sexual. It was something she was eager to do herself, however, so she supposed that boded well for the endeavor's success.

"Now you've heard my whole sordid story." He shook his head with a smile, his cheeks definitely pink. "So what do you say, Lily Tyler? Think we can be friends?"

"Friends? Sure," she said, but the words didn't exactly ring with conviction. She couldn't help thinking something was missing. This outgoing, charismatic guy wasn't the type to just swear off women altogether. Besides, you didn't *have* to swear off women altogether just to avoid jumping into bed with someone. That was absurd.

No, it had to be her. It had to be that he didn't want any involvement with her and was going out of his way to make sure she understood that.

The question was: Why did she care?

He held up both hands. "I promise I won't jump you again. Scout's honor." He crossed his heart, then held up three fingers and grinned, tilting his head. "As long as you promise not to answer the door in nothing but your bathrobe again."

She made herself smile. "It's a deal."

They looked at each other for a long moment, then both shifted their eyes away.

"So tell me about this guy you're seeing," Brady said, and cleared his throat. "Is it the one who was over the other night? That Jerry guy?" He leaned back in the stool and regarded her, his expression more relaxed now, his hazel eyes smiling.

He was relieved, she thought. Was that insulting,

or was this feeling she had something else? Something disturbing, like disappointment?

"Yes, Gerald. He's—he works with my father," she said, turning her mind to Gerald with some effort. It was hard with Brady right in front of her, suddenly seeming like a good guy. A good guy with no interest in her.

Oh brother, was she that fickle? Liking the boy who was in front of her, the one she couldn't have? She didn't want Brady, she wanted Gerald, she reminded herself. The man of her dreams. Her Mr. Knightley, for goodness' sake. Brady was simply the distracting Mr. Churchill, the self-avowed rogue.

She lifted her chin and assumed an expression of confidence. "Gerald is a brilliant lawyer. He even impressed my father, which is hard to do. I've had kind of a crush on him since the day I first met him, in my father's office."

"A crush, huh?" Brady's eyes narrowed. "That's hard to imagine. You don't seem like the crush type. How long has that been going on?"

She fingered her glass, running a fingernail along its sweaty exterior. "I guess I met him about two years ago. Two and a half."

"Wow, and it's taken him this long to ask you out?" Brady got up and headed for the refrigerator. He opened it and took out the pitcher of tea. "I mean, I know you're intimidating and all, but come on, buddy. Show some guts."

Lily cocked her head. "You think I'm intimidating?"

He chuckled. "You have your moments. At least with me."

She couldn't help a small smile. "I intimidate you?"

He shot her a sideways glance. "I'm going to plead the fifth on that." He took up his glass and poured himself more tea, then paused, looking at her sheepishly. "I'm sorry, is it okay if I help myself?"

Lily laughed. So he had some charm, she could resist that.

"It's fine," she said. "In fact I prefer it. That way I don't have to remember to be a good hostess."

"Hey, don't ever stand on ceremony with me."

As he stood there next to her at the counter, Lily couldn't help being aware of how big he was, in the same way she had the night of the kiss. Not big in the bulky sense, but in a masculine way. His presence took up more room than his body. She felt like she was being touched even when he stood three feet away.

At the same time there was something comforting about his nearness, as if he were some kind of predatory animal who was dangerous to everyone but her. To her, he was protective.

Okay, she thought. *Yes. I can be friends with him.*

She took up the pitcher of iced tea, poured herself another glass, and turned her thoughts inward.

She had to remember what she loved about *Gerald*, and how that had come to be. And she had to make herself tell Brady Cole all about it.

"Gerald caught my eye first of all because he's tall," she said, remembering back to that long-ago day she'd gone to have lunch with her father. That day when Gerald had stepped out of his office and captured her heart with his deep, dark, sensual eyes. Something about those eyes, framed with luscious black lashes, had drawn her in right away and had not let her go.

"He's six-foot-four," she continued. "Well, you saw him. And he dresses *impeccably*. And . . . there's this way he moves, with a kind of aristocratic grace. Maybe that's it, the aristocratic thing. It's like he's from a different era, in a way. He's unfailingly polite, courteous, a perfect gentleman. A *classic* gentleman."

"Huh," Brady said, sitting once again at the island. "Sounds like something of a throwback."

"Kind of," she said. "I have thought of him as a character from *Emma*, my favorite Jane Austen novel. From the early nineteenth century."

He nodded. "Yeah, I've heard of it."

"Really?"

He shrugged one shoulder. "I was nearly dragged to the movie by a date. You know how it is with guys and chick flicks."

She smiled and reached back to the counter behind her. *See?* she thought with some smugness.

He wasn't even literary. Gerald had actually *read the book*. She grabbed another slice of lemon and turned back toward Brady to squeeze it into her glass of tea. When she was done, Brady held out his hand and she gave it to him. He squeezed the rest into his glass.

"But what really captured my attention," she continued, "at least at first, was how respectfully he was treated by my father. *My father*, who treats friends, associates, even family, as if we're only there to serve the needs of whatever moment *he's* in, he actually asked Gerald's opinion. Then he made a point of introducing him to me. At which point Gerald makes this totally lame joke, and my father slaps him on the back like it's the cleverest thing he's ever heard and walks off, saying something about letting us 'young people' get to know each other better."

Lily shook her head in wonder.

"Well, I guess you'd have to know my father to know how strange that is," she added. "But it was as good as if he'd put his stamp of approval on Gerald's forehead and handed him over to me. What sold me on Gerald, though, was the fact that after his lame joke and my father's unwarranted laughter, he looked at me with this ironic, amused expression, and we both laughed. Like we were instant conspirators."

She smiled, remembering the feeling.

"Ever since that moment," she continued, "Gerald

has treated me like I was one of his very good friends. He always made a point of talking to me when I stopped by, he'd get off the phone if I strolled by his office, or break off a conversation with a colleague to show me some attention. And when he looked at me, as clichéd as it sounds, he made me feel as if I were the only woman in the world."

She was silent a moment, thinking about how special that had made her feel for so long.

"That's got to be a pretty good feeling," Brady said after a while.

She glanced at him. He was studying his glass of tea, spinning it in the condensation on the countertop.

She sighed. "Yes. It was that quality that kept me believing, despite the fact that he continuously turned down invitations from me for dinner or drinks, that he privately *was* interested in me, but was held back by some . . . external reason."

He lifted a brow and looked up at her without raising his head. "And was he?"

She laughed lightly. How *relieved* she'd been when Gerald had finally told her the truth!

"Yes. I found out because one day I gathered all my courage and asked him, point-blank, if I should stop asking him out." She paused, recalling the disastrously expensive *Phantom of the Opera* tickets she'd bought that precipitated this course of action. "And he told me he was waiting to make partner.

That he found me 'completely desirable and charming,'" she smiled wistfully, "but that he did not want to get ahead by dating the boss's daughter. Not only did he not want my father to get the idea he was using me, and not only did he not want his colleagues thinking he was taking advantage, but most of all—and he said this while giving me this intense look and taking my hands in his—that he didn't want *me* to get that idea. When he asked me out, he said, he wanted me to know that he was asking because he wanted to be with me and for no other reason."

Brady was silent a moment, nodding. Then he said, "So I guess he made partner."

Lily sighed and moved around the island to sit on the stool next to Brady. She turned it around so that it faced the rest of the room and leaned back, wondering if the whole world saw that discrepancy immediately except her. Though she hated to admit it, she had to consider that maybe Georgia was right—that Gerald hadn't tired of waiting for *her* so much as waiting to make partner. Because though Lily had chalked it up to romantic fervor at the time he'd asked her out, their dates had since proved so tepid in the fervor department that she now had to rethink it.

But she wasn't about to tell Brady any of that.

"No, he hasn't. Not yet," she said finally. "But he's right on the verge. I think he just got tired of waiting. Like I did."

She didn't dare look in Brady's direction, didn't want to see the skeptical look he was probably wearing.

"I can certainly understand that," he murmured.

Lily dropped her head, looking at the glass in her hands, and told herself to ignore the thrill the innuendo in his words produced in her. No doubt he didn't mean it the way it sounded, but for Lily it brought back the same sensation she'd felt that night he'd stopped by, the night of the kiss. That sensation of desire, of nearly irresistible attraction.

Was she crazy? She had to let that go, she told herself firmly. Now that she knew how completely Brady agreed with her that the kiss had been a mistake—despite its being the most passionate kiss Lily had ever experienced—she knew she had to make clear to both of them that she had no expectations of him except friendship.

"I'm sure that now, after so much time," she said, "Gerald figured out that my father wouldn't be influenced by whether we were dating or not."

Brady frowned and looked at the counter. "No, no you're probably right."

Lily glanced over at him. He was working hard not to say something, she could tell. The effort nearly made her laugh. Instead she said, "You don't really believe that, do you?"

He looked up at her, surprised. "What do you mean?"

At that, she did laugh. "I can tell by your face.

You think he got tired of waiting for the partnership and decided to use me after all." She shook her head at him. "You should never play poker, Brady."

He laughed with her. "Lily, come on. I don't even know the guy. And like you said, he's been working with your father for two years now. I'm sure he's realized that your dad knows what he's doing."

"He certainly does." She turned in her seat and knocked the side of one fist sternly on the counter. "And believe me when I say my father has *never* been one to be influenced by his family in any way. Not even about something as simple as coming home for dinner at night. So I don't think he'll be handing out any partnerships based on who's dating *me.*"

"Why, Lily," Brady said, a teasing glint in his eye. "Do we have some 'issues' with our father? Should I get my brother on the phone?"

She laughed. "It must be awful having a psychologist for a brother."

"Oh he's not a real one. He just plays one on TV." He shook his head ruefully. "Which is a joke, but not all that far from the truth. He writes a sitcom about a shrink."

"He does? That's fascinating," she said. "Which one? Would I have seen it?"

"I don't know." He pushed one hand through his hair and shrugged. "Some cable show. Called *Sex at Midnight* or something like that."

Lily raised her eyebrows. She'd heard of that

show, but she got the feeling Brady didn't want to talk about his brother's success.

"What about your parents? Where are they?" she asked.

Brady hesitated. "Well my dad . . ." He laughed curtly and held his hands palm up. "Who knows? I never met him. And my mom's in a nursing home in New Jersey."

"I'm sorry," Lily murmured, amazed at the transformation in his face. From teasing and laughing one minute, to closed up and sober the next. He really *shouldn't* ever play poker.

He glanced at the clock on the wall. "Holy cow, is that clock right?"

She looked up at it, too. "Yes. Why? Are you late for something?"

"Yep." He placed both hands on the counter and pushed his chair back. "It was great talking to you, Lily," he said, smiling again. "Thanks for understanding about . . . everything."

She smiled back. "Sure. Thank you, too."

"So . . ." He held out a hand to her. "Friends?"

She nodded once and took his hand. Her breath caught in her chest as he gently squeezed, his palm enveloping hers.

"Friends," she said.

He didn't let go immediately, instead looking into her eyes an extended moment, a half smile on his face. She'd never noticed before how like warm, glowing embers hazel eyes could be.

"Friends," he said again, in the voice that sent trills up her spine. "I think I'm going to like this."

He headed back out the hallway to the front door but paused by the hall table. Picking up the pillowcase, he said, "Is this mine?"

Lily, who'd followed him, felt herself color at the sight of it, as if he could read the thoughts she'd had about him when she'd held it earlier.

"Yes, Megan gave it back to me. I wish I'd seen you get Doug into that."

He chuckled. "It was a trick, all right." He wadded the fabric up in one hand and opened the door with the other. "See you later, Lily."

"Yes, see you around."

Lily kept her eyes on the material in his hand as he walked out the door and wished for no good reason she could think of that she'd put the pillowcase someplace else before he'd arrived.

"Hi, Brady, come on in," Megan said.

He'd arrived at the Foley house to ride to the airport with Sutter, his bike seat being out of commission. Foley had offered to send the car for him but Brady didn't want the limo to pull up in front of his house and make Lily feel worse than she already did about Doug's destruction. Around Brady's calves a yellow mutt sniffed and wagged happily, looking up as Brady reached down to ruffle its ears.

Megan Rose was the kind of woman Brady

considered low-maintenance. Ironic, considering her boyfriend, his boss, was a man who could afford the highest-maintenance woman ever born. Pretty in a vivacious way, Megan also had a way of looking at you that made you think she was figuring out exactly who you were. There was no falseness in her, and no tolerance of falseness in others.

"Hello, Megan," he said, entering the foyer of the house on Washington Avenue. He'd made the mistake of calling her Mrs. Foley the first time they'd met, only to be corrected by a peal of laughter. Seemed his boss was living in sin with this free-spirited woman. "Thanks again for yesterday. You saved me; I was afraid I'd killed that damn dog."

Megan laughed. "Nobody would have held you accountable for that, Brady. That would have been death by sheer vindictiveness. Doug has a little problem with men, you know."

"So I've learned."

"Come on in," she said, leading him through the house to the huge kitchen at the back. "I'm just feeding Belle. And Sutter ought to be ready in a few minutes. Can I get you a cup of coffee while you wait?"

Brady said sure, and sauntered over to where Belle, Sutter and Megan's one-year-old daughter, sat fingering a flotilla of Cheerios on the tray in front of her high chair. When she saw him, she smiled and held one out.

Brady took it and pretended to eat it.

"Belle," he said to Megan, "that's a good South-ern name." He took another Cheerio from the child and made a show of pretending to eat that one, too.

"It seemed appropriate, since she was some-thing of a wake-up call for both Sutter and me. So how's Doug doing?" she asked.

Brady looked up to find Megan smiling at the two of them. "Lily said he's doing fine. She was remarkably calm about it, too. I thought she'd be hysterical. I know she's pretty attached to him."

Megan set a cup of coffee down on the table in front of him, and Brady sat. "Yes, we dog people can be a little nuts about our animals. Ask Sutter; he learned that the hard way."

She looked affectionately at her older dog, a tri-colored bear of a dog, lying flat on the cool tile of the kitchen floor. Brady's entrance elicited little more than a wave or two of that dog's tail.

"I've never had a pet," Brady said, sipping the coffee.

"Never?" Megan repeated, eyes wide. "Not even a fish?"

He shook his head, laughing.

"No gerbil? Hamster? *Nothing?*" she persisted.

"Not even a lightning bug in a jar," he said. "We moved around a lot when I was a kid. My mom, she's got a dog now. Or she did, before she went in the nursing home. My brother's got it now, thank

God. It's a pain in the ass. Some kind of yappy little thing."

"I can't believe you've never had a pet," Megan said. "That just scandalizes me." She opened a jar of baby food and sat down opposite Brady and next to her daughter. "There's nothing like having a pet, something that loves you no matter what and is always happy to see you."

"I count on my employer's kids for that," he said, making an exaggerated happy-face at Belle and receiving a wide smile in return. He laughed.

"My friend Penelope," Megan said, "has a Labrador retriever who she calls her fur husband. She says if he had thumbs, he would make her dinner."

"Yeah, but what would they have?" Brady asked, sliding a Cheerio toward Belle, then moving it quickly back when she went for it. This earned him a more tentative smile, so he let her catch it the next time.

Megan laughed. "Good point. But it just illustrates how tough it is to be single in Fredericksburg when a girl as pretty and successful as Pen has to settle for a dog, even as great as Wimbledon is. Did anybody warn you about the dating scene here before you took this job?"

He shot her an ironic look. "The subject didn't come up. But that doesn't matter to me. I'm not dating right now anyway."

"Really. That's an interesting comment." Megan

spooned something orange from the jar into Belle's mouth. Belle's eyes never left Brady. "Because Lily and I were talking just yesterday about how perfect Penelope might be for you."

This caught Brady's attention, and his eyes shifted to hers. "You were, huh?"

"Yes. She's beautiful—I mean, really beautiful. And she's smart and nice, and she owns her own business here in town. I just know you'd like her."

Brady sat back, much to Belle's disappointment, and looked at Megan. "And Lily thought this was a good idea, too, did she?"

"Absolutely." Megan nodded. "We were a couple of witches on the subject, plotting over our cauldron." She grinned at him.

Brady took up his coffee cup and sipped. Lily was matching him up with someone else. Why did this surprise him?

Because he'd felt something else from her. Not just during the kiss—the kiss she had *obviously* wanted to turn into more; there was no denying that, though he wasn't going to press her on the issue—but even during their talk yesterday. He'd gotten the distinct impression she was telling him all that stuff about Gerald to convince herself as much as him that she wasn't interested in Brady.

Could he have misread her so completely? He'd felt so sure . . . and it had given him hope that if he could be friends with her first, be smart about this attraction, that maybe something better could develop between them.

Apparently he'd deluded himself. Now that he thought about it, it seemed obvious that a woman like her wouldn't be interested in a guy like him. At least, not beyond the physical. She was a brain, an intellectual. A college professor, for God's sake, when Brady had never even been to college. She likened her dates to literary characters. Brady was about as far from a literary character as he could get. Comic book character, maybe. Flyboy. Adventure boy. Noncommittal boy.

"So I guess you and Lily haven't suffered too much from the tough single life in Fredericksburg. You've got Sutter, and she has that guy Gerald." He took another sip of coffee and watched her.

Megan tilted her head, considering. "I've never met Gerald, actually. I've only just heard about him." She gave him a sly look. "It's a little hard to believe he's quite the paragon she describes, but I'll keep an open mind. At least until I meet him."

"Yeah, I had the same thought. I mean, what's wrong with the guy that it took him two years to ask her out?"

Megan looked surprised. "She told you that?"

"Yeah. We had a real good chat yesterday, after she got back from getting Doug. She told me all about Gerald."

Megan sighed. "Well, that's Lily for you. Always

ready to champion her man. I hope he knows how lucky he is."

Brady's eyes narrowed. "Something tells me he doesn't."

Megan glanced at him. "Really? Why not? Did she say something?"

"It was nothing she said." He shook his head. "It was the facts. He works for her dad, he wasn't going to ask her out until he made partner, but then he goes and does it anyway. Even though he'd already waited two years. I mean, what's up with that?" He lifted his coffee cup again.

"Maybe he got horny?" She sent him an impish grin.

Brady nearly spewed his coffee, swallowed hard, then burst out laughing. "My goodness, Dr. Rose. Now I'm scandalized."

"Oh sure. I bet you thought the exact same thing." Then she shrugged, and said, "But to tell the truth, I'm not so sure that was it." She spooned more orange stuff into Belle's mouth.

Brady leaned his elbows on the table. Belle reached a sticky hand out toward the four captain's stripes on his shirt.

"No, no, Belle." Megan guided the little hand back toward the Cheerios. "We can't have Captain Cole going out dressed in mashed sweet potatoes."

Brady picked up another Cheerio and handed it to Belle. "Not that it's any of my business, but if it wasn't . . . ah . . . let's call it 'desire' that made Gerald ask her out, what do you think it was?"

Megan looked at him with interest, and he knew he was close to tipping his hand. "What a gossip you are, Brady Cole." She laughed. "As am I, apparently." She gently scraped sweet potatoes off Belle's chin with the tiny spoon. "I just happen to know that he hasn't been acting like desire was his primary motivator. And that's all I'll say on the subject."

"Are you spilling state secrets?" Sutter asked, entering the room with long strides and flipping one end of his unknotted tie over the other. He bent to kiss the top of Belle's head, then Megan's, and continued tying the tie.

Megan looked up at him and laughed. "Yes, but not yours, don't worry."

"Good," Sutter said.

Brady felt a pang of something like regret that he'd never been in a relationship where a woman looked at him like that. Then he threw back the rest of his coffee like a shot of whiskey and stood, chiding himself for going soft. It just went to show, when you castrated yourself you turned into a girl.

Sutter reached out a hand and shook Brady's. "Morning, Brady. You ready to go?"

"Whenever you are, sir," he said.

"We'll be back tomorrow afternoon, Megan," Sutter said. "You want anything from Zabar's this time?"

"Oh yes!" She got up and, winking at Brady, plucked a piece of paper off a pad to hand to Sutter. "I made a list."

"Shopping," Sutter muttered to Brady, but the smile he wore—not to mention the solid kiss he gave his girl—told Brady he didn't mind at all.

They headed for the door.

"Oh, and Brady?" Megan asked. "You are coming to our party on the fourteenth, right?"

"You bet," Brady said, with a businesslike nod.

"Great." Megan beamed. "Penelope will be here, too."

"Ah-ha," Sutter said, with a laugh. "I see it really is time to go."

Brady turned with him to the door and sent Megan a noncommittal smile, thinking there was little doubt that Lily, also, would be at the party.

Eight

 "Megan was telling me about your pilot," Penelope said, one hand stroking the silky black head of her dog, Wimbledon.

Lily had the feeling she'd been building up to the subject for several minutes now. Circling around the subject of neighbors, men, dates.

"She said the two of you thought we'd be good together," Penelope continued. "I told her you'd already said he wasn't right for me, but she thought you'd changed your mind about that . . ."

The question was there, in her tone, and Lily couldn't ignore it. She picked up a twig and tossed it for Doug, who chased it, pounced, then stood over its motionless form, looking disappointed.

Lily and Penelope sat on the picnic table at the dog park. It was a warm day, so the dogs were a bit listless, and only one other person with her dog was there, all the way on the other side of the enclosure.

If she had any guts, Lily knew now would be the time to tell Penelope about kissing Brady. Neither Georgia nor Megan was at the park with them, and Penelope was not yet emotionally invested in Brady.

The problem was it would require so much explaining, and so much humiliation. Why would Lily be kissing Brady if Gerald was as important to her as she'd been claiming for so long? Besides, they had just been talking about Gerald, and Lily had waxed rhapsodic about the fact that he was taking her to dinner at Augustine's tonight, the most fancy, romantic restaurant in Fredericksburg, in Lily's opinion. To say now, *oh by the way, I made out with the pilot the other day* would render suspect everything she said about Gerald.

"Well, I've gotten to know him a little better," Lily said, though that was something of an understatement. "And I think, you know, after all, he's actually a nice guy." Maybe if she kept talking, she'd get around to spilling the beans. "Which is surprising, after that whole Tricia scene. But he made a point of explaining about that, and it really wasn't his fault, and ultimately he just seemed . . . nice."

"That's what Megan said!" Penelope turned a bright face to her. "She said she gets a really good feeling about him, and you know how intuitive Megan can be. And she said he's *so* handsome. Do you think he's handsome?"

"Well, sure," Lily said, envisioning Brady's eyes, that warm, intimate look he gave her sometimes. Did he look at all women that way? So that heat stole up their skin and caused flutterings inside their breasts? How could she feel this way about somebody whom Penelope might date?

Then again, how could Lily burst this balloon for her friend? Poor Pen had had so little reason to be excited lately, and she needed this so badly, what with her ex-husband getting remarried and having a baby.

"She even said she mentioned it to *him*," Penelope added. "That we might be good together."

Lily sat up straight on the bench. "She did? She said that? To Brady? What did he say? I mean, was he, uh, open to the idea?"

Penelope beamed. "Yes! She said she thought he was, even though he gave all that guy bluster they always spout about being set up. But she said she told him about me and . . . he seemed interested." She lifted one shoulder, trying to appear casual.

Lily shifted her gaze away from Penelope's, afraid her friend would see the odd turmoil suddenly roiling inside of her. "He did, huh?"

So much for all that *crap* about a date diet. *I don't want to get involved right now . . . I'm too old to make snap decisions . . . I'm tired of playing around.*

What a *crock*!

"She asked him if he was coming to her party, and he said yes," Penelope went on. "And she said 'Good, because Penelope will be there, too,' and she said he smiled!" Penelope laughed. "Oh God, am I pathetic or what? I've never even met this guy, and I'm excited because he smiled. This is sick. I need to move."

Despite herself, Lily laughed. "Would you quit saying that? You can't move and leave me here alone. Even if Brady doesn't work out, there are other guys in this town. We just have to find them."

"*You* don't have to find anyone. You've got Gerald. Do you think he has something special planned for tonight, going to that fancy restaurant and all?" Penelope gasped. "Oh! Maybe *tonight's the night*! Maybe he's planning to, you know, make his move."

Lily's heart gave a little leap at the idea. Thank God. That had to be a good sign. If she could feel excited about Gerald "making his move," then the Brady thing really was just an accident, something that happened because she was in a weird state of mind that night, and he just happened to be next door. Except she'd felt it again, that strong attraction, at her house when they were talking. She suddenly realized that must be what people meant when they talked about "animal magnetism."

Too bad Gerald lived so far away. No doubt proximity had a lot to do with it.

"I don't know," Lily said. "But it does seem interesting that he's made a reservation at Augustine's of all places. I've never even mentioned it to him. I don't know how he found out about it."

"Ah, he did a little research," Penelope said. "Another good sign. So what are you wearing?"

A breeze rustled the trees around them, and Lily pushed the hair up off the back of her neck. Summer was definitely coming. Though it was only May, it was already hot.

"I thought I'd wear that blue dress I have. The one I wore to Susan McNally's wedding last summer."

"Oh no!" Penelope protested, shaking her head. Then she tipped it to one side. "I mean, that's a pretty dress. And you look gorgeous in it. But you want something sexy for tonight, Lil. You want to give him the signal the moment he sees you that you're on his wavelength. That *tonight's the night.*"

The thought of it made her stomach flip. Was she ready to try to seduce Gerald? And if she wasn't, after two years, what did that say? Maybe they'd waited too long, that's why she was so nervous about it. They should have just leapt on each other the moment they met, like she and Brady had.

"Oh God. I don't know if I'm ready for this. I

suddenly feel so unprepared." Lily dropped her hair, put her face in one hand, and rocked forward. Maybe she should wear her bathrobe; it had worked for Brady.

She really needed to tell Penelope about the kiss, she thought. Now, in this conversation, before things got any more awkward. If she told her later, Penelope would always wonder why she hadn't said anything in this conversation.

But really, the devil on her shoulder counseled, did anything *really* have to be said? It wasn't as if she and Brady were *involved*. Not now. It was just their little secret, hers and Brady's. A momentary lapse. He wasn't going to tell, and neither was she. So maybe it was just as well to let it lie.

For one thing, she'd bet her bottom dollar that if she told Penelope about it, Pen would back off and ruin a good shot at a nice guy.

Because of course Brady would be interested in Penelope. Why wouldn't he be? She was beautiful, and smart, and available.

"Lily? Hello? Are you still with me?"

Lily sat up and pushed her hair back off her face. She glanced apologetically at her friend. "What? I'm sorry. I just got to thinking. About tonight, what to wear. What did you say?"

"I said"—Penelope laughed—"that you *are* prepared. I've never seen anyone *more* prepared. You've been waiting for this moment forever, Lil. When it happens, it's going to be wonderful. Trust me."

"I hope so," she said, thinking *It had better be.* If it weren't, how in the world would she stop thinking about Brady?

"But you should wear that little red dress," Penelope continued, "the one you had on at Georgia's barbecue last year. That was adorable. And make sure you lower those spaghetti straps! That dress was made to show cleavage, which you have got, girl!"

Lily laughed nervously. She couldn't imagine Gerald being interested in cleavage. She couldn't even imagine him naked, now that she thought about it. He was Mr. Knightley. He dressed impeccably and was the perfect gentleman. What in the world would Gerald be like, naked? It seemed too . . . improper.

"Maybe you're right. Maybe I need to rethink things," Lily said, feeling trepidation hit her like a Mack truck.

She couldn't picture her boyfriend naked. What in God's name did *that* mean? It meant she had better see him naked soon, or he was going to take on the form of a neutered Ken doll in her imagination, and that wouldn't do either of them any good.

She stood. "I better go, Pen. I've got to shower and change and feed Doug." She looked at her friend. "Thanks for listening to me go on about this."

"What, are you kidding? I can't wait to hear

what happens! This is a love story I've been following for a long time." Penelope smiled, reached out, and squeezed Lily's hand. "I just know it's going to be wonderful."

Lily smiled past her guilt. Penelope wouldn't have held back on her. She was as open as a child, wearing her emotions on her sleeve and wanting the best for everyone around her. She would have told Lily if the situation had been reversed.

But then, Penelope really *did* deserve to meet this guy, unencumbered by Lily's mistake. She never needed to know. Why spoil it for her?

"Are you all right?" Penelope asked.

Lily shook herself. "I'm fine. Sorry. Just . . . I've got myself all wound up about tonight. Listen, I'll call you in the morning. Have a good night, Pen."

She rounded up Doug and went home, feeling like the worst kind of friend. It was just so hard to know what to do. Part of her thought telling was the right thing to do and keeping it secret a cowardly pretense. The other part thought keeping quiet was right and telling just a selfish unburdening that would ruin Penelope's chance at possible happiness.

It was impossible to tell which was correct.

Once home, Lily went upstairs to pull out the red dress. Looking at it, she wondered if even it was seductive enough to jolt Gerald out of his sexual malaise. It looked a little too pert, too flirty.

She needed something with serious sex appeal. Something that said *Take me, you fool, I'm a mature woman with needs.*

She thought again about the bathrobe, and felt her insides rise to her throat as she remembered the bone-melting feeling of being kissed by Brady. What would have happened if he hadn't stopped it? If they had gone upstairs to her bed, as she had wanted to, and consummated the act? Would she still have gotten that speech about the date diet?

She closed her eyes and sat on the side of the bed. Probably. And it would have been that much harder to hear, knowing that she'd kicked up her heels like a ten-cent floozy and taken him, a virtual stranger, into her bed, only to be rejected later.

No, she had to concentrate on Gerald. He was the one she wanted. He was the one she pictured at the altar—gorgeous in his tux—at Christmas dinners with her father, holding out his hands for their toddler to walk into. She could even picture their family photo, sitting on her father's polished mahogany desk at work. It was too perfect. She couldn't give up now, not because she'd gotten stupid with some hotshot pilot who happened to live next door.

She tried to insert Brady into the mental picture frame on her father's desk, but she couldn't. For one thing, she couldn't get him out of that stupid bomber jacket, so he clashed with her classic suit and the kids' dressy clothes. No, a man like Brady would never make it onto that mahogany surface.

Not that it was all about how he *looked*, of course. She wasn't being shallow about it, just realistic. He was not the right type for her. And the picture frame merely encapsulated the fact that she couldn't imagine even one conversation her father could have with the likes of Brady Cole.

Lily stood and undressed, then pulled the slippery red dress over her head. She turned to the mirror. She'd forgotten how slinky the material was, how it clung to her breasts and hips, making her look slim and curvy all at the same time.

She raised her hands to one of the spaghetti straps and let it down. Then she did the other. Cleavage abounded, and she blushed. Gerald would think she was loose. He wasn't the type of guy to be drawn in by revealing clothes, was he? She dropped her hands. She couldn't shake the feeling he'd like the blue dress better, the conservative wedding-guest one.

Still, this was a special occasion. And she'd be damned if she'd settle for that little peck again tonight. She left the straps long and turned away from the mirror.

Once she'd applied her makeup and done her hair, she went downstairs to the kitchen. She was wound up. Alternately nervous and full of dread, excited and apprehensive about what the evening held in store. She decided to pour herself a glass of wine and sit on the front porch. The weather had turned unseasonably warm, but she had yet to turn on the air-conditioning. The front porch would be the best place to wait for Gerald's arrival.

Sure enough, the porch was cool, and a nice breeze stirred the leaves on the trees in the front yard. Lily sat on her porch swing and sipped her wine, concentrating on the fact that she was here waiting for a date with Gerald Lawson, the man she'd pegged as her future husband the first time she'd seen him. And nothing in all that time— nothing for *two years*—had shaken that conviction except for that one stupid kiss. She was giving it way too much importance.

About halfway through the glass of pinot grigio, Brady's door opened and out he stepped, clad in blue running shorts and a white tee shirt. Before she could stop herself, Lily's eyes scanned his body, taking in his muscular legs, his tight behind, and his obviously toned torso in the light tee shirt. Her mouth went dry.

Brady stood on his front stoop, his eyes on the ground, looking for something. He held one shoe in his hand and his eyes seemed to be scanning the floor for the other one. He moved to the railing, gazed into the front garden, then around to the side. Then he cursed and headed back inside.

A few moments later he returned, wearing an iPod around his arm and different shoes on his feet. With one hand on a porch column he proceeded to stretch his leg muscles, first by bending one knee and grabbing the ankle with his hand, then the other, then leaning on the railing and pressing his heels back. All the while he looked out into the street, oblivious to her presence, listening to something through the earpieces.

He and Pen would look good together, Lily thought. He had a strong profile, upright carriage, and a confident way of moving that would complement Penelope's supple grace. Penelope was athletic, too, both a runner and an excellent tennis player.

Lily frowned, staring at Brady's thigh muscles. Those thighs had almost been under her sheets. If she'd had her way that night, she would know them intimately now, right down to how the skin felt on her palm and the weight of the legs across hers.

It took Lily a minute to realize those thighs were facing her. When her gaze rose up over his shorts and tee shirt to Brady's face, she found him looking at her with a smile quirking his mouth.

He pulled the earpieces from his ears.

"How long have you been looking at me?" she asked, blushing.

"Just a second. Why?" His smiled turned to a grin. "How long have you been looking at me?"

She shook her head. "I wasn't really looking. I was thinking. Just sitting here."

He stepped easily over the railing that separated the two porches. "You been out here long?"

"Oh, a little while." She took another sip of her wine and hoped the bulb of the glass hid her pink cheeks. She'd been caught gawking, and he didn't even attempt to hide the fact that he knew it, and liked it.

"You look—nice," he said, propping himself on the railing and tilting his head. His eyes strayed down to her cleavage and hung there long enough for Lily to feel like squirming.

She scoffed. "Just nice?"

He drew his eyes back up to hers, their expression serious. "Well, yeah. What were you hoping for? Bad? Sloppy? Ugly?" He shook his head and smiled. "Sorry, doll."

She laughed.

"I was going for sexy," she admitted, for no reason she could fathom.

Except . . . maybe Brady could help her with this. Maybe he was the perfect person to tell her how to seduce Gerald. After all, they were supposed to be friends now. She should ask him, and see how he liked being "friends" like that.

He crossed his arms over his chest. "You're always sexy," he said, eyes crinkled amiably.

"Yeah, right." She took a deep breath. "Gerald's taking me to Augustine's tonight. It's a very romantic restaurant. And my friend, *Penelope*," she said pointedly, "suggested I wear this dress."

He didn't move but continued to regard her with friendly, contemplative eyes. If she'd been hoping for a reaction, it appeared she wasn't going to get one.

"Good call," he said finally. "It's a great dress."

They looked at each other a long moment before he stood up and moved toward her. Lily tensed.

"But if you really want to look sexy," he said, standing before her. He held out a hand, flipping his fingers up and down a few times. "Come on, stand up."

She frowned up at him. When he didn't relent, she put her hand in his and let him pull her to her feet.

"Then you need to do this." His hands on her upper arms, he turned her around so her back was to him.

She repressed a shiver, then jumped as she felt one of his hands at her shoulder, taking hold of a spaghetti strap.

"May I?" he asked, his voice so close to her ear she felt the hairs on the back of her neck stand up.

"I—I don't know," she said. "What are you doing?"

"You'll see." He tightened first one strap, then the other, then put his hands on her shoulders and turned her back around to face him. He let his eyes graze her—chest to knees—then adjusted one of the straps a little higher. The dress had moved up a crucial inch, concealing that cleavage Penelope had talked about.

Lily placed a hand to her chest. "Did I look like a hooker?"

"Not at all." He took a step back, his smile smug. "But *now* you look sexy. It's always best to make the guy's imagination do some work."

She raised a brow in his direction. "I thought you said I always looked sexy."

"Sex*ier*," he amended, grinning.

Dimly, Lily became aware of a car pulling into her driveway. She tore her gaze away from Brady's and felt startled at the sight of Gerald's black Jaguar, pulling up behind her old Mercedes in the driveway.

"Damn, it's a regular European auto club here," Brady said. "I'm surprised you don't both have the same taste in nationality, though."

Lily shot him a glance. "I didn't pick mine out. It was a hand-me-down from my father."

"Ah, that explains it." He smiled.

For a second she was completely confused. To have all these scintillated feelings for someone other than Gerald was so foreign to her, after two years of concentration on that target, that she had what felt like an out-of-body experience, watching Gerald pull up while she stood next to Brady on her porch—*their* porch.

Which was the real man? Why was she going

somewhere with Gerald when Brady was right here? And why was she here with Brady when Gerald was coming to get her?

"The man of the hour," Brady said, as Gerald got out of the car. "Don't let that dress make you do anything I wouldn't do."

She cut her eyes toward him. "And just what would that be?"

His mouth curved, but his eyes weren't in it this time. "I think I laid that out the other night."

"Uh-huh," she said skeptically. "Which night would that be?"

Brady laughed. "Touché!"

But before she could add something about how she wasn't only talking about the night he kissed her or the night he put her off, but the time he talked to Megan about Penelope, Gerald was coming up the walk.

"Good evening," Gerald said, flashing a brilliant white smile at her, then turning to Brady. "Hello. Brady, isn't it?"

"Yes, sir," Brady said, reaching out to shake hands, just as Gerald's foot hit the first step. "Good to see you again."

The two of them stood within two feet of each other—Gerald tall and elegant; Brady athletic and vibrant. She felt like she was looking at the all-male version of yin and yang. Gerald comprised all that had been civilized, Brady was all instinct and testosterone.

"Nice to see you, too," Gerald said. "Off for a run, I see. Or are you just back?"

"I'm a little sweatier than this when I finish." Brady laughed. "I'm just heading out now. You kids have fun."

With that, he took the stoop in a single bound and ran off down the street.

Lily couldn't help it, her eyes followed him.

"You look wonderful," Gerald said.

She refocused on her date. He looked wonderful, too, as usual. And he was every bit as handsome as ever.

He bent to kiss her cheek.

"Thank you," she said. "I'm really looking forward to tonight. This is one of my favorite restaurants in town."

"I know." He grinned, one dimple creasing his right cheek. "Your father told me."

"My father!" She looked at him, mouth agape.

"Yes, he said this is where he took you." He reached out and took her hand. She couldn't help comparing his long, soft palms to Brady's hard square ones. "And I thought, if it's good enough for Jordan Tyler to take his daughter, it's good enough for me."

"I can't believe he even remembered," Lily said. "That was about three years ago. He doesn't get down here very often."

Gerald winked at her. "Maybe we can get him down here again before too long."

Lily's insides jittered at his easy use of the word "we," not to mention the implication that there might be a special *reason* to dine with her father. Her mind spun with the possibilities.

"That would be lovely," she murmured.

He gave her a short bow, dark eyes shining. "Are you ready to go?"

She couldn't help an answering smile. Something was definitely up with him. He seemed more relaxed than she'd known him to be on a date. Butterflies awakened in her stomach.

She looked around the porch, decided she could leave her wineglass on the table, and picked up her purse. "Ready." She smiled. And she was. Penelope could have Brady.

They were seated at the most secluded table in the restaurant, the one in the corner with the fish tank on the wall and the giant fern screening them from the rest of the room. Lily slid onto her seat feeling as if the night was about to burst with the fulfillment of all her dreams.

They chatted easily over the menus, decided on courses that complemented each other—hers fish, his prime rib—then Gerald chose a bottle of wine.

"Darling," he said after the wine steward had poured and left. He leaned across the table and took one of her hands in his.

Lily would never have believed she could hear

someone call her *darling* and keep a straight face, but when Gerald did it sounded right. More than that, it made her feel warm all over, as if the word brought out the sun, and she had only to bask in it.

"I have some news." A smile played about his lips, and Lily thought, *This is it. He's made partner.*

"Your father," he continued, "has entrusted me with a tremendous project, one that will assure my future with the firm in no uncertain manner. It is an opportunity for an origination, by that I mean a chance to make some money for the firm, that is far too good to pass up, so I've told him I will take this project on. But I wanted to talk with you about it first."

Lily ignored the fact that he said he'd already taken on the project, despite wanting to talk to her about it first. Clearly this was the partnership! And he wanted her to know that this meant their future was *now*.

It all made sense. *Of course*, that was why he'd been holding her at arm's length. He'd still been waiting on the partnership. How could she be so dense? He'd known it was close, so he'd asked her out, but he hadn't gotten it yet, so he'd kept their relationship nonsexual.

He'd been protecting her! He wasn't impotent. Just wait until she told Georgia.

"This sounds very exciting." Lily leaned toward him, her eyes intent on his. She squeezed his fingers, felt his squeeze back. "I know my father thinks the world of you. It doesn't surprise me at all that he'd entrust you with something big."

"This is big, all right." He chuckled low.

She imagined herself reaching out to stroke his face, hold his cheek in her hand. *Congratulations, darling*. She'd love to be the type of woman who could say that.

"However," he said, his visage going mock-stern, "it's going to take a little sacrifice on both of our parts, I'm afraid."

Hell, I'm used to that. That's the kind of thing she was the type of woman to say. Though she didn't.

"You see," he said, "the project is in Hawaii. I'll be gone about six, maybe eight weeks. Just until the end of the summer. But darling, after that we'll have everything we wanted, everything we've planned on. I'll be able to court you properly then. And I'll be on the track I've been working toward my entire career. Your father as much as promised me that. Lily, are you as excited as I am about this?"

"Hawaii?" she repeated, the word stuck in her head like a clog in a drain. "*Hawaii?*" she repeated. "As in *the middle of the Pacific?*"

He chuckled but looked worried. "That's the one. Maybe, if things are going well, you could come out for a weekend. It's a beautiful place, you should see it. I wouldn't have much time to show you around—this project is going to be very intense—but you could stay in the same hotel, and we could have dinner together."

"So . . . you haven't made partner?" she said, still stuck on her own expectations. His big news had been that he was *leaving town*? This whole fancy dinner had been about abandonment, not attachment?

He sat back, his expression clouding. "Not yet. But don't you see? This project will guarantee it. If I come through on this, your father as much as promised me the partnership when I return."

"In six, maybe eight weeks," Lily said, repeating, "*Weeks.*"

And in the meantime, she'd be living next door to Mr. Testosterone.

"That's right." He nodded. "Don't you think that's wonderful news? We've been patient this long, Lily. Surely we can be patient a little longer, don't you think?"

Lily pressed her lips together and looked at her plate. "Forgive me, Gerald, but it seems to me that being patient has been a lot easier for you than it has been for me."

"What on earth do you mean?" he asked, sliding his hand out from hers and leaning back.

"I mean," she said, fixing him with a hard look, "that you don't seem . . . *frustrated*, at all. While I've felt . . . *frustrated*!" She threw a hand up in the air, disgusted with her inability to communicate. *Hawaii? Six, maybe eight weeks?* She couldn't get the words out of her head. They circled like vultures, feeding on any other thought. And he'd looked so pleased as he'd said them.

He leaned toward her then, and took her hand again, squeezing hard. "I don't pretend not to know what you mean, Lily," he said, his voice low and intense. "Trust me, I feel the same way. Maybe you don't see it—I didn't want to act precipitously and scare you off—but believe me, those feelings are there. I just don't want to do anything we might later regret."

She leaned toward him then, too, so that their faces were mere inches apart, their voices hushed. "But what would we regret? Gerald, if we both want the same thing, I don't understand all the waiting. Especially now, with you going away. Is there something you're not telling me?"

Gerald's dark eyes seemed to swallow her whole. His chiseled face was so sober, she wished for a second she hadn't asked the question.

"Yes, in fact there is." Gerald's hand held hers so tightly now it was nearly painful. "Lily, my feelings for you are . . . of the most cherished variety. I don't think I speak out of turn when I say that I believe you and I are on what I'd call a marriage track, as surely as I'm on the partner track at Tyler, Andersen and Jones. But I don't want to make any mistakes. Count my chickens before they've hatched, as it were. So I'm taking things one step at a time, as best I know how. Can you help me do that, Lily? Can you help me assure our future together?"

Nine

Lily walked up to her front porch in a daze, Gerald at her side. He held one elbow gently, guiding her as if she might fall over at any moment. And truth be told, she thought she might.

When had everything gone so wrong? How had it all gotten so messed up? Was it Brady, was that why she was so thrown by this? It was just six, maybe eight weeks. She could wait that long. Heck, she'd waited ten times that long already.

It was just . . . Brady hadn't been right next door all that time.

And why was she so disturbed by Gerald's delivery of the news? After all, he'd spoken of marriage! Why wasn't she *thrilled* with that? The way he'd put it: that they were on the marriage track, that he was working for everything they'd planned on . . . that he needed her help to assure their future. Did that mean they were kind of . . . *engaged* now?

On the plus side, Gerald had agreed to go to Megan's party with her next weekend, as he wasn't leaving until that following Monday. So at least her friends would have a chance to meet him.

But still she felt . . . confused. Afraid and discontent and somehow worried that she was suddenly committed to something she hadn't bargained for, in a way she'd never imagined.

They stopped at her front door and Gerald turned her toward him.

"Darling, I'm so sorry if I've upset you." His eyes were kind as he looked down at her. "I thought my news was good, but I see now that you feel it contained some bad as well."

"No, no," she protested, looking away. "I'm just surprised, that's all."

"I understand. But I know this is the best thing for both of us," he said. "You're going to have to trust me on this, darling."

How had that endearment gone from charming to chafing in one short evening? Lily would bet it wasn't even ten o'clock yet.

"Gerald," she said, "I do trust you. But I have

to admit I am a little disappointed. I mean, you wouldn't want me to be glad you were going away for six weeks, would you?"

"Maybe eight," he said, with a tilt of his head. "And of course you're right. I'm glad you're going to miss me. As I will miss you." He ran his hands up and down her arms. He didn't seem to be imagining her cleavage, covered or not.

"I didn't say I was going to miss you," she said petulantly, looking up at him through her lashes. "I don't see you enough to miss you. What I'm missing is more the *idea* of seeing you. I was really looking forward to this summer with you."

Gerald chuckled and pulled her into his arms. "Oh my sweet Lily." He kissed the top of her head.

She wondered if that was to be the extent of her kiss good night.

Suddenly, she was so fed up with the situation, so tired of being put off, that she put her arms around him and pulled him tight, breathing deeply of his scent through the suit—light cologne, clean summerweight wool, and cotton fabric. There was no scent of Gerald himself.

His arms tightened around her.

"I'm just so . . ." she began against the material of his suit. "Frustrated," she finished, unable to find a better word. "We were only just starting to get close." She pushed back and looked up at him. "I don't want to have to start all over again when you get back. It's the summer, I have a lot of time off. Maybe I *should* come out for a week. I could probably even make it two, if you wanted."

Gerald gave her a gentle smile. "We'll see."

Lily was transported back to the days when her father would tell her the same thing. He'd be going on a business trip—one of the many he made while she was growing up, leaving her with Ruth, her nanny—and she would beg to go with him, or just to visit him on the weekend when she didn't have school. *We'll see*, he always said. And after a while Lily did see. He never wanted her there.

Was she acting like that child now? Was she not understanding that serious men with serious jobs had to keep their personal lives regulated? Her father always made it clear that he cared about her, but he had duties that she didn't understand. Was that what was happening now?

Lily must have looked so crestfallen that Gerald took her face in his hands. She looked up into his eyes again, drinking in the sight of him so close. As he leaned in for the kiss, her heart began to hammer.

This was what she wanted. Just this. A little *passion*, for goodness' sakes. She rose onto her tiptoes to receive the kiss, wrapping her arms around his neck.

His mouth opened wide, as if to devour her, covering hers and moving from side to side. Lily tried to adjust, moved her head this way and that with his, and touched his lips with her tongue, searching for his. But there was nothing but a great, gaping cavern. It was as if he wanted to inhale her, not kiss her.

It was . . . awkward.

Was she doing it wrong? Had she been doing it wrong all these years? Was French kissing *not* about tongues, as well as mouths and lips?

Awkwardly, she tried to move beneath the onslaught, taking his bottom lip gently in her teeth, but he simply covered her mouth again with his, moving, tongueless, along her skin.

It was the strangest kiss she'd ever received. She was so distracted by the method that she didn't even notice where his hands were until well into it. They had moved up to press against her breasts, kneading them as if they were two cans of Play-Doh that needed softening.

Finally, he ended the vacuum, pulled back, his hands on her upper arms, and beamed at her as if he had just bestowed the kiss of a lifetime. She gave him a tentative smile and resisted the urge to wipe her face.

He leaned toward her again and nuzzled her ear, saying, "Trust me, Lily, there's much more where that came from. We just have to be patient. Just a little while longer."

He pulled back again, gave her that chaste peck on the cheek she was so familiar with—lingering a little this time—then turned and sauntered down the walk toward his car.

She stared after him. Her elegant, polished, experienced Mr. Knightley. The worst kisser ever born.

Slowly, in a daze, she entered her house and wiped her mouth with the back of one hand. Doug jumped up from the couch and ran to greet her. She bent and picked him up, stroking his warm, solid body and kissing the top of his head. She felt like taking a shower. Scrubbing her face with cleanser. She wanted to return to that naïve girl she was not so long ago who believed with all her heart that Gerald Lawson was The One. Unequivocally, without a doubt, for sure.

But now, at this moment, she felt as if he had deliberately turned her hopes and expectations upside down by, in a weird way, giving her what she thought she'd wanted.

She sat down on the couch and tried to think, but her mind only spun in the same directions, over and over again. The dinner conversation, his leaving, that awful kiss.

There was no way that she'd been kissing wrong all these years, she thought, because that kiss with Brady had felt as natural as breathing. Even if it was breathing air that scorched her skin and ignited her insides.

Gerald's kiss hadn't had her thinking about dragging him up to the bedroom, as Brady's had, so much as dragging his head back by the hair and saying *What the hell are you doing?*

What in the world was she going to do? She didn't even know what to think.

Then it came to her. There was only one person she could talk to about this. One person who would understand the problem, the battle of carnality versus reality, emotion versus desire. One person who would get how important and disconcerting passion could be.

Georgia.

With another kiss on the head, she deposited Doug on the floor and grabbed up her purse again. She headed out the door, slamming it behind her.

As she turned to lock the dead bolt, a voice from the opposite porch said, "You're home early. Dress not do the trick?"

Lily froze, then swallowed hard. Brady.

She looked in his direction but could barely see him in the dark. "Not exactly."

He scoffed lightly. "The man's a fool."

"I've got to go," she said, and spun on her heel, practically running to her car.

"I should have called first, I'm so sorry," Lily said, when Georgia opened the door. She was dressed in a silk peignoir, her blond hair mussed and her giant Great Dane, Sage, standing behind her like a bodyguard. In her hand was a book, one finger holding her place.

"Good *Lord,* honey, what on earth happened to *you*?" She stepped back from the door and motioned her in. "Come in here and tell me what has you in such a state."

Lily put a hand to her face. "Do I look that bad?"

Georgia laughed, and the sound—confident and familiar—soothed her. "Just a little wild-eyed. Come on in and let me pour you somethin' to drink. I was havin' a margarita myself."

"That sounds perfect," Lily said, giving Sage a long stroke and laying her hand on his back as he leaned toward her. "Make it a big one."

"Is there any other size?" Georgia asked, heading for the kitchen.

Lily exhaled slowly, very glad to be there. This was just what she had to do. She didn't know why she resisted it before. Talking to Georgia was going to be the best relief she could get.

Granted, Georgia had never liked the idea of Gerald, but she was the only one who'd understand the dilemma Lily now found herself in. Georgia admitted that she succumbed to passion on a regular basis, often to disastrous effect. Of course, Georgia didn't worry about it the way Lily did—she was more likely to laugh about her indiscretions—but at least she'd understand how desire could be completely divorced from emotion. And, Lily was betting, she would comprehend in a way that neither Megan nor Penelope would how you could fall into a kiss with someone you *knew* wasn't the man for you, even while hating the kiss from the one who *was.*

"Here we go," Georgia said, reentering the room carrying a huge saucerlike glass rimmed with salt. Her pink-and-white peignoir flowed around her as she walked, alternately exposing shapely legs and fluffy pink, kitten-heeled slippers. "This'll calm you right down and make the world a rosier place. I suggest you down half of that before you even begin."

"Thank you." Lily took the glass, sipped from it, and leaned back on the couch. "You have no idea how badly I need this."

They sat in companionable silence a minute, sipping their drinks, before Georgia said, "So you look sexy as all get-out tonight, Lil. Have a hot date?"

Lily sighed. "Sort of. That's what I wanted to talk to you about."

She swallowed and wondered how to begin. Was the kiss bad because Brady's had been so good? Or was it just bad? What did Brady have to do with her confusion about all that Gerald had said? Nothing? Was Gerald's lack of passion, lack of *perception* about her feelings, the whole problem?

So she began at the beginning. The night Brady stopped by when they'd fallen into that kiss.

Georgia's eyes widened during the tale, but she didn't say anything, just continued sipping her

margarita, looking like a blond Buddha in a flow-
ered dressing gown.

Lily moved on to the date with Gerald and all
that he'd said about the marriage track, racing
through her story right to its disastrous conclusion with that terrible kiss on her front porch.

When she finished, Georgia looked at her a long
moment, then said, "Honey, there's a lot of things
I could say here, but since I know you'd just blow
off most of it and not take my advice, I'll tell you
two things I think you might actually pay attention to."

Lily straightened in her seat and looked plead-
ingly at Georgia. "Thank God, I knew you'd know
what to do. Please, tell me. I've never been so confused."

"First, if you're *sure* there's nothin' there with the
pilot except animal need—and believe me, I know
what that's like—don't tell Penelope anythin'. For
one thing, she might be the only person on the
planet who doesn't understand animal need. And
you know she'd write him off faster than you could
say *It was just a kiss!*"

Lily laughed, despite herself. "I know. You're
right. I'd thought the same thing exactly."

"Good. Second. Lily, you've got to *let Gerald go*.
Let him go off on this little business venture of
his, do what he needs to do, make Daddy happy
and all that. And while he's gone, you try to forget
he even exists."

"But Georgia, I can't do that! For one thing, the way he was talking, it's like—does he think we're engaged? Or preengaged? I mean, did I agree to something already? I can't just pretend that conversation never happened."

"Why on earth not? What did he give you, after all? Nothing but a bunch more wait-and-see blather." Georgia waved her hand in the air. "Let me tell you one thing, Lil, until that ring is on your finger you don't owe him a goddamn thing. And remember *this:* He doesn't owe you anythin' either. You don't know what he'll be doin' out there in Hawaii, with all those women in thongs and whatnot. Think about *that* the next time you want to kiss your pilot."

Lily recoiled. "I will *not* be kissing the pilot again—"

Georgia raised her glass. "Well, that's good, because we just decided to let Penelope have him."

"And second, Gerald would never cheat on me. I mean, he could have been cheating all this time up in Washington, and he hasn't been—"

"Are you sure?" Georgia raised her brows.

"Well of course I'm sure. Why else would he be down here talking about the marriage track with me?"

Georgia chuckled and looked at her pityingly. "Because, sweetheart, men love to have one catch already on the line when they go off to another part of the pond. It's the classic scenario. They pick the woman they want to marry, but the woman they want to *be* with is a whole 'nother story."

Lily felt the bottom drop out of her stomach. "Are you *trying* to make me worry? Do you really think Gerald might go off and find someone else? Or already has? I mean, it's true, we don't have a formal commitment. So I guess there isn't anything that would stop him from finding someone else . . ." She stared at the coffee table, wondering what she would do without her dream of Gerald. How empty the world would seem.

"A minute ago you were worried you'd accidentally gotten engaged. Or preengaged, though God only knows what that is. So which is it? You want him or not?"

Lily sighed, miserable. "You know I want him. I've wanted him for . . . forever. I just want him different than he was tonight."

Georgia laughed, her big boisterous laugh, making Lily smile though she secretly wanted to burst out crying.

"I know what you're going to say, so don't even say it," Lily said. "I just wish everything were as clear-cut now as it was a month ago."

"And do you know why they're not?" Georgia asked, the teacher with her slowest pupil.

"Everything I just told you," Lily said. "That kiss with Brady, this weird night. Gerald's awful kiss."

"No." Georgia shook her head, her eyes steady

on Lily. "It was clear-cut before because none of it was real. Hopes and dreams can be very specific. In fact, I'd venture to say they get more specific the longer you've had 'em. But life doesn't work that way, my girl, and you should know that by now. Life is messy, complicated, and hormones and sex and bad kisses and stupid conversations are all part of that."

Lily reached out and grabbed a handful of nuts from a bowl on the coffee table, picking through them for the cashews. "All right. You're right." She gave her friend a frown. "I agree with all you've said. So tell me one of those things you thought I wouldn't agree with."

Georgia smiled. "Well now, I'm not sure I want to ruin my battin' average. I seem to be hittin' home runs right now."

Lily smiled wryly. "Even if you might get through to me on something new?"

Georgia lifted her glass. "Aha! You know me too well. All right, here's my impression of your conversation with Gerald tonight. And don't you interrupt me to tell me you misrepresented him or I'm not bein' fair or anythin' like that."

Lily crossed her heart with one finger. "I promise."

Georgia nodded once. "All right, then. I think Gerald treated you abominably tonight. He spoke to you like you were a child—ah-ah-ah." Georgia lifted up a palm just as Lily took a deep breath to interject something. "He made all the decisions, made some wallopin' assumptions, did a disturbin' amount of talkin' down, and generally gave you the verbal equivalent of patting you on the head and sayin' *don't you worry your little head about it, princess, I'll figure it all out for you.* If that doesn't show you he's got a significant lack of respect for you, then I don't know what would."

Lily shook her head and looked at her hands. "Well, you were right. I don't necessarily agree with that. I mean, he was a little high-handed, or at least I can see how he would sound that way, but it's because up to this point I've left the ball in his court. But I won't argue with what you say. In fact, I'll think about it. But maybe after you meet him next weekend you'll see how he is. That that's just how he talks."

Georgia's brows rose. "We're meeting him next week, are we? He's coming to Megan's party?"

Lily nodded. "Then he's leaving on Monday."

The two finished their drinks, filled up another, talked about other topics, and called it a night around midnight. Lily felt better leaving Georgia's, glad that she'd unburdened herself and gotten some impartial advice. At least, as impartial as she was likely to get from someone who would listen to her story.

She went home, was relieved to find both front porches empty, and let Doug out of his crate to pee one last time. She was just heading for the back door when a face—white and ghostly—popped up in the back-door window.

Lily gave a little shriek and felt pinpricks travel like mercury along her skin, before recognizing the face as belonging to her next-door neighbor, Nathan.

She opened the door. "Oh my God, Nathan, you scared me half to death."

Doug bolted out the door, growling, and grabbed onto Nathan's pant leg. Nathan jumped back, holding himself against the house as Doug, sounding fierce as a weed whacker, revved himself up and pulled against Nathan's jeans.

"Doug, *no!*" Lily scolded, reaching down and swatting the dog smartly on the behind.

Doug, shocked at the contact, gave a yip and let go, looking up at Lily as if she'd kicked him.

"Go on," she said sternly, pointing to the yard. "*Go!*"

Doug slunk down the back stoop and into the yard, becoming nothing but a ghostly figure himself in the moonless night.

"I'm sorry about that," Lily said. "I'm working on him, but he's still not very fond of men, though he's gotten a lot better around Gerald. Do you want to come in?"

Nathan nodded emphatically. "Sure, yeah, thanks."

They went back into the kitchen, Lily closing the door firmly on Doug.

"So what were you doing out there?" Lily asked. "It's the middle of the night."

"I know," Nathan said, scratching his scalp and making his curly hair jump with the movement. "I saw you drive up and wanted to tell you something."

Lily went to the cabinet, got a tall glass, and filled it with water. She held it up to Nathan. "Want some?"

He shook his head.

She downed half of it on the spot. Her head was beginning to hurt from the margaritas and her tongue felt dry as leather. "So what did you want to tell me?"

Nathan seated himself at the kitchen table. "Did you have a date tonight?"

Maybe it was the margaritas, but she was feeling especially annoyed at Nathan right now, popping up in her window and now being all weird about whatever it was he wanted to say.

"Yes," she said slowly.

"With Gerald?"

"Yes," she said again.

Nathan nodded and swallowed; she could see his prominent Adam's apple rise and fall with the effort.

"Were you, uh, out all night? Or did you come back here? Maybe . . . have a drink or something?"

"We came back, briefly. Then I went out again. Why?"

He swallowed again and looked at the table. "Nathan—"

He raised his head, his face all puppy-dog eyes and unguarded feelings for her, cutting off what was about to be a curt *get on with it* from Lily.

"I thought I saw someone outside your house tonight," he said finally, rushing the words. "Trying to get in the back door. I'm really sorry. I don't mean to scare you or anything, but I wasn't sure what or who it was. I just thought you should know. I'm sorry."

Lily's blood froze in her veins. Someone trying to get in the back door. So it *hadn't* just been the wind that night. Something strange really had been going on.

"Who was it? Someone—a man? What did he look like?" she asked.

"It was a man, I don't know who. He—he was looking in the windows first, then came to the back door. It was hard to see just what he was doing. It was only about an hour ago, so it was dark. But I could swear he was trying to jimmy the lock or something. He was kind of . . . bent over." Nathan hunched his shoulders and held his hands in front of him as if trying to pick a lock.

"Why didn't you call the police?" Lily demanded.

Nathan blushed. "Be—because I thought, uh, that is I saw you go on your date and I, well, at first I thought maybe it was the guy you went with.

Maybe he'd come out into the yard or something, to I don't know, to get away from Doug maybe."

Lily laughed dryly at that.

"It wasn't until he heard me open my door and kind of rushed off into the darkness that I thought it was really suspicious. He went back toward the trees by the alley, so I knew he wasn't a guest. That's why I came out and watched a while, to make sure he was gone. And I checked out your door, but it looked okay. Then I waited for you to get home."

Lily sat down at the table across from Nathan, both hands circling her water glass. How in the world would she ever get to sleep tonight?

"Do you think I should call the police now?" Nathan asked.

Lily sighed. "I don't know. I don't know what they could do now. The guy's been gone at least an hour. And you said yourself the door looks normal."

"Yeah, that's kind of what I thought. But maybe they could send a patrol car. You should just—"

At that moment, a loud bump sounded on the back door, and both Nathan and Lily nearly flipped out of their skins. Doug's yelping told them immediately that he'd tried to enter and discovered the dog door locked.

"Dammit." Lily got up and opened the back door. Doug skittered on the back stoop for a minute like Fred Flintstone starting his Stone Age car, then shot into the room like a ballistic missile. Without a sideways glance at Nathan—who'd raised his feet up onto the chair at the sight of his nemesis—he headed for the stairs, and Lily heard him trampling up them as if the very devil was after him.

"Oh my God," she said, gaping at the wake he'd left. She hadn't seen him that scared since the night of the wind.

Nathan scooted his chair back and craned his neck to look out the back door. Then he bolted to his feet, chair overturning behind him, and hit the kitchen light switch.

As darkness swept the room, Lily spun. "Nathan, what the he—"

"*Shhhh!*" he hissed at her. "*Who's that?*"

Ten

Brady crossed the darkness of his backyard, unaware of the two pairs of eyes in Lily's kitchen following his every move, and headed toward the porch. It was a warm night, and part of him wished he had a hammock, so he could sleep out-doors.

No doubt Lily's wretched dog would eat him alive first thing in the morning, though.

He was barefoot, because he couldn't find his other flip-flop, just like he couldn't find his other running shoe the other day, and the new grass felt cool on the soles of his feet.

He looked off across the yard, toward Nathan's yard and beyond. He'd just freed a cat he'd found tied to a tree, and it had bolted in that direction. He'd lost him in the dark as soon as the animal had leapt the fence between his yard and Nathan's.

Who in the world would tie a cat to a tree? he wondered. Had it been some kid? Somebody who'd found the cat and hoped to talk his parents into letting him keep it? It had been tied with twine attached to a cheap plastic collar, but there hadn't even been a bowl of water nearby, so whoever was trying to keep it in one place had done a pretty bad job of it. The thing had been yowling its head off, which was how Brady had found it in the first place. Just over his back fence in the tree-lined lane behind the row of houses. The lane used to serve as an alleyway for deliveries. Now it was just an overgrown, underused pathway.

As he crossed the lawn he looked up at Lily's side of the house. All was dark. He wondered where she'd gone after the early demise of her date. He also wondered what was wrong with that Gerald guy for bringing her home so early, then leaving, even though she'd looked like a million bucks.

He'd have said the guy was gay, since he was such a snappy dresser, but Brady didn't get a gay vibe from him. It was more that he seemed asexual. With a giant stick up his ass.

Brady reached the back porch and sat on the old rocker that had come with the place. He leaned his head back, gazing at the sky, and thought about Lily Tyler.

She was a bundle of problems, that was for sure. She fancied herself in love with Mr. Snappy Dresser, had a dog who hated men, and a father with a rather large, if figurative, shotgun. Add to that a body that wouldn't quit and the passion to go with it, and you had a woman that a man running away from Crazy Tricia would be a fool to get involved with.

He should write her off, he thought, and see about this Penelope woman Megan Rose had talked about. Except that he wasn't supposed to be seeing *any* woman, not until he could form a reasonable friendship with one. And try as he might, he couldn't characterize what he had with Lily Tyler as a friendship. There was too much sexual tension in the mix.

Brady must have fallen asleep in the chair because he awoke with a start to the sound of lowered voices. He slid slowly upward in the chair and looked across the porch to see two figures in the dark, whispering.

One was Lily. And the other—though this was hard for Brady to believe, and he actually blinked hard several times in order to make sure—was Nathan from next door.

The most shocking part of all: They were embracing.

Lily rode the elevator up to her father's office, reliving the surreal scene of the evening before. She wished she hadn't had so many margaritas at Georgia's. For one thing, she liked to be on her toes when she met with her father. For another, she wished she could remember exactly what had led to that bizarre embrace Nathan had given her when she had walked him out the back door.

In the wake of the scare about someone trying to break into her house, and Doug's bizarre behavior, Nathan had made the generous—if frightening in and of itself—offer for Lily to come stay with him and his mother. What that would accomplish, Lily had no idea, though it was obvious Nathan thought it would lead to something like domestic bliss.

But as she'd tried to put him off that idea, he'd blurted something about being so worried about her, then he'd latched on to her like some kind of monkey spawn afraid of losing its mother. She'd had to pry him loose and shoo him home before things got even more awkward.

The elevator doors opened, and Lily stepped off, waving to the receptionist as she made her way down the long, richly carpeted hallway to her father's corner office.

Jordan Tyler wasn't an exceptionally tall man, but he projected tallness with an immaculately tailored air of power. His high-ceilinged, wood-paneled office with velvet drapes and leather-upholstered furniture, imposing bookcases, and discreet, but full, bar might have dwarfed another man, but Tyler's ice-blue eyes and nerves of steel made him the most intimidating thing in the room.

He was direct, no-nonsense, and so sure of his superior intellect that others almost invariably questioned their own in his presence.

Including his daughter. Early on, Lily had learned to disguise her intimidation, knowing there was nothing her father loathed more than someone he wanted to respect succumbing to his domination. Still, something inside of her would quiver when her father got angry, try though she might to suppress it.

"So how are things in that frightening little 'burg you moved yourself to?" he asked, leaning back in his chair and interlacing his fingers across his stomach.

They tried to meet once a month for lunch, to eliminate the risk of losing track of each other altogether, Lily assumed, but it was frequently canceled due to her father's demanding schedule. It was canceled again today, but not until she had arrived, so they were doing an impromptu catch-up in his office before the important meeting he'd had to schedule.

"I don't know why it scares you, Daddy. Just because it's small, doesn't mean it's small-minded." She crossed her legs at the ankles, the way her eleventh-grade etiquette tutor had taught her. "And things are fine. Work is going well. I've got several very popular classes, including the one on nineteenth-century authors for freshmen that I proposed. I just finished grading the finals, and almost all of them did well. The students really got into it."

"Excellent, excellent," he said, nodding, his cool blue eyes bestowing approval on her.

She couldn't help but feel good under the approbation, even though she felt pathetic for still needing his approval.

She took a deep breath. "So, Daddy, Gerald told me about Hawaii. That he's having to leave for a few weeks. I understand it's a great opportunity for him. And it was your idea?"

"In a way, yes, I suppose it was. But mostly he was chosen because he's done business with this company before, when he was in the West Coast office, you know. So he has the contacts."

Lily nodded, steeling herself. "That's good. Although . . . I have to say I'm a little disappointed. He's going to be gone practically the whole summer. And we were just starting to get to know each other. You know, as . . . on dates, I mean."

Her father nodded and leaned forward, his elbows on his desk. "I know that. I even mentioned that to Gerald, was concerned myself on your behalf, but he didn't seem to have a problem with it. Is everything going all right with you two?"

Lily blushed. She knew her father wanted this relationship almost as much as she did. And she hated to disappoint him, hated it more than disappointing herself sometimes. What made this worse, however, was that just a few weeks ago she'd been so excited about Gerald's asking her out that she'd gone on and on to her father about what a great future she believed they could have.

And maybe they still could. He was, after all, talking about marriage. It was just . . . that awful kiss, that weird date.

"Everything's going fine," she said, as calmly as she could. She couldn't even imagine talking to her father about the merits or import of a good or bad kiss. "As a matter of fact, on our last date Gerald said a lot of positive things about our future. He . . . he said he thought we were on 'the marriage track.' "

Her father beamed and leaned back in his chair. "Excellent! I like that in a man. Planning, foresight, open discussion. I hope you told him you thought so, too." His brows rose, and those cool blue eyes fixed her with their anticipated response.

"Well, of course." She swallowed and looked down at her hands, knowing she had not done so, exactly. Hadn't really been given the chance to give her yay or nay to the idea. "I know you and I have talked about how I feel about that. Gerald seemed to think, though, that this opportunity in Hawaii was too good to pass up, even though I registered some disappointment that he was going away for the whole summer."

During which time she'd be living next door to Temptation Incarnate.

"It is a good origination for him," her father said, nodding. "It'll be quite the feather in his cap, you know. And I'm not the only partner who needs to be impressed before he can be brought into our ranks."

"Oh please, Daddy, you know as well as I do that you're the only one who counts. Whatever you say, goes, and everyone knows it." She smiled. "But, I'm just wondering, aren't you impressed enough with Gerald already? I guess I'm not clear what's holding up his partnership. You do nothing but sing his praises to me."

"I am very impressed with Gerald," he said. "And I'll be more impressed after he lands these clients in Hawaii. It doesn't hurt a man to have to work hard for what he wants."

Lily sighed, thinking that he should have to work harder for her too. "I'm sure that's true."

"It probably won't hurt you and Gerald any, either. Let distance stoke the fire a little, honey. There's no need to rush into this."

Lily couldn't help it, she rolled her eyes. "Daddy, I'd hardly say waiting two years for a first date is 'rushing into' anything. We were just starting to know each other as, as romantic prospects." She bit her lip. "And now he's going to be gone for a month or two. It's just bad timing, as far as I'm concerned. I don't know why it couldn't have waited."

Her father raised an eyebrow and gave her a look that she knew made other men quail. "I know you're unhappy about it. But you've got to let the man make his own decisions, Lillian."

She looked down at her lap, smoothing the fabric of her skirt. "I know that. Of course I know that. And he *has* made his own decisions." Along with a few of hers, apparently.

"Don't you respect that? You don't want a man you can walk all over, do you?" He gave her a gentle smile.

She laughed slightly. "No, I really don't. And I do respect his decisions. I'm just . . . worried, I guess. I don't like having to stop things in midcourse." She squeezed her hands together until her knuckles turned white. "And . . . you know, Daddy, I feel a little like I've done nothing but respect his decisions. I've *waited* on his decisions. Based my *life* around his decisions and when he's going to make them. I can't help thinking: When is it going to be *my* turn?"

She was suddenly angry, but at whom? She wasn't even sure. At Gerald for being so self-assured? Her father for being so subtly, yet powerfully, involved? Herself for letting these men walk all over her? She knew that her father didn't deserve this outburst, but she couldn't help it. Didn't she have a right to express her anger?

Of course, it wouldn't do to make *him* mad.

The phone buzzed. Lily exhaled silently. She

needed to pull herself together. Her father respected control more than anything.

He picked up the receiver. "Yes." He paused, listening. "Tell him I'll call him back in five minutes. And get me that file."

He hung up and studied Lily a moment. "Listen, I understand what you're feeling, Lillian," he said. "But you need to get over this idea that marriages are something to rush into. Isn't that a lesson you learned a long time ago? Don't overlook your own experience in these matters. Gerald obviously feels that he has things to do, important things to accomplish for his career, before going ahead with a relationship."

"And career always comes first," she said, her anger flaring despite her best efforts to quell it.

Her father sighed and, perhaps sensing the depth of her agitation, said, "Honey, it's not that the job comes first, necessarily, it's that it's a balancing act. I myself underwent a tremendous amount of career pressure before I could marry your mother. She understood, and that went a long way toward convincing me that she was the right woman to be my partner in life. Your relationship with Gerald is not going to implode just because he goes away for a few weeks. Take a deep breath and calm down. You've got time. You're, what, twenty-eight, twenty-nine?"

"I'm thirty-two, Daddy," she said, with a look that told him what she thought of his mistake.

"And I'm not trying to rush into marriage. If anything I'm trying to do the opposite. He's talking marriage, and I feel like we hardly know each other. Not in the context of a romantic relationship."

"You'll have time to get to know each other," he counseled calmly. "He'll be back before you know it. Even after an engagement there's time, you learn a lot about your intended in the months leading up to a wedding. Personally, I believe in long engagements, and I told Gerald so myself. It gives a couple the opportunity to come to grips with the promise to be made, the import of the commitment."

Lily took a deep breath. He was right, she knew that. In so many ways, he was right. Maybe it was just her recent doubts—that kiss, that date—that had her feeling so frantic about Gerald's departure. But it was, as her father said, only a few weeks. What *was* the big deal?

"Okay. I see what you're saying." She gazed into her father's face. He cared, she knew that. He just didn't understand what she felt was at stake here. She felt compelled to add, "It's just . . . well, Daddy, I don't want to disappoint you. And I don't want to disappoint myself either. But I never realized how little Gerald and I know each other after all. Two years of chatting in the office and the occasional shared cup of coffee gave me little insight into who he is in a relationship."

Not to mention that the contrast between what she felt with Brady—a complication that sprang up from nowhere and was probably the universe's way of telling her to think twice—and what she felt with Gerald was too confusing and convoluted to figure out when one of the parties was missing for six, maybe eight weeks. Not that she had any hopes or expectations when it came to Brady, but that kiss with him had been a wake-up call. She was not feeling what she should for Gerald.

She wished she could get this across to her father, explain to him what not seeing Gerald could do to her hopes—and her father's expectations—about a future with Gerald. She needed to get to know him *now,* before living next door to Brady Cole ruined her future.

But of course her father wouldn't understand that. Something told her he didn't give in to any sort of passion, least of all ones that didn't make sense and led nowhere. Because nothing was a bigger dead end for her than Brady Cole. He just didn't *fit.* He didn't belong in that picture frame she'd constructed in her mind, with Lily and Gerald and their two beautiful children.

Not to mention that being in that picture frame was probably the *last* thing he'd ever want. He didn't exactly strike her as the marrying kind.

"You couldn't possibly disappoint me, Lillian." He tilted his head, looking at her kindly. "But don't be too quick to judge him, all right? You know Gerald in one context, and now you're getting to know him in the other. But it's the same thing, in the same way that Gerald is essentially the same man at work that he is at home. It's his character that matters. And his character is consistent. I've known him for several years now, and you can trust me that he's a good man, and a good man for you." He picked up the phone again and dialed. "Doris? Never mind, I have the folder right here." He hung up.

A second later the door opened and Doris, a paralegal in the firm who had to be six feet tall and looked like a model, with dark hair and eyes and dramatic features, entered holding a sheaf of papers.

"I thought you might need these, too," she said, doing her runway walk to Tyler's desk and handing them to him. She glanced impassively at Lily, and said, "Please excuse me for interrupting."

"No problem," Lily said, feeling tiny.

"Excellent," her father said, scanning the documents, "thank you, Doris."

Doris pivoted with *Vogue*-worthy precision, and strode out the door, closing it behind her.

"I wish we could have had lunch today," Lily said. "In a restaurant. So you weren't so distracted by your papers and your phone calls and whatever else you've got piled up here." She gestured toward the paper-strewn surface. "I don't think you're quite understanding what I'm saying. I don't *want* to rush into something with Gerald, and making a commitment based on your recommendation of his character would be doing exactly that. Not that I don't trust your opinion, Daddy, but marriage has to be based on more than objective qualities, don't you think? I have to *feel* something, the *right* things, before I can commit."

He dropped the folder on the desk, and his gray eyebrows descended. "Raw feelings are less to be trusted than the opinions and considerations of those whom you respect. I honestly regret the day that arranged marriages became passé, because more awful unions have been produced by passion—what you might refer to as the *right feelings*—than by rational assessment of a situation by concerned, yet objective parties. You should know this better than anyone."

Lily slumped back in her chair. "I know what you're referring to, and it's not fair."

"Now, now, I'm not trying to be unfair. And I'm not throwing anything in your face. I know you've grown and learned a lot since then. But I think it's relevant to bring up the last time you let passion make a relationship decision for you. There's a reason precedents are so important in law; it is the same in life."

Her father had never forgotten the betrayal of her ill-advised marriage, to Duane, the plumber, even though she occasionally convinced herself that he had. He didn't bring it up often, but when he did it always surprised her. Sometimes even now that act of rebellion at age twenty seemed so breathtaking that she was astonished at herself all over again.

Where had that girl gone? she wondered now. The one with the nerve and the confidence to do something like that even though it had ended up being a colossal mistake.

"I told Gerald about that, by the way," she said. "And he understood completely."

Her father sat back in his chair, expelling a breath of air as he did so, and looked at her in surprise. "You *told* him? About the plumber?"

Lily nodded, noting his disbelief. "He was fine with it. He understood."

And thank God he had, because she'd *had* to tell him.

"Well, there you have it," her father said, letting his confusion shift to confidence. He beamed. "More evidence of Gerald's good character. Only a man of great integrity would be able to overlook such impulsiveness in a woman."

Lily flushed. "Unlike yourself?" The words popped out before she could stop them.

Her father regarded her with steely reserve for so long a moment that Lily literally squirmed in her chair.

"I'm sorry you think that about me," he said finally. "I have always wanted only the best for you.

And you have to admit that Duane was not the best. Far from it."

"I know." She sighed. "I'm sorry. You didn't deserve that."

He shook his head, dismissing the slight. "I know you're upset. But listen to your old father for a minute. I know it's hard to believe, but I do know a lot about life. Just because you haven't got sweaty palms or butterflies in your stomach, or whatever it is you girls think you're supposed to have when you choose a man, doesn't mean that he is not right for you. Those things pass eventually anyway. Choose wisely. Choose someone with a future. Choose someone strong and steady and reliable. I can assure you, Lillian, you don't want someone you can boss around like some uneducated plumber. I know you. You need a strong man. A man like Gerald."

Why did this discussion about Duane make her think of Brady Cole? He wasn't anything *like* Duane.

But he was the exact same kind of mistake, she thought. Or would be, if she—or he—let anything come of it.

"I want you to know, Daddy," she said, calmly, "that I'm not likely to make a mistake like Duane again. This thing with Gerald . . . I know we've talked about it before, and we've both hoped something would develop. Now that it looks like something *is* developing, I just want to be sure it's right. You understand that, don't you?"

"Of course I do," he said. He gave her a smile, forgiving her. "It's just that *I* know it's right. I can tell, sweetie. You just have to trust me."

She shook her head, suddenly feeling as if she might cry. "*You* need to trust *me*, Daddy."

"And I do. Of course I do." They looked at each other a long moment before her father shifted his attention to the folder on his desk. "Now, let's not talk about this anymore until there's something concrete to say on the subject. I'm sure there's no need to quibble over something that's going to resolve itself in the end anyway." He smiled confidently at her. "If Gerald can wait the few weeks this project will take, then surely you and I can, too."

If Gerald can wait, Lily thought. Of course Gerald could wait. Gerald had no trouble waiting for anything, apparently.

She hated that all she could think about was the way she and Brady had come together like Velcro the night they'd kissed. *I want you*, she'd said, and even now she could not forget how very much she'd meant it. Her body had been like a beast possessed. Carnal and voracious. She'd never known such loss of control.

Why didn't Gerald feel any of that passion? Why didn't she feel any of that passion for Gerald? When he'd taken her in his arms there'd been none of that . . . that *desperation* to touch, that physical need that she'd felt with Brady. Indeed, thinking back on that horrible kiss she'd shared with Gerald, she had felt quite the opposite.

"Good idea," she said at last. "We'll just see what happens."

And we'll hope that in the meantime Lillian didn't do anything impulsive in the passion department. She couldn't think of a bigger way to disappoint her father. Or herself.

A slight smile played on her father's lips. "Good. And you know, this is probably a beneficial lesson for you, Lillian. If you want to be married to a partner, then you're going to have to understand what the job demands. Of both of you."

She made herself smile. "If I didn't already know that from growing up with you, Daddy, I don't know what Gerald could possibly teach me about it."

He laughed. It was what she always resorted to with him. Laughter. If she could make light of her issues, then he would not be burdened by them. And she would seem reasonable and smart.

So why did she feel so powerless when she did it? Was it because he didn't understand her, and she didn't make him? She just did what she could to smooth things over.

She wondered, would a life with Gerald make her feel like she was in the same kind of position forever? Or would it be an entree into her father's world on her own terms, where she could finally assert her own will?

"By the way," her father said, still studying the file folder in front of him, "how's that pilot working out?"

Lily stood up abruptly. "He's great. A nice guy."

Her father looked up at her in surprise. "What's the matter? Are you leaving?"

She shook her head, willing away the blush that had hit her cheeks. "Nothing's the matter. I just realized the time."

Whatever she did, she couldn't let on to her father that there was anything between her and Brady other than neighborly friendship. It wouldn't take her father long to make the leap from Duane to Brady if he suspected anything else.

He glanced at his watch. "Yes, I have some papers to glance at before my meeting."

She nodded. "And about the, uh, pilot. I think he's going to ask out my friend Penelope." She picked up her purse and turned for the door.

"That's nice. Isn't it?" her father said, his eyes registering far more perception than she would have liked. Why couldn't he have been as perceptive when she was talking about her problems with Gerald?

She walked to the door. "It's great. They'll be perfect together. And remember, Daddy, next time let's go to a restaurant."

"Certainly," he said, still eyeing her. "Give my secretary a call and set up our next luncheon. I promise I'll get us out of this office."

She flashed him a smile and departed, praying to God her guilt and self-consciousness about Brady had been obvious only to her.

Doug's work was never done. It was a full-time job, figuring out how to manage the lives of all the lesser beings around him, but it was a job he loved. Lily was a human worth protecting, and the others . . . well, they were usually fun to mess with.

It wasn't hard keeping them in line. Look at the guy from the house next door, the Timid One. Doug could smell sweat on him every time he saw Doug enter the room, which was rather enjoyable. But the Timid One almost never came over anymore. He just stood at the fence looking at Lily like she was in heat and he was crated.

The other one who came around every now and then, the tall one he thought of as Smelly Man—it was something he put on himself that Lily seemed to like but gave Doug a headache—wasn't worth his time. Not to mention that nothing he had on would taste good, not with that awful, unnatural odor attached to it. So he left him alone, knowing he would disappear on his own before much more time passed.

Doug headed out the dog door into the warm summerlike air. Lily was going to be gone all day.

He knew because that's when she left the dog door open for him. She did this despite the fact that she'd been so displeased by his alterations to the New Guy's vehicle. Based on subsequent stomach rumblings and discomforts, he had to admit that she was right. It had been a bad idea.

This new idea was better. He trotted up to the New Guy's porch and sniffed around. Nothing there worth noting, really, but he was just warming up. He had all day, a fact that gave him the most contented feeling of relaxation.

He stretched out on the back porch for a while in the shade. He napped. Then stretched, rolling onto his back, his side, then flattened on his belly. He napped some more. Dreamed about a squirrel that had gotten away from him the day before. Then he got up.

The air smelled of cut grass and baked dirt. A lovely smell. He'd have to do some rolling in it once he was finished with his task.

New Guy's back window was open, as usual. Doug didn't like taking out screens, but he'd done it before. It was mostly a matter of getting a toe-nail or two in the right spot and digging like the window was fresh topsoil and you had the biggest bone in the world.

Eventually he got it open. He knew just where to look for his quarry, too. These humans were nothing if not predictable. Not like another dog who might hide his belongings anywhere, if the yard was big enough. He went upstairs and headed down the hallway to the room that was in a similar spot to Lily's. Sure enough, once in the room he saw beyond an open door the place where the New Guy kept his footwear.

Doug began the day's task.

One at a time, picking one shoe from each pair, he trotted down the stairs, took each to his special place, then came back for the next.

It was exhausting, but he had some cowhide to work off.

Eleven

Dammit, where was his other shoe?

Brady dug through the pile of shoes and belts at the bottom of his closet, looking for his other loafer.

After a second he sat back on his heels, staring at the mess.

Where were *all* his other shoes?

He leaned forward again and, one by one, pulled shoes from the closet. One blue Nike running shoe. One white Nike running shoe. One Asics running shoe. One New Balance running shoe. One black dress shoe. One brown dress shoe. One Wilson tennis shoe. One Teva sandal. One loafer. One boat shoe. One of those godawful

Mexican things that weren't even comfortable.

He had only one shoe from each pair.

This was too weird. It couldn't be that he was just losing his mind. There was no way he could have so meticulously lost one shoe from each pair. In fact, he couldn't think of a time when he'd ever actually *lost a shoe*. How would he even do that?

He remembered the flip-flops on the back porch. One of those had been missing, too. He'd have to cobble together a makeshift pair of something and go buy another pair of loafers. His boss's party was tonight, and there was no way he could show up wearing mismatched shoes.

He turned and looked at the clock. *Dammit*, he thought again. He only had an hour.

Brady rose and went down the stairs. Rounding the newel post at the base of the steps and heading for the kitchen, he thought about who might play such a trick on him.

Naturally, his mind sprang to his first and foremost tormentor: Tricia. It wasn't her usual style, but then, if she'd branched out from insane screaming fits into silly pranks, he'd welcome the change. He hadn't heard from her in a while. She was about due for another assault.

If it had been Tricia, how had she gotten in? Would Lily have let her in?

The thought of Lily made him pause. She'd looked incredible last weekend. So incredible he could hardly believe how early her date had left. At first he'd hoped *she'd* cut it short, indulging the ridiculous fantasy that she'd realized Gerald was a putz and that he, Brady, was a worthwhile guy who might possibly make a good friend—which could easily lead to more—despite his needing to be on a date diet. But then Megan Rose had called during the week to make sure he was still coming to the party, and he knew the setup with that woman, Penelope, must still be on. Lily clearly didn't want him if she was trying to scrape him off on her friend. Why couldn't he get that through his head?

In any case, it didn't make sense that Tricia would come here and mess with his shoes, especially without leaving some kind of calling card. She wasn't one to do things without getting credit.

He crossed the kitchen, noticed the open window, and decided to close it. Springtime, he thought, you never knew when it might thunderstorm. It wasn't until he rounded the kitchen table that he saw the broken screen on the floor by the wall. Something had pushed against the mesh until it bulged in the middle; then it had obviously popped out of the frame and into the house. The thing was bent nearly in half. Then whoever it was had climbed in through the window.

Brady picked up the screen and examined it. No, they hadn't pushed the screen in, they'd scratched, dug, and torn at it first. Whatever had come in had possessed some kind of claws to destroy the screen first. Fine, talon-shaped runnels were impaled on the wire mesh, as good as a bloody fingerprint.

Tricia would never ruin a manicure doing something like this.

His eyes shifted from the screen to the window to the backyard beyond. Lily's dog lay on his back under a tree, feet straight up in the air as his body writhed on the lush spring grass.

Brady narrowed his eyes. *Doug.*

He stared out the window at the dog. The animal had had it in for him from the moment he'd moved into the house. What was impressive was how stealthy and creative he'd been about making the point.

Brady could be stealthy and creative, too, however. Eyes on the dog, he pushed the window shut and considered.

If he went out there now, all he'd get was a barking fit, followed by the swift retreat of the culprit through the dog door into Lily's house. Besides, it didn't look as though the dog had eaten all those shoes. His belly wasn't distended like it was the day he'd consumed the seat of Brady's motorcycle, and there were no telltale pieces of leather lying around the grass nearby.

No, Doug had done something with them. Something that Brady could figure out when he had a little more time. Right now the dastardly little dog could wait. Brady didn't have time to deal with him properly, because he had to buy some shoes.

He'd have time tomorrow, though, he thought, staring holes in the ugly mutt's back. And when he did, he'd track the little bastard and find out where he'd buried the damn shoes. They'd no doubt be unwearable at this point, but he wasn't going to let the dog win. He couldn't. His pride was at stake now.

Lily moved listlessly around the store, fingering this fabric and that, occasionally lifting a hanger to look at and mentally discard a dress, and could come to no conclusions.

"Here's a nice Ellen Tracy," the saleswoman said. "Very fun, very sexy, and perfect for this lovely summer weather we're having. And everyone looks good in aqua."

Lily stared at it and sighed. Fun. Sexy. Gerald was immune to those things. He was allergic to cleavage and put off by sensuality. She might as well put on a housedress and accessorize with a spatula, since everyone seemed to be assuming that's what she wanted anyway.

"Thanks," she said to the saleswoman, "but I think I'm just going to wear something I already have."

The woman shrugged and turned away. Lily was sure she'd pissed her off, taking up her time, then not buying anything. The saleswomen in this store were notoriously snooty, but Lily hadn't had time to go anywhere else. This shop was the closest one to her house, and it wasn't until she'd pulled out the blue dress she'd worn to Susan Mc-Nally's wedding that she'd decided she wanted something new for tonight. Something that might give her confidence.

She turned and headed out the door, opening it with such force that the bells jumped and tinkled wildly, like tiny birds in the path of a tornado. She hadn't meant to hit it that hard, she just couldn't contain her frustration, with everyone from Gerald to her father. Mostly, though, she was frustrated with herself.

A month ago she'd known exactly what she wanted and essentially how to get it. Gerald had asked her out, and it had seemed that she was finally on track.

Now, though . . . now everything was so confusing. That weird date with Gerald had started it.

No, that wasn't true. The kiss with Brady had started it, damn him to hell. But the weird date hadn't helped any, and the awful kiss with Gerald had only sealed the deal. She didn't want to buy a new dress for Gerald, she thought, because she didn't want to invite another kiss. She also didn't like the fact that he considered himself so secure in her affections that he hadn't expressed the slightest reservation at leaving her for the entire summer. Had she made her desires that obvious to him? Did he think she had no other options? Did he believe she'd wait for him forever, until he decided it was convenient to take her up on a relationship?

Of course he did. She'd made sure of it for the last two years.

What was strangest about the situation was that she still didn't have any trouble thinking about him in the abstract scenario of her future, as she always had, but when it came down to having another conversation like last weekend's or even just standing in front of him tonight and hoping for a kiss . . . that desire just wasn't there.

Which frightened her. What would she do without the idea of Gerald? Her relationship with him protected her from so many other mistakes.

She kept thinking she had to make it work because she'd invested so much in this already, but did she really?

She was just on the verge of figuring something out when someone stopped short on the sidewalk in front of her.

The first thing she noticed, since her eyes had been downcast, was that this person was wearing one loafer and one flip-flop. She raised her gaze.

"Brady," she said, her eyes reaching his face. She wished it didn't look so welcome to her baffled heart. But tonight was the night he was to be introduced to Penelope, and by all reports he was looking forward to it.

She mentally pulled herself back. "What happened to your foot?"

"Nothing. I'm just wearing what's left of my podiatric wardrobe," he said. "Why, what are you wearing to the party?"

She looked back down at his feet. "Well, at least two of the same shoes. I know that much." She sighed. "Other than that . . . I was just looking for a new dress but . . ." She reached a hand out to gesture at the store, behind her, then let it drop.

His face grew concerned. "Something the matter?"

"No." She sighed again. "Maybe. I don't know."

"I couldn't help noticing you were back early from your date the other night. Romantic dinner not go as planned?" he asked.

"Actually," she said speculatively, "it was romantic, in a way. Kind of. At its, uh, heart." She frowned and shook her head.

She didn't want to think about that night anymore. She should be thinking about the future, about the way Gerald would be as a husband, as the guy in that picture frame on her father's desk.

But she couldn't think straight with Brady right in front of her. He looked so good, in khaki pants and a white polo shirt. Even with the silly combination of shoes. How had he gotten so tan already? Wasn't it interesting how his sun-bronzed face made those hazel eyes stand out so golden? And how amazing was it that he could stand there completely nonchalantly in mismatched shoes and still look incredible?

She glanced away, down the street.

"So it was romantic, but ended early." Brady nodded. "Okay."

"Oh God," she muttered. "I really don't want to talk about it."

"Oh. Sorry. I guess it's none of my business anyway."

She laughed slightly. "No, it's not that. It's just . . ."

She looked up at him again and thought how lean and athletic he looked. It must have been the running, that's why he was so tan. He went on the longest runs. She'd see him leave in the morning with his iPod strapped to one burly biceps, and he wouldn't return for an hour or more. Not that she was watching for his return or anything. She just liked taking her coffee on the porch, or in the front room, near the windows.

"So," she started again, attempting to put some pep in her voice, "you're meeting Penelope tonight. Are you looking forward to it?"

His eyes narrowed. "Ah-ha. I thought you were in on that. Megan told me about your plot to get us together."

"Oh, it wasn't my plot," she clarified. "It was Megan's, all the way. I just . . ." She shrugged. "Went along with it. Besides, you two would look good together," she finished miserably.

He tilted his head, studying her, and she looked at the ground. "Are you okay, Lily?"

"Of course!" She couldn't let him think she was down because of him and Penelope. That would be pathetic. "I'm sorry, I'm just preoccupied. You see, Gerald and I, we, ah, actually we talked about marriage the other night!" The very words put panic in her heart, and she looked up at Brady, a desperate clog in her throat. "Isn't that great?" she squeaked.

He pushed his hands into his pockets and looked to the side, where a large truck groaned by, belching exhaust. It passed, and he looked back at her.

"Great," he said. "You must be, um . . ." His eyes rose heavenward as he inhaled, evidently searching for a word.

"Oh I am, I am." She nodded vigorously. "So . . ." She sighed again. "What are you doing down here? Shoe shopping?" She glanced back down at his feet and laughed.

"Actually, yes." He pulled his left hand from his pocket and looked at his watch. "And I better go. Don't want to be late for the party, you know. You going?"

"Oh yes. With Gerald."

He wasn't looking at her, was gazing just past her down the street. "Well, great. You guys can talk more . . . marriage. See you later, then."

Without looking at her again, he strode past her.

"Yes," Lily said, "see you there."

She turned and watched him go. Was it just her, or was something bothering him, too?

She watched him turn into the Comfort Shoes four doors down, one flip-flop smacking smartly as he went.

"My God, the boy does give off some heat," Georgia said, sidling up to Lily at Megan's party.

They stood by one of the many tables of food—the one in the dining room that had sushi and tempura, Thai spring and summer rolls, and teriyaki chicken. Outside there was one grill with filet mignon and aged sirloin steaks served up by a bona fide chef. Next to him was another grill chef preparing steamed oysters, clams, and lobsters, and sweet corn. In the parlor was vegetarian fare including falafel, barbecued tofu, couscous, tabbouli, and vegetable wraps. The living room held a table overflowing with shrimp cocktail, and from the kitchen came every imaginable hors d'oeuvre along with orders of french fries and onion rings, baked potatoes and hush puppies.

And, of course, in one corner of every room was an open bar.

"Who gives off heat?" Lily asked, loading her plate with California rolls, spicy tuna rolls, unagi, and maguro sushi.

She knew just who Georgia was talking about; Lily had spotted Brady the moment she'd arrived at the party and was rarely out of range to see him again. Not that she was trying to keep him in sight. It just happened that way.

Georgia eyed her, Lily could tell, but she wouldn't return the look. "Brady Cole," Georgia said. "Maybe you've met him. Good-looking guy? Pilot? Great kisser?"

Megan came up beside them. "Are you guys having fun?"

Lily jumped. "Yes! It's great!" she said, relieved to see her. For the first time she started to wonder if telling Georgia about the kiss had been all that wise. Not only was there the possibility that she'd be indiscreet, but there was something about Georgia's knowing look that could unnerve a girl.

"Honey, this is the nicest party I've ever been to," Georgia said, giving Megan a quick squeeze around her waist. "And Sutter is in fine form this evenin'. I've never seen him so relaxed. Did you tune him up beforehand with a margarita or two?"

"You just haven't seen him enough, Georgia," Megan said. "He's way more relaxed now than he used to be."

"Are *you* having a good time?" Lily asked her.

Megan blew out a lungful of air. "Sure. But I am keyed up! Maybe it was all the preparation, but I'm just full of nervous energy."

"Well, it's a fabulous party. Don't you worry about a thing." Georgia waved a manicured hand.

"Thank you. Oh, and Lily," Megan said, turning a smile on her, "your Gerald is a doll! He's been *such* a gentleman, getting drinks for people and mingling like a professional. I can't tell you the last time I met someone so accomplished, socially."

"He's a social lubricant, all right," Georgia said. "Sliding around the company like he's covered with K-Y." At Lily's glare, she added, "But I like him!"

Megan laughed and leaned toward Lily. "I like him, too. Really. And he's so handsome."

Lily breathed a sigh. She was worried they'd find him too formal. "Do you really like him? Have you talked to him? He can seem a bit conservative at first, but he's really not. And he is handsome, isn't he?"

She didn't know why, but she'd been finding him just a little too formal this evening herself. It was probably just her concern about her friends' opinions.

"He's great," Megan reassured her.

"He's handsome, all right," Georgia said. "And he positively reeks of success. *Reeks.*" The way she said it, Lily wasn't sure she meant it as a compliment. "Must be the suit."

"Has anyone seen Penelope yet?" Megan asked. "I'm dying to introduce her to Brady. And he was just asking about her."

Lily's senses went on high alert. "He was?"

"He looks damn good tonight, too," Georgia said, sounding more sincere than she had talking about Gerald. "Don't you think he gives off heat, Megan? He's like some kind of sexual supernova.

I felt explosions going on just walkin' past him."

"He does look good," Megan said.

Lily had to agree with them that he did, in the most amiable way she could, while taking in his easy stance by the archway into the dining room, beer in hand, lean face clean-shaven and those warm eyes smiling into those of some short-haired woman in a business suit.

"Who's he talking to?" Georgia asked.

Megan grabbed a glass of champagne sporting a strawberry in its depths from a passing waiter. "That's Montgomery. One of Sutter's VPs. I hope Brady's flirting with her because she needs flirting with like no other woman I've ever met. In fact, I think she's forgotten she's a woman and not just some asexual corporate drone."

"Maybe Gerald would like to talk to her," Georgia suggested.

"Why do you say that?" Lily demanded.

"Their suits match," Georgia said.

"Do you think I should call Pen?" Megan looked around the room. "It's not like her to be late. Ah! *There* she is." She flashed a smile at Georgia and Lily. "Excuse me. A matchmaker's job is never done!"

She flitted off.

"What is up with her?" Georgia mused, watching Megan go. "She's nervous as a cat, though she looks pretty as a picture, doesn't she? I love that color on her. She should always wear coral."

"She does look beautiful," Lily murmured, but she couldn't take her eyes off Penelope, who looked incredible. Brady was going to fall flat on his ass when he met her. Her long dark hair was loose, flowing over her shoulders onto a white sheath dress that draped perfectly over her slim body. She'd cinched it simply at her waist with an apricot-colored silk scarf. She looked like a million bucks.

Lily glanced down at her own dress, the pale blue one she'd worn to her friend's wedding the previous year. She thought Gerald would like the conservative cut, and he had seemed to. But Brady had barely looked at her all night.

And now all eyes were on Penelope.

Brady surreptitiously glanced at Lily. She didn't look happy. And she didn't look comfortable. For one thing, she was dressed like she was going to a baptism instead of a barbecue. For another, her date had abandoned her the moment they'd walked into the party. He'd been trying to get to her ever since—just to see if there was trouble in paradise— but Megan kept introducing him to people, and Lily was a moving target.

At this moment, she was staring toward the door. He wondered if she were contemplating dumping her date, who was paying elaborate amounts of attention to the women in his conversational circle. Brady knew guys like him. Guys who projected a refined air that women loved but who were privately scum-sucking pigs. Gerald was definitely not a man's man. In fact, every man here probably saw right through the guy. He was the type to come off as a gentleman but was really flirting his ass off with every woman in the place.

Lily deserved better.

He glanced back toward where Lily was looking, expecting to see Gerald, but instead spotted Megan as she approached a stunning woman in a white dress. They hugged each other, as women did when they hadn't seen each other for more than an hour or so, and then they both turned toward him. Megan's eyes sparkled.

Brady's brows rose in surprise.

Good God, he thought. *Is that Penelope?*

Twelve

Lily didn't know what else to do. She saw Megan and Penelope heading for Brady, and all she could do was act. She beelined across the room for them, leaving Georgia in midsentence.

"Penelope! Where were you?" Lily asked when she reached them, leaning in to give her a light hug. "We were starting to get worried."

"I was just telling Megan," Penelope said in a hushed voice. "You wouldn't believe who stopped by just as I was getting ready to leave."

"Who?" Georgia asked, coming up from behind Lily. She shot Lily a speculative glance before turning her attention back to Penelope.

"My ex-husband!" Her eyes were wide.

"Glenn?" Georgia said the name as if it were something in her mouth she needed to spit out.

"I only have the one," Penelope said, feigning exasperation, but she smiled. "He said he needed to talk to me. And he looked really upset about something."

"Anythin' that man has to be upset about should have nothin' to do with you, honey," Georgia said, putting her foot down so hard her drink sloshed. "I hope you kicked him out like the ill-bred cur that he is."

Penelope shrugged, but inhaled tensely. "I had to. I was late coming here. But what do you think he could want?"

"Best not to wonder, sweetie," Georgia said. "That's how they get you. They make you wonder, then the next thing you know you're up nights thinkin' about 'em, wonderin' what they're up to, what they're thinkin', what they want from you. Then they've got you right where they want you. Rat bastards."

"Georgia's date canceled," Megan explained to Penelope and Lily.

They nodded with looks of understanding.

"So what did you tell him?" Lily asked. "Are you going to see him again?"

"I told him I'd meet him tomorrow. For brunch." She smiled wistfully. "We used to love to go to brunch. We'd play tennis early Sunday, sometimes with our friends, Terri and Jeff, but mostly just us. Then we'd go home, shower, and head to Andrew's Mediterranean Bounty for that fabulous buffet they have on the weekends. I loved that ritual."

"Well, *get over it*," Georgia said. "Your future is here, darlin', not behind you. Do you see that guy over there by the dinin' room?"

They all swiveled as one toward Brady, except Lily, who kept her back to him, facing Penelope.

"The one with the pecs to die for," Georgia continued, "and the ass that could stop traffic? Well, you can't see the ass, but trust me. It's fine."

Penelope peered around Lily, trying to look discreet. "The guy standing next to the woman in the suit?"

"The very one." Georgia put her hand on Penelope's forearm. "*That's* your future, honey. That's Brady Cole, and he is hunkier than anyone I've laid eyes on in years." She glanced at Megan with a grin. "Except Sutter, of course." Silence reigned for a minute. "Oh, and Gerald," she added grudgingly.

Penelope gave an excited gasp. "Oh *Gerald's* here. That's right! Where is he?" She looked around.

Lily started to point but Georgia interrupted.

"Penelope, did you not *see* the delectable man I just pointed out? That's Brady! If he doesn't knock Glenn completely off his perch in your mind, then there is somethin' seriously wrong with you."

Penelope glanced back across the room like a chastised child and nodded, giving Georgia an appreciative look. "He *is* handsome."

"That's it?" Georgia protested. "Handsome?"

"Are you not interested in meeting him?" Megan asked. "Does he not look like your type? He was asking where you were earlier, but if you aren't interested, don't worry about it. I just hope I didn't set someone up for disappointment."

"Of course I'm still interested!" Penelope said. "I'm sorry. I'm just so distracted by Glenn's visit. I can't imagine what he wants to talk to me about. We haven't had a real conversation since the divorce papers were signed, something like five years ago."

"Who gives a damn?" Georgia said. "Glenn," she scoffed. "Been there, done that."

Lily, Megan, and Penelope all gaped at her.

"Not *me*." Georgia laid a palm to her chest and looked affronted. "*Penelope* has, for God's sake. What is the matter with you all? You know I'd never poach anybody's ex."

They looked at her dubiously.

"Anybody I'm *friends* with, that is," she amended, with a roll of her eyes.

They laughed.

"Okay," Penelope said, "first things first. Which one is Gerald?"

"Over there," Lily said, pointing toward the hallway. "The tall one, in the suit."

"Oh, he wore a suit," Penelope said. "How elegant."

"Some might say too elegant for the occasion," Georgia said. Then, apparently feeling Lily's eyes upon her, added, "But they'd be jerks for saying so."

"He looks quite the Southern gentleman," Penelope said reassuringly. "And handsome, from this angle, but I can't quite see his face."

Lily gazed at Gerald. He was leaning forward to hear what the woman across from him was saying, so that she didn't have to raise her voice. The musician in the next room was a little loud if you were standing in that hallway. Gerald was nothing if not courteous.

"Let me get him," Lily volunteered. "I can introduce you."

"Not right now, okay, Lil?" Megan said. "Brady just escaped Montgomery. This would be a perfect time to introduce Penelope."

Penelope gave Lily an apologetic look but turned immediately to Megan. "Lead on," she said with a bracing breath. "I'm as ready as I'll ever be."

"No problem," Lily said vaguely, as Megan took Pen's arm and led her away.

She watched them cross the room toward where Brady stood by the shrimp cocktail table. She watched as Megan got his attention, then introduced Brady to His Future. She watched as Brady's smile got broad, and those hazel eyes turned to embers as he looked at her. She watched as Penelope and Brady—perhaps the most attractive couple on the planet—were created.

"Have you tried the falafel?" a voice said beside her. *Gerald*, Lily thought with a sigh. "I'd never had it before, but that woman over there, the one with the frizzy hair, recommended it, and I have to say it's quite tasty. A delicious little morsel, one might say."

Lily turned and looked up at him. He was examining what was left of the "delicious little morsel" on his plate, a slight frown of concentration on his face.

"I wonder what in the world it's made of," he added.

"Chickpeas," Lily said.

"Ugh, God," Georgia muttered behind her. "Chickpeas give me gas."

Gerald's gaze rose to rest on Lily's. "Chickpeas? You're joking."

She shook her head. "I'm pretty sure."

"Me too," Georgia said.

"Gerald, have I introduced you to my friend Georgia?" Lily made a half turn and put a hand on Georgia's upper arm, drawing her with subtle force into their conversational circle.

Gerald extricated his attention from the falafel and gave Georgia his signature smile, along with an outstretched hand. "Georgia, hello, I've heard so much about you."

"All of it scandalous, I hope," Georgia said, one brow raised.

"Every last bit." He laughed.

Georgia smiled, pleased. Lily's heart warmed toward Gerald for the first time all day.

"Feel free to spread it around," Georgia added, grinning. "I live for being the object of heated whispers and unfounded rumor."

"You're going to have to do something about the 'unfounded' part, then," Lily said.

Gerald laughed and put an arm around Lily's shoulders. "She does speak her mind, doesn't she?"

Lily wasn't sure if he was talking about herself or Georgia, but he was at ease and charming and—she could hardly believe it—quite possibly winning over her most difficult friend.

"So tell me, Gerald," Georgia said, "are you having a good time?"

"Oh absolutely. The food is divine. The company uniformly friendly and interesting, and I even think I've made some valuable business contacts. Not that that's the object, mind you, but it does come up in conversation, as you know."

"Oh yes," Georgia said, looking skeptical again. "It does, doesn't it? So tiresome. Just when I think I've escaped the tedium of dog breedin', someone brings up Sage's sperm. Sage is my champion Great Dane, you understand. You just can't imagine how *fatigued* I get of talkin' about his *sperm*. But, of course, it was in the news not so very long ago because my ex-husband and his new wife stole some of it—we have it on ice at a sperm bank, you see—and after that it was on everyone's lips. So to speak. You know how people love to talk about things like sperm."

"Ah, yes, I, ah, suppose so," Gerald said, glancing at Lily.

Lily couldn't suppress half a smile. There was nothing Georgia loved better than shocking people, and shocking Gerald was no doubt something she'd been wanting to do for years.

It was no mistake, either, that Georgia's volume had risen with the topic.

Sure enough, one or two of the people nearest them turned to see who was talking so loudly about sperm.

"It invariably happens at these sorts of soirees," Georgia went on, waving a hand at the company around them. "I'll be chattin' with someone when some dog owner with a bitch in heat will up and want to know all about Sage's reproductive history! Oh sure, they ask about his title and pedigree. Sometimes they want to see pictures. But mostly they want to know how many inseminations there've been, how many pups he's sired, who the bitches are. You know, that sort of thing. Now I ask you: Who can remember so many bitches' names?" she finished, gazing up at him with her wide baby-blues, making clear the question was not rhetorical.

"Ah, I, um, I couldn't say. Just how many have there been?" Gerald asked tentatively.

"Dozens and dozens!" Georgia boomed. "I mean, there are all the ones he actually mounted himself, back in the days before his knees got so fragile. You know how tough sex can be on the knees, I'm sure."

"I—I—I—" Gerald's face went beet red.

"Well it's no different for dogs, let me tell you. Maybe worse, because it's always, you know, doggy style." She let out a girlish laugh. "Tough for the bitches' knees, too, as I'm sure you can imagine. I mean, who among us hasn't woken up with rug burn on our knees a time or two?"

Gerald looked around as if desperate for escape.

Lily glanced back over at Brady and Penelope. They were turning toward the French doors at the opposite end of the dining room, obviously intending to go outside.

"Excuse me a moment," Lily said, turning a smile on Georgia and Gerald. "I'll be right back."

"I'll go with you," Gerald said quickly.

"No, no," Lily said, "I'll only be a minute. Just going to the restroom."

Lily headed that way, went down the hallway—amazed at how the lights preceded her as she walked, illuminating as she approached and going out as she departed; what would it be like to live this luxurious life?—past the bathroom, through the back parlor, and into the kitchen. The huge room was bustling with caterers who pulled trays from the enormous Sub-Zero refrigerator, loaded and unloaded cooking sheets from the three convection ovens, and artistically laid out delicacies on an array of ornate trays on the granite countertops. The caterers smiled at her even as they questioned with their eyes why she was there. She made her way quickly through to the dining room, then out the French doors onto the back patio.

She spotted Brady and Penelope immediately by the koi pond and went to the bar to get herself another white wine. She could see them from there, but couldn't hear what they were saying. All she knew was they each looked engaged in the conversation and not about to break away for food, drink, or mingling with anyone other than the one right in front of them.

She looked around the backyard. This was silly, to be stalking her friend and neighbor when Gerald was inside hopefully impressing the rest of her friends. She should go back in, she thought, but she really didn't want to. Instead, she wandered across the grass to where Megan's older dog, Peyton, lay in the shade of a large tree.

An hour later Lily sat miserably on a chaise longue in the backyard, nursing yet another wine and fingering one of Peyton's silky ears, having lost track of Brady completely. He and Penelope had talked for a long time, and they'd both looked as if they'd enjoyed it. It wasn't until Georgia had come out that Lily realized how pathetic she was being. Watching Brady as if she had anything at stake other than the fact that he had admired her once, and now was going to fall in love with one of her best friends.

She and Georgia had talked a while, and Georgia had even tried to cheer her up about Gerald, telling Lily that she had found herself *liking* him, as he'd ended up handling the sperm conversation with some actual aplomb.

Georgia had just gone off to get another drink when Brady emerged from a group of people near the fence line and crossed Lily's line of sight.

"Can I get you another beer, honey?" he called back to someone.

Lily followed his gaze to see a tall, gorgeous woman with sun-streaked hair and the toned body of a professional athlete. She looked like a racehorse come to life, all sleek and powerful and ready to move.

"Thanks, Brady," she said with a smile. Her eyes were ice-blue.

He'd called her "honey," Lily thought. Who the hell was this woman that he was already calling her "honey"? Had Brady brought a date?

No, she shook her head. He knew he was here to meet Penelope. So maybe this was some woman he'd just picked up. *The sleazy pig!* Lily felt anger flare to life and told herself it was on behalf of her friend, who'd been looking forward to meeting him for weeks. Now here he'd gone and picked up somebody else, right under all their noses. And him supposedly on a *date diet*. She scoffed to herself.

She watched Brady stride to the bar, his gait confident, even cocky. Having women all over you would do that, Lily surmised, ignoring the fact that his gait was always confident. When he turned around to return to that group, he caught her looking at him, raised one of the beers in her direction, and smiled at her.

Lily scowled. How dare he? Did he think he could come over here and give *her* all that macho "honey" crap, too, and get away with it?

"Here you go, honey," he said, handing the blonde the beer, then he turned and headed for Lily. "Hey," he said as he got close. "What're you doing, sitting over here all by yourself?"

He pulled Georgia's lawn chair a little closer and sat down next to her.

"I can't believe how you just spoke to that woman," Lily said, watching the blonde to see if she was watching Brady. "Did you just meet her today? Because that's pretty condescending, don't you think?"

"What?" Brady looked confused and glanced behind him. "What woman?"

"That blonde!" Lily said, indicating the woman

with a twitch of her head. Vaguely, in the back of her mind, she knew she was irked all out of proportion to his actions. "Not to mention that it's pretty tacky trying to pick up another woman even though you are here expressly for the purpose of meeting Penelope. Poor Penelope, who certainly doesn't deserve this!"

Brady gave her an incredulous look. "What the hell are you talking about? That blonde is my copilot. I'm not trying to pick her up. We *work* together, for one thing."

"Your copilot?" Lily repeated, momentarily stunned. Then she sat up, swinging her legs over the side of the chaise because being offended while reclined was unconvincing. "But that's even *worse*! You work together. *She* works for *you*, and you're calling her 'honey'? Oh my God, that's just so—so *sexist*, I can hardly believe it. You'll be lucky if she'd doesn't sue you for harassment."

"Good God, Lily, what in the world has gotten into you?" he asked. "Should I get you another drink, or have you had too much already?"

"I have had just enough, thank you," she said, wondering as she said it what she meant. "I didn't take you for a chauvinist, Brady. And I have to say I'm very sorry to discover it."

"Lily," Brady said, leaning forward so his elbows were on his knees and his face was intent on hers. " 'Honey' is her name. Honey Miller. I'm not picking her up, and I'm not sexually harassing her. I'm calling her by her name."

He leaned back in the lawn chair and looked at her speculatively.

"What is it, Lily? Are you not having a good time? No more marriage talk today?"

"What's that supposed to mean?" she asked defensively. What a fool she was making of herself. His copilot? He *worked* with that beauty? Why didn't she just shut up when something was none of her business?

He gave a one-sided smile, his eyes lazy. "Just what I asked. I saw Gerald in there, schmoozing his way around the crowd. He not paying you enough attention? Is that why you had to leap all over me for calling my copilot by her name?"

"First of all, I did not *know* that was her name," Lily said, infusing her tone with more import than the words deserved. "Second of all, Gerald pays me plenty of attention. More than I want, even. Sometimes." She frowned. That wasn't what she meant to say. Was she drunk? "More than you do, anyway."

"Well, I would hope so." He tilted his head.

"Yes, me too." *Good Lord, I'm not making any sense.* "So, what did you think of Penelope? She's great, isn't she? Don't you like her?" Her tone was combative, though she hadn't meant it to be.

"Of course I like her," he said. "What's not to like?"

"Nothing! There's nothing not to like. She's perfect." Lily threw up her hands and leaned back in the chaise again. "I just hope you're not only falling for her beauty without a thought to what's behind it. Because there's a lot behind Penelope. She's a dear, dear friend, and I would appreciate your not hurting her."

He shook his head, laughing slightly. "How would I hurt her? We only just met."

"For one thing," Lily said, leaning toward him, one elbow wobbling on the arm of the chaise, and lowered her voice, "by telling her about that kiss."

He leaned in, too, his eyes sparkling. "What kiss?" he whispered back.

She narrowed her eyes. "You know what kiss. The one you and I had, a few weeks ago."

"Ohhhh." He leaned back in his chair and smiled like the cat that had swallowed the canary. "That kiss."

"Yes, that kiss, and I'd appreciate it if you'd quit talking about it. I don't want anyone to know." She glanced around them like she was talking to Deep Throat, and everyone else was wearing a wire.

Brady's brows rose. "I'm not the one who brought it up. In fact, I'd nearly forgotten about it."

Lily gasped and straightened so fast she almost pulled a muscle in her neck. "You'd nearly forgotten about it!"

Brady grinned, then laughed out loud. "Don't

be ridiculous, Lily. Of course I hadn't forgotten it. It's been the highlight of my year so far, if you want to know the truth. And it's good to know you haven't forgotten it, either."

Lily knew she was being toyed with, and knew she was handling it badly. She had to relax. She had to sober up.

She paused a long moment. "You know, Brady, I would really appreciate it if you would get me some water," she said finally, after taking a deep breath. She'd have gotten it herself, but she wasn't at all sure that if she got up out of this chair she wouldn't topple off her heels and into the grass.

Brady placed his beer bottle on the ground and stood up, a smile on his face. "With pleasure, honey."

Lily's eyes shot to his, and he laughed.

A moment later he was back with a bottle of water and a cup of coffee.

"I don't need any coffee," she said. She wasn't *that* drunk. Just a little tipsy.

"It's not for you," he said, taking a sip. "So tell me, Lily, why are you with Gerald? Or rather, if you're here with Gerald, why aren't you *with* Gerald? Where is he, anyway?" He looked around the yard, eyes scanning the crowd.

She took a generous swig of the water. "I don't believe a couple has to be joined at the hip at a party."

"You two don't seem to be joined at all," he said.

She frowned at him. "We were just in there moments ago, talking about falafel." She gestured toward the house.

"Falafel."

"That's right. It's made from chickpeas."

He made a face.

"It's very good for you," she said piously.

"Maybe. But it doesn't sound like good conversation. I hope he did better with all the other women he was talking to."

Lily nearly choked on her gulp of water. "What are you trying to say, Brady? Are you attempting to make insinuations about my boyfriend? Because if you are, you can give that up right now. Gerald may converse easily with others, but he would never cheat on me. Of that, I'm sure." She sighed heavily, thinking it might be a little too true.

Brady took another slow sip of his coffee. "I'm just wondering, and maybe you can help me out here, why are you with that guy, Lily? He doesn't even seem like your type. In fact, you seem like you're having to do some work to be *his* type." He scanned her dress with his eyes. "What kind of guy wears a suit to a cookout, for instance? And you look like you're going to a wedding."

Lily looked down at her dress, dismayed at his perception.

"Living next door to you," Brady continued, "I happen to know that you usually dress real well, like, in an appropriate way for a situation. But today you look like a Stepford wife. Is it just because Daddy likes him? Because I met your dad, and sure, he's a tough nut. But he didn't seem like the type of guy who'd want his daughter to marry someone who didn't make her happy."

Lily was sitting up so straight and tense the cords on the front of her neck began to hurt. "Gerald *does* make me happy. And who are you to tell me about my father?"

"I'm just curious about you, Lily Tyler. You seem like a together sort of woman, and you're certainly feisty enough to handle anything thrown your way. Yet you're driving your daddy's old car, you're living in your daddy's house, and you're doing everything you can to sell yourself to a partner in your daddy's firm. Tell me, Lily, is there anything about you that isn't a product of what Daddy wants?"

Lily glared at him, mouth agape. "That's—not true."

"What's not true? That you're living like someone who has no respect for herself?"

Lily's head began to spin, and she suddenly felt as if she might throw up.

"Darling?" Gerald's voice floated out of the crowd beyond Brady.

Lily looked up into Brady's unreadable eyes, heart pounding hard, her face flushed.

Brady leaned in close just before Gerald arrived and his words, low and intense, sent a shiver up her spine. "Better quit talking about that kiss."

Thirteen

"Megan has asked us all to come outside for a moment," Gerald said, oblivious to the electricity arcing between Brady and Lily. "I believe she has an announcement to make. What do you suppose it's about?"

"I'm getting another beer," Brady said. "Gerald, good to see you."

He slapped Gerald once on the back and strode off, leaving Lily standing in the wake of his unreasonable irritation.

Why had he gone after her like that? She didn't deserve all he'd said. It was just that he'd seen her in that fancy blue dress, with her fancy-suited man, and he'd thought, *Who is that woman?* Not the one who'd answered her door in a bathrobe and given in to passion that was a bolt from the blue for both of them, that was for sure.

He was scowling when he reached the patio and headed straight for the bar, where he ran into Megan.

"Sam Adams," he told one of the bartenders, then turned to Megan, trying like hell to school the expression on his face into something resembling nonchalance. "So, an announcement, huh? Belle expecting a little sister or brother?"

Megan regarded him silently a minute, a curious smile on her lips. "I know this is none of my business," she said finally, "but were you and Lily just fighting?"

"Fighting?" he repeated, disingenuous as hell.

"Because it looked like you were fighting," Megan went on. "Which is curious since in my experience people who are relatively new to each other don't get into subjects that put a look on someone's face like the one that was just on yours."

"We might have had a little disagreement." He wrapped a cocktail napkin around the wet beer, put his spare hand in his pocket, and made himself look Megan directly in the eye. "The look on my face is probably due more to the fact that I'm not used to drinking much, but Sutter said we won't be flying until at least Wednesday." He gave her what was probably an unconvincing grin. "So cheers."

"Your champagnes," the other bartender said, holding out two glasses for Megan.

Brady looked from the glasses to Megan. "Two-fisted. I guess the announcement isn't about a sibling for Belle then, huh?" He laughed, the sound coming out less than spontaneously.

"Brady, can I ask you something quite bluntly?" Megan asked.

"That question there's rather blunt all by itself," he said, looking around the yard in an effort to avoid her frank gaze.

"It's not really my business except that I don't want to lead anyone on in any specific direction if those directions are not open for, uh . . . traffic?" She laughed at herself. "Jeez, that was convoluted. Let me put it plainly. If you're not interested in Penelope, because, say, you're interested in Lily, it would be better for everyone concerned if I said something to defuse the current plan."

Brady's hand gripped his beer bottle hard. "I like Penelope," he said, noncommittally. "But the thing is, and I should have told you this before, I'm not dating right now. Anybody. I'm taking a break from that whole . . . effort."

"Why's that?"

He looked at her and grinned, for real this time. "You are the most *direct* person I've ever met."

She laughed. "I get that a lot. I'm also persistent. And not easily distracted. So—why are you taking a break from dating? Bad breakup? Broken heart? Poor dating choices?"

Brady opened his mouth to say all of the above, but was saved by Sutter's appearance by Megan's side.

"We've got the whole lot assembled," he said. "Shall we wow them with our news?" He turned his smile from Megan to Brady.

Megan handed Sutter one of the glasses of champagne. "I'm sorry. I just got caught up here." She turned away with Sutter but shot Brady a parting glance. "We're not finished!" she said to him, and there was something about her smile that made her relentless prying completely charming.

Sutter and Megan moved to the steps that led down to the lawn and stood quietly. Someone began tapping a piece of silverware against a glass, quieting the crowd. Before long, everyone had silenced, and the two stood looking out over the assemblage of most of their friends and family.

"We have an announcement to make," Megan said, her clear voice sailing high in the summery air.

She looked happy, Brady thought, as did Sutter. They stood close but not touching, as if so confident of the other's presence that they needed only proximity to be secure.

Megan turned to Sutter, and said, "You go ahead. I'm suddenly too nervous."

Sutter laughed and raised his glass. "I'll make it short and sweet. Please join me in raising a glass to my lovely fiancée, Megan Rose, who has taken pity on this poor soul before you and agreed to marry me."

The two beamed across the crowd as voices rose in delighted congratulations, and glasses *tinked* together repeatedly.

Sutter and Megan looked at each other and smiled, their expressions speaking volumes about their happiness. Sutter bent down and kissed his fiancée.

Brady's eyes strayed from the happy couple across the lawn to where Lily stood by the chaise longue, Gerald beside her lifting his glass. Gerald's eyes were still on the happy couple, but Brady's were on Lily. She had a hand to her forehead and was looking at the ground. He felt a moment's unease and took a step forward. He was way too far to do anything, however, when a second later she slowly crumpled to the grass beside Gerald, landing in a pile of fancy blue dress.

Brady dropped his beer, vaguely heard it smash on the flagstone patio, and raced across the yard, heedless of the people who had no idea what was going on and got in his way.

Heart pounding in sudden fear, he wasn't sure what he'd do once he got there. He knew only that he had to get to her, pick her up, make her all right.

Gerald was just figuring out that the brush against his leg was not the dog but his girlfriend hitting the turf when Brady skidded to her side, immediately on his knees. Gerald turned and gave a startled cry.

"Lily! Good God, what's happened?" Gerald said, lowering himself to Lily's other side.

Brady lifted her shoulders and laid her back against one of his arms, straightening her dress with his other hand. He gently pushed the hair from her face.

"Lily," he said, staring into her face. He lightly tapped her cheek with his palm. "Come on, now. Come back to us. Lily?"

Her eyelids flickered, and Brady took a huge breath, the first one he'd taken since he'd vaulted off the patio toward her.

Then she inhaled sharply and opened her eyes wide, jerking her limbs when she realized she was on the ground.

"Don't move for a second," Brady said, holding her tightly, keeping her from rising. He stroked the hair at her temple. "Just lie still for a minute. You're all right."

"What? Brady? What happened?" Her voice was soft, and she looked at him almost tenderly. She tried to sit up again, then focused on Brady's face and leaned back into his arms. "What's going on?" She clutched his shirtfront with one hand.

"Darling, you fainted," Gerald said, prying her

hand from Brady's shirt and taking it in his, while bestowing a withering look on Brady. "Come here, sweetheart."

Gerald reached in and pulled Lily from Brady's arms, moving her toward him. But she foiled them both by extricating her hand from Gerald's and pushing herself to a sitting position on her own.

"Oh my God," she said, sinking her face momentarily into her hands. Then she lifted her head, pushed the hair from her face, and looked up into the crowd around them. "This is so embarrassing."

"Lily!" Megan pushed through the crowd; behind her were Sutter, Georgia, and Penelope. "Is somebody calling nine-one-one?"

Five people with cell phones raised them up. "On it!"

"I am!"

"Got it!"

"No!" Lily said. "Please don't. I'm *fine*. I just—I don't know what happened."

"Stand back," Sutter said to the people surrounding them. "Please, we mustn't crowd her. Lily, it's best if you're seen by a medic. I know we'd all feel better."

"Yes, Lily, please let them come," Penelope said.

Lily put a hand to her forehead again. "No, I'm really okay. It's just that I'm not used to this heat. And I think I had a bit too much wine."

Georgia pushed past the others to kneel by her

side, her shoulders infringing on Gerald's space, to his obvious annoyance. "Are you tellin' us you passed out from wine?" she burst. "That's ridiculous. I've never seen you drink that much in your life."

Lily gave a weak laugh. "No. I'm not drunk. But . . . I don't think I ate enough. Please!" She held out a hand to the cell-phone crew. "Please tell them not to come. I don't need the paramedics. I'll go to the doctor Monday, I promise."

She turned pleading eyes from Megan to Sutter. "Tell them to stop. I'm *fine*. Really. I don't want to ruin your big day."

Brady saw tears gather in her eyes and passed her a napkin he'd folded in his pocket from one of his beers.

She took it with a grateful smile.

"I think she's all right," he said. "I can look in on her later tonight, too. Make sure she's still feeling okay. And I'm right next door if she needs anything." He looked at her again, his heart still laboring to return to a normal rhythm. "Anything at all."

"Excuse me, but *I* can do that," Gerald said tersely.

Brady turned cool eyes upon him. "Of course you can. And I'm sure you'll be right on the case until you turn into a pumpkin at ten o'clock. I can handle things after that. And I can get her to the doctor on Monday."

"Congratulations!" Lily burst loudly above their two voices. She gave an embarrassed smile to Sutter and Megan. "This is all very unnecessary and we're distracting everyone from the real point here." She gave both Brady and Gerald a pleading look. "Sutter and Megan are getting married! Let's celebrate!"

She started to push herself to her feet. Brady helped her up with one arm, Gerald grabbed the other.

Megan laughed and reached out for one of her hands. "Thank you. And thank you, too, for breaking up that awkward moment after the announcement. We weren't sure how to get off the stage."

Lily laughed but gave a pained look. "I'm so sorry."

"Don't be silly," Sutter said. "Megan was serious. We hadn't thought beyond the announcement. You were the perfect denouement."

Nobody else but Sutter with his impeccable British accent could have uttered that word without sounding gay, Brady thought.

"I think you're looking a little better," Penelope said, reaching one hand toward her forehead.

"Yes, your color's back," Georgia concurred, elbowing Gerald out of the way and taking Lily's arm. "Why don't we go into the house a minute and get you straightened up?"

"Good idea," Penelope said.

Brady backed up a step as Penelope slid into his place. He let go of Lily's arm reluctantly.

He could not keep his eyes from Lily as she moved away from him unsteadily. She had fallen with the grace of a ballerina, like a wounded bird, toppling lightly from a tree branch. It had scared him like nothing had ever scared him before.

And . . . he wasn't sure if it was his imagination or not, but he could swear Lily squeezed his hand before letting it go.

"Gerald, it's all right," Lily said, one hand flat on his chest where they stood at her front door. "I'm fine. I think I just need to get in bed and go right to sleep."

"But I'm worried about you," he said, his dark velvet eyes the very picture of concern. "Perhaps I should put off my trip Monday. I'm sure they could wait an extra day for me. That way I could stay here tonight and tomorrow and make sure you're all right, then pack on Monday and leave Tuesday."

Lily's brows rose in surprise. "You'd do—?"

"Oh no, wait." He smacked a hand to his forehead. "Meeting with Keller Monday night. Can't cancel it, he'll think I'm not committed. He's like that, you know. I'll be dog tired, too, from that long trip, but with the time change in their favor they expect you to hit the ground running." He shook his head. "But I can stay tonight."

Lily looked at him in wonder.

"Gerald," she said firmly, this time with a slight push on his chest. He backed up a step over the threshold. "It's all right. You go. There's no reason to rearrange your schedule. Don't worry about me. Really. We'll talk once you get there, and I can tell you all about how the doctor said I was perfectly fine."

"Perfectly perfect, is what he'll say," Gerald replied, taking her upper arms in his hands and running them up and down. He gave her a reassuring smile. "Did I tell you how beautiful you looked today? Even sprawled out on the ground?"

She laughed. "Oh yes, nobody ever looked better passed out on the lawn."

He caressed her arms a few more times, looking at her tenderly. "All right. I'll let you get to sleep, now. But darling, are you sure I should leave? I could stay until morning, just to be sure you're all right, that you don't need anything. I'll sleep on the couch!"

Lily made herself smile. He meant so well, but she wanted him gone. And soon.

"I am *fine*. I just need some sleep." She rose up on tiptoe and gave him a quick peck on the mouth, telling herself it was appropriate and not just because she wanted to avoid the sucking chasm of a kiss like the other night's. "Go home, get your packing done tomorrow. We can talk in the morning if you want to."

He stepped forward and took her in his arms, pulling her close. Lily leaned into him. Despite everything else, he did give a nice hug. She laid her cheek on his lapel and inhaled his scent. A Dior scent, he'd once told her. Really for women, but he liked it better than the men's colognes. She smiled into his summerweight wool. No wonder Doug liked him. He smelled like a girl.

He started to pull away, dipping his head to come in for a kiss.

Lily stepped back abruptly. "You go on, now, Gerald. Enjoy Hawaii while you're there, and we'll discuss everything when you get back. All right? Let's not worry about anything else right now. You've got to concentrate on your work, and I've decided to teach summer school. It's best that we get on with it. Right now." She smiled to temper her words.

Gerald looked confused, and Lily was sure it was because, after two years of besotted devotion and unrequited affection from her, he was suddenly sensing her withdrawal.

"Good night, Gerald," she said.

"I'll—talk to you tomorrow?" he said, holding on to her hand until he had just her fingertips. "Make sure you're okay?"

"Of course," she said reassuringly.

He bent toward her again. She turned her face to the side. And, for once, when he left she was happy to have gotten only the chaste peck on the cheek.

Lily closed the door behind him and went into the kitchen, Doug at her heels. With a sigh of relief, she got herself a glass of water and leaned on the counter, looking out the back window at the black night. She turned on no lights, just stood in the darkness, sipping her water and thinking.

She had made a huge mistake. She was so suddenly sure of it she could hardly believe she'd never noticed, never even *questioned* it until this moment, this fateful evening.

She had fallen for a man she had mostly invented. Gerald wasn't her Mr. Knightley. He was a nice man from her father's office, who dressed well and had a *GQ* face, but who didn't understand her or truly care for her. Nor did she understand him, beyond what she'd projected onto him.

Doug went to the back door and looked up at her expectantly, panting lightly.

"Okay," she said, and opened it, stepping out onto the back porch with him.

Doug trotted happily out into the yard, sniffed the air, and promptly darted for the back fence, a favorite haunt of his lately.

Lily sat down on the back stoop, water in her hand.

Her father . . . she could barely stand to think about him. What would he think? That she'd flaked out on him again. He'd had his heart set on Gerald, and now she knew he would believe she just couldn't wait those eight weeks Gerald might be away. That she was too impulsive to put the time in. He'd never understand that she'd simply had a revelation that Gerald was not *the one*.

The one was someone she'd put out of reach, someone of whom her father would never approve, someone who did not fit in that imaginary picture frame she'd placed on her father's desk.

She was such a fool, falling for Mr. Churchill instead of Mr. Knightley, but what could she do? She was no Emma.

"Are you feeling better now?"

The voice from the darkness startled her, but for some reason she wasn't completely surprised to hear it. From the shadows of his side of the back porch—a mirror image of the front porch—Brady walked down the steps and around the center railing to put one foot on her stoop. Both hands were in his pockets. He'd changed from his khakis and polo shirt into jeans, an untucked tee shirt, and no shoes.

"I feel," she said, "remarkably normal."

Except for this fluttering in my chest whenever you're near, and the dampening of my palms, and sadness in my heart. Because Brady didn't want her, she knew. He didn't even respect her. He'd made that clear this afternoon. When you got down to it, she didn't think much of herself, either. She'd agreed with all he'd said. Why *would* he respect someone who'd turned a schoolgirl-type fairy tale into her life's ambition? He'd seen right through her, to the false hopes, the pompous assumptions and the shallow reasons for wanting to marry Gerald.

"You scared the shit out of me, you know," he said, his voice neutral, unreadable. Was he still annoyed with her? Should she be annoyed with him? "I thought you'd had a heart attack or something."

She laughed once. "I'm getting old, Brady. But I'm not that old."

"You know I didn't mean that," he said quietly.

She sighed. "I know."

Silence held sway a few moments. A breeze lifted her hair from her cheek and ran its fingers along her skin. Brady sat down on the bottom step and leaned back against the porch column.

"I'm sorry for what I said this afternoon," he said finally. "It was totally uncalled for. I didn't intend to hurt you."

She shook her head, though he wasn't looking at her. "Don't worry about it. I'm all right."

She swallowed over a lump in her throat. A foolish, childish, don't-say-mean-things-to-me lump. She disliked herself for that, too.

He lowered his head, picked at some grass beside his feet with one hand. "I just . . . I wish I hadn't said it. Any of it."

"We'll forget about it," she said, feeling tired.

He chuckled mirthlessly. "I won't."

They sat in silence a few more minutes, Brady's discomfort obvious. She knew he was sorry. He wasn't a mean person. It wasn't his fault that everything he'd said had been true.

"You're awfully brave to be out here with Doug on the loose," she said finally.

"Damn, is he out here?"

The fact that he didn't leap up from his seat told her he wasn't afraid of her dog the way Nathan was, but she knew he didn't like Doug. That had been the most perfect thing about Gerald, the fact that Doug had actually liked him. And vice versa! She'd considered it a sign, but was it?

Or was the sign the fact that Brady obviously disliked Doug, no matter what the dog felt? It bothered her, his dislike, more than anything else. It felt like . . . judgment.

"He's down by the fence," Lily said.

She saw Brady's silhouette nod.

Lily took a sip of her water. "Look, I'm sorry to have scared you, but I'm okay now. There was a nurse at the party who said it's not all that uncommon for women to faint if they've had nothing to eat."

Plus she'd just finished her period and was a little anemic, but she wasn't going to get into that with Brady.

Besides, she knew the real reason she'd fainted. She had stopped breathing. Just before the faint, that was. As Sutter and Megan were making their announcement, as the two of them stood up there so obviously in love, so obviously connected, so obviously meant for each other, Lily had come to the realization that Gerald—the Gerald who had for so long embodied her Mr. Knightley—was a figment of her imagination. He wasn't a real, solid, flesh-and-blood soul mate like Sutter was to Megan.

With that realization came the breathless certainty that she'd been kidding herself for *years*, that she'd been blind to what had been right in front of her face for all that time.

She wasn't in love with Gerald. And he most certainly wasn't in love with her. They were both playing the same game—with themselves and with each other.

Her father had somehow, without even trying, made it clear that he wanted them together, and obedient children that they were—Lily his biological daughter and Gerald his ergonomic son—they went along. They told themselves they belonged together. And Gerald still believed it, apparently.

As Lily saw it now, the faint was the line of demarcation between illusion and reality. She been existing in illusion for years and had been so shocked by reality that she had stopped breathing. Stopped until she lost consciousness. As if she had to erase all that had gone before. She'd gone down the moment she'd realized that the myth of Gerald was just that, a myth, and she'd woken up with the certain knowledge that he was not the right man for her.

"If fainting was normal," Brady said now, "you'd see women dropping like flies everywhere you went. I hope you're still planning to see a doctor on Monday."

She smiled at his severe tone. "You're sounding like an old mother hen, Brady. Who would've guessed you had that in you?"

"Not me, that's for damn sure," he said dourly.

From the back of the yard, a chunky white wraith emerged from the trees bordering the alley and raced up the lawn, suddenly stopping halfway. Nose in the air, Doug turned in a circle, onto some scent more distracting even than an actual man on his back porch.

"You have the weirdest dog I have ever known," Brady said. "Yesterday I saw him licking your back door."

Lily looked from Doug to Brady. "Maybe he wanted to get in."

Brady laughed. "I'm not surprised you didn't hear him knocking."

"All dogs have idiosyncrasies."

Brady shook his head. "Not like that one. He's a menace. Did I tell you he's been stealing my shoes?"

"What?" Lily tilted her head toward him. "Stealing your shoes?"

"Yeah. I'm missing a whole bunch of shoes."

"Doug wouldn't take them!" she said, instantly on the defensive.

Talk about a mother hen. Doug was a lot of things, but shoe thief wasn't one of them. Lily was tired of people blaming him for things he couldn't possibly have done. Nathan's mother was always complaining that he dug up her flower beds and defecated in her garden, despite the fact that Doug never left Lily's yard.

"How do you know?" Brady swiveled on the step to look at her.

"How do you know he did?"

"Because the screen on my back window was clawed out of its frame, and it was obviously done by an animal."

"So? It could've been a raccoon. Or a squirrel. Or a *person*. Look, Brady, I know you don't like Doug. But you don't have to make things up about him just to prove the point. It's okay. Lots of guys don't like Doug. And vice versa," she said pointedly, as if the fact of Doug's animosity could possibly be an insult. Crazy as it seemed, though, Lily still thought it was.

To have Brady hate Doug, however, made her so upset she could hardly stop herself. Now that she realized she could never be with Gerald, and that Brady not only didn't like her dog, but he very likely didn't like her either . . . well, it was all just too much.

"I'm not making anything up," Brady said, his voice edged with indignation. "The damn dog's been taking my shoes. In fact, he's taken one from every damn pair I have."

Lily laughed cynically. "Are you telling me my dog has figured out which shoes go together, and has taken one of each? My goodness, what fashion sense he has. I never realized."

"He's demonic, that dog," Brady said heatedly. "I have no doubt he's capable of figuring out which shoes go together. Look at him." He threw a hand out toward where Doug was now periodically standing up on two back feet, paddling his front feet in the air and sniffing the breeze. "What the hell is he doing? Tracking bats?"

Lily frowned, watching the dog's antics. He did do some strange things, she had to admit, but that was part of his charm. Brady would never understand that.

"I don't know," she said. "But I do know he doesn't steal shoes."

She stood up. She didn't need to sit out here and listen to him belittle her dog, proving with every word that he and Lily were nothing alike, had nothing in common, and could barely be good neighbors, let alone anything else.

Brady stood too. "Come on, Lily, we both know he hates me. I'll get the screen and show you. It was obviously him."

"That wouldn't prove anything. How do you know it wasn't Tricia? Huh? Doesn't that seem more likely to you? That the woman you drove insane came and stole your shoes? Maybe she's sleeping with them under her pillow. Maybe you drive every woman you meet insane. Did you ever think of that?" She spun on the step and grabbed for the back door.

With one step Brady was beside her, hand on her arm, turning her back around.

"It wasn't Tricia. And I don't drive every woman I meet insane."

Even in the dark his eyes were fierce. The feel of his hand on her arm was hot, tight, and compelling.

Lily swallowed over another lump in her throat. He hated her dog. He thought she was stupid and immature. He—he was looking at her like . . . like . . .

Brady stepped in and slid his other arm around her waist. Before she could say a word, his mouth descended onto hers.

Fourteen

The kiss was delicious. She fell into it like a pool of warm water, let it envelop her, sweep her under, drown her. Their tongues touched and twined, their bodies melded, her hands reached up to his head, and her fingers dove into his thick, soft hair.

Their bodies were a symphony, their coming together a tango, the kiss a perfectly balanced blend of lips, tongues, breaths, hands, and bodies. She felt as if she were spiraling upward toward the heavens, and downward toward the white-hot center of the earth.

She was embraced by a body at once protective and potent, and the sensation was heady.

Her hands grabbed his torso, spreading wide as they traveled up his ribs, feeling the solid, muscular mass of him.

His hands swept up her back to bury themselves in her hair. He pulled back slightly, bending his knees and moving his head to trail his lips down her neck to that spot—oh God that *spot*—on the side of her neck that shot shivers up and down her skin. She grabbed his arms, wanting skin, then held his head, her fingers clutching his hair.

He backed her up against the door, his lips taking hers again. His body pressed against her, his hips on hers, grinding her against the wall. It was hard and painful, and she couldn't get enough.

There was no hesitation this time. No pulling back. He wanted her, that was obvious. And he was going to get her unless she did something drastic.

Something she was not about to do.

"Let's go inside," she said.

Her skin was on fire, her nerves electric. She felt as if she were eating cake with icing that made the roof of her mouth tingle with sugary sweetness—decadence, extravagance, too much and not enough.

"What's the matter, Lily? Never done it outside?" He smiled against her lips and took her mouth again in a commanding kiss.

Laughter bubbled up within her—laughter borne of adrenaline, of power, of lust.

"I'm not sure you're aware," she said between

kisses, holding his face in her hands, "that the moment Doug gets bored with whatever he's doing, he'll be all over you."

Brady didn't need any more prompting. He reached past her, opened the door, and they stumbled back inside. He kicked the door shut behind them with one foot, and they came together again like a clamshell, no air between them.

Mouths, hands, bodies reached, touched, moved like synchronized parts of a clock.

Brady's arms encircled her, pulling and holding her to him as he moved them through the kitchen. She opened her eyes to see him watching where they were going and giggled through the kiss.

She knew where he was headed. She pulled away and took his hand.

"Come on," she said.

She led him up the stairs to the bedroom. They arrived breathless, almost startled to find themselves there.

"Do we need to talk about something?" Brady asked.

Lily paused, looking into his eyes. But neither his expression nor his question gave away what he was thinking.

"I don't know. Do you need to talk about something?"

Brady paused, staring back. Illogically, Lily shivered under the heat of his gaze.

"Not if you don't," he said finally.

They each laughed quietly, nervously. Then Brady moved forward. His hands slipped around her waist and she felt again how large his presence was. Almost as if his hands could span her waist and lift her to the ceiling with ease. She was light as a feather, he was strong as a titan, they were producing an energy together that was otherworldly.

I want you. The words sprang to Lily's mind but she dared not speak them. Her hold on this moment seemed so tenuous.

She should be thinking . . . of someone . . . of something . . . else. But she couldn't think of anything but Brady, here before her. He was looking at her in the way she'd always dreamed of being looked at. As if he saw her, recognized her soul. He understood her, she felt, in ways she didn't even understand herself.

"Lily," he said softly, his lips brushing her cheek, moving softly to her ear.

She closed her eyes, let her hands rest on his upper arms, feeling the bulge of his biceps, the tension in his touch. She inhaled, and the sound quivered between them.

He trailed his tongue down her neck while his fingers moved to the zipper at the back of her dress.

"Can I take this off?" he asked. The question was so quiet she felt as if she might have dreamed it.

Afraid of speaking and waking from the moment, she turned her back to him, felt the zipper descend, felt the fabric of the dress loosen and fall to her feet.

Brady's arms came around her and his lips pressed against the muscle between her shoulder and neck, then moved to her nape. She inhaled again, closed her eyes, dug her fingers into his forearms enveloping her.

"I've wanted to do this since the first moment I saw you," he said.

She smiled into the darkness, inhaling deeply with the words. Could he mean them? Did he feel that way about her, always? Or did he just say this sort of thing . . . ?"

She turned in his arms, putting her hands to his face and pulling it down to hers. Their lips met. She moved her fingers to his shirt, sliding down until she was at the hem of his tee shirt, and pulled upward.

"Can I take this off?" She echoed his words, smiling with them.

He stepped back a fraction and held out his arms.

She pulled the shirt over the waistband of his jeans, up his torso, watching as the tightly muscled stomach was revealed. Then the well-defined chest, the muscled shoulders, flexed and long as he held his arms over his head.

She whipped the shirt over his head and tossed it to the side, letting her hands trail his lean, toned body. Who knew this was what resided beneath all those sweaty tee shirts he ran in? She knew he had nice legs, but this *body*. She palmed his skin, ran her hands down his chest to his waist, fingered the subtle line of hair that emerged from just above the button of his jeans.

"Let me help you with those," he murmured.

She shook her head. Then she pressed her lips to his chest, sucking the skin just hard enough to leave a mark, a temporary one, while her fingers flipped the button open, and pulled the fly down over the hardness beneath.

One of Brady's hands reached behind her and flicked her bra open, easy as if he'd flicked a fly off the wall. She laughed and dropped the garment on the floor between them.

Once she had his fly open, she pushed the flaps wide, then, slowly, placed her hands on his hips and pushed his jeans and boxers, along with her panties, down, down, down until they reached the floor.

She rose, running one hand up his hardness as she did. He stepped out of the puddle of clothing, and they were naked together.

Lily stepped close and sighed as skin touched skin for the first time. Her breasts against his chest, his legs against hers, the soft, hard, private, shared desire pressed between them, generating a heat that grew exponentially with each second.

Brady kissed her again, and Lily felt the length of her body become his. She was fluid and soft, yet relentless. There was no stopping her now, his body was hers. She took him by the hand and led him to the bed.

She leaned back, he knelt forward, and they were kissing again. He pressed her into the bedclothes, his body atop hers, his fingers probing the apex of her thighs. She opened to him, clutching his back, wrapping her legs around his thighs.

Brady rose up on his arms and looked down at her. His muscles flexed, his chest hardened, and she ran her hands across it.

"Lily," he said, and she knew the question in the word.

She nodded, and reached between his legs, cupping his desire, feeling it throb in her hand. He inhaled sharply as her hand stroked its length, and she guided him to her center.

His hips pushed forward, urging himself toward her. He pressed gently, once, twice. She held him tightly and raised her hips, feeling herself open in near anxiety, so eager for his penetration.

He touched her again, moving his hips, and ran his tongue down the side of her neck.

She groaned, wanting—needing—him inside of her. Her hips pressed upward, but he backed away slightly, touching her, moving just slightly inside, teasing her.

"Brady," she breathed, pulling at his hips with both hands.

As if his spoken name released him, he dove

inside of her, filling her, making her gasp with surprise and sudden gratification.

He was not gentle then. He entered her swiftly, strongly, again and again. No more were the kisses soft, the tongue tickling and teasing down her neck. His body pounded into hers, and she answered his every thrust. His mouth found hers and they went after each other ravenously, hungry for the kiss, devouring each other's breath.

Lily spiraled out of control, her head spinning and her body wild. She clutched at him, digging her fingers into his back, hanging on for dear life and still not getting enough, never enough. He was as deep as deep could be, and he moved as if possessed, until she splintered and gasped, her world exploding into a million shards of ecstasy dancing under her skin. She arched stiff and threw her head back, muscles contracting and her heart bursting with exhilaration.

She felt Brady's body stiffen seconds afterward. As she sank back into the mattress he thrust one final time, expelling a breath of air, and pushed into her deep, and hot, and throbbing. Then he sank above her, canting sideways so that their bodies meshed together in a damp, satisfied heap, connected, fulfilled.

Brady wasn't sure how much later it was when Lily sat bolt upright in bed.

He looked at her in the dark, her hair wild around

her head, her body still sheened with sweat from their lovemaking. He wanted to take her again, God help him. He felt like he'd been wrung out and whipped dead, but by God he could do it again in a heartbeat.

"Doug," she whispered.

Brady pushed up onto one elbow, taking a strained moment to remember that Doug was not some other guy, but her fiendish, possessive dog who had somehow missed an excellent opportunity to castrate Brady.

"What is it? What about him?" Brady asked. His voice emerged husky. The result of a spent body.

She pushed her legs to the side of the bed and got up, moving swiftly to the closet. She pulled forth the fluffy pink robe he remembered so fondly.

"It's Doug. I left him outside, and now he's barking." She turned to Brady in the dark and though he couldn't see her face clearly, for some reason he was sure she looked panicked. "He sounds scared."

Brady could hear it then, too, the shrill, constant yips. A cross between a cry and a bark.

Lily spun and ran for the stairs.

Brady leaned back and sighed. He could think of better endings to this evening. Like, for example, it being morning and the two of them waking up together. But leave it to Doug to screw up what Brady would like.

He'd also like two matching shoes.

Reluctantly, he pressed himself up to sitting, then swung his legs over the side of the bed. He felt consumed, exhausted, and thoroughly content. How long had it been since he'd had sex?

How much longer before that had it been since he'd had sex with someone he cared about? Lily was incredible, a firebrand, a hellcat, a body of passions the likes of which he'd never before known. At the same time she was tiny, a princess, a delicate cloud of emotions needing protection. She produced in him the strangest set of feelings he'd ever had. He needed to fight her and protect her.

What kind of weird shit was that?

He pulled on his boxers and jeans and followed her down the stairs. When he found her in the kitchen she was holding a trembling Doug and cooing in his ear.

"He okay?" Brady asked.

The moment the words were out of his mouth, the dog exploded with barks and growls, his paws freestyling against Lily's arm in an effort to get at Brady.

Brady backed up, worried about Lily's safety while she tried to calm the little beast.

"Should I go?" he asked. The dog could inflict actual damage on Lily in trying to get to him. "Would it be easier . . ."

She didn't look at him. "Yes, I think it would."

He backed out of the kitchen a couple of steps,

trepidation suddenly taking hold. He meant should he go back upstairs, but he had the feeling that she meant he should leave. Go home.

Was she regretting what had just happened? Had this been another "mistake"?

Brady suddenly found it difficult to breathe. He turned and headed upstairs. He would get his shirt, he thought. He would get it slowly, and maybe she would put the dog somewhere and come up . . . ask him to stay . . . tell him she wanted him to stay, wanted to wake up with him, as he wanted to do with her.

But as he reached the bedroom, he knew that she would not be up. She was down there, placating the wretched dog, soothing it after the trauma of finding a man who wasn't Gerald in the house with her.

Maybe soothing herself from that very same trauma.

Brady felt anger well up within him. He was not some substitute for a guy she couldn't get to sleep with her.

So he wasn't a lawyer with umpteen million years of schooling behind him. So he wasn't on the "partner track" making five hundred thousand dollars a year. So he didn't wear a suit to a barbecue.

He would *never* do that.

He was who he was, and if she didn't want *him*, Brady Cole, imperfect, badly behaved, poorly educated, flawed but *trying,* dammit, then he didn't want her.

He grabbed his shirt up off the floor and pulled it over his head. Then he went down the stairs—glancing into the empty living room and down the hall to the kitchen, but he didn't see her—and went out the front door.

No good-bye—the dog might get upset—no eye contact to confirm that she wished him gone, wished him *Gerald*; no *see you around* to establish that this had been another mistake, that she was another entrée on his list of forbidden fruits. He had, accidentally, had another one-night stand.

But this one broke his heart.

Penelope! She'd forgotten all about Penelope! Or had she? Maybe she'd blocked her out, not wanted to confront that question on the heels of realizing what an idiot she'd been for so long about Gerald.

Now she was not only an idiot, but a terrible friend. And a slut. And a bad dog owner.

Lily heard the front door close behind Brady and she sat down at the kitchen table. She placed Doug on the floor and wept into her hands.

Doug licked her calf, whining softly from the floor.

She was so exhausted. So confused. She'd gotten what she'd wanted tonight, but only for tonight. She and Brady weren't a good couple. They wanted each other, but other than that, what did they have in common? And even if she didn't care, she was sure that he had no intention of turning this into a relationship. Not after what he'd said to her that afternoon. Not Brady Cole, self-made man. He'd never settle for a Daddy's girl.

But even if he did, and even if she was the type of person to go after him no matter what he might think of her, she couldn't just pursue what she wanted and say to hell with Gerald and Penelope, could she? Of course not. She could not be that bad of a person.

Did it make her a bad person to *want to*, though? To really, really want to?

The tears came harder and she pushed herself up from the kitchen table. She stumbled through the living room and up the stairs and threw herself into her bed, surrounding herself with covers mussed and wrinkled from her body and Brady's, inhaling deeply of the pillow upon which his head had lain.

She was in trouble. Worse than any she'd ever been in before.

With that thought, she fell asleep.

Lily awoke the following morning to a sharp bark from Doug, next to her bed. He sprang to his feet and trotted to the hallway. Whatever he heard must have been either terribly bad or terribly inviting, because Lily heard him trundle down the steps.

She turned onto her back and put her fingers over her eyes. They were swollen and gritty from crying. She was sure her face was blotchy, too. She felt as if she'd been beaten up.

A few minutes later she heard footsteps coming up the stairs. She pushed herself up in bed, panicked.

Had Brady come back? She looked too awful to see him! Who else could it be? And what had scared Doug so badly last night? Surely it wasn't coming up the stairs now, without another peep from him.

"Rise and shine, cupcake!" Georgia's voice sang out. "It's ten o'clock. We waited as long as we could!"

Lily exhaled and sat back on her pillows, inordinately glad to see Georgia and Megan come through her bedroom door.

Doug trotted behind them with a grin on his face, like a happy butler showing them in.

"See?" Megan said to Georgia. "I told you we should have given it another half hour. I'm so sorry to wake you up, Lily. We just came to see how you were."

Lily smiled and felt tears of sentiment prick her eyes. She was so lucky to have such good friends. She blinked the tears back. "I'm fine! What a great surprise to see you guys. How did you get in?"

"The back door was open," Georgia said, sitting on the end of the bed.

"It was her idea to try it," Megan added.

Lily ran her hands through her hair and sat up straighter. "Let me get dressed and make you guys some coffee. Have you had breakfast?"

"We were goin' to ask you the same thing, but it's obvious you haven't. We've got coffee brewin' and muffins in the oven," Georgia said. "All you have to do is get your lazy ass downstairs and tell us all about what happened last night when Gerald brought you home."

Lily flushed. "I can't believe you guys brought me breakfast! And after I ruined your party, Megan."

"What? Don't be ridiculous," Megan said. "I'm just glad you're all right. And Sutter sends his best. He wants to pick up the tab for the doctor visit and wants me to tell you to make sure you go for *his* sake. He doesn't like to worry. And you know he always gets his way." She grinned.

"Does he, now?" Georgia smirked.

"I can't believe you're getting married." Lily sighed.

"You can't?" Georgia laughed. "I can't believe they haven't already. Sometimes I forget they're not."

Megan chuckled. "We thought we ought to do it before Belle could actually say the word *illegitimate*."

"People don't say things like that anymore, do they?" Lily said. "I mean, nobody who saw you and Sutter together could think she was conceived in anything but love."

"Oh, that's what they all say," Georgia said. "Love, lust, what's the difference? If you get married, it'll shut up all the matronly old biddies, and nobody'll think Sutter's afraid you're going to steal his millions."

"They don't think that!" Lily protested, shooting a mortified glance in Megan's direction.

Megan laughed. "Don't worry, Lily. I'm sure a lot of people do think that, but I know Sutter doesn't, so let them talk. Gives them something to do, I imagine."

"God, I wish I could brush things off the way you do," Lily said, then she gasped. "Is that *the ring*?" She pointed to Megan's left hand and reached out.

"Oh, yes! I guess you left before I could show it to you. Can you believe it?" Megan held out her left hand and a fine blush hit her cheeks. "I told Sutter it was way too much, not even my style. Which, let's face it, would be something along the lines of a Cracker Jack prize. But I can't help it, I *love* this thing."

Lily held Megan's fingers in her hand and gazed at the square-cut diamond with two giant baguettes on either side.

She sighed. "It's the most gorgeous ring I've ever seen."

"It is, isn't it?" Georgia agreed, leaning over Megan's hand with Lily. After a second Georgia's eyes strayed around the bedsheets, from pillows to top sheet to the foot of the mattress where much of it had come untucked.

"You had sex!" she said finally. Her eyes widened. "Oh my God, did *Gerald* stay over? Did he give you a good-bye boink? Is that what happened?"

"Georgia!" Megan gasped, laughing. "Oh my God. You never fail to amaze me. Don't answer any of those questions, Lily."

Lily felt her face heat like a burner on the stove. She was sure she could fry eggs on it if she tried.

"*No!*" she protested hotly, hoping to hide the true situation with vehemence. "Good God, no. And I wouldn't have let him stay even if he wanted to. I'm not going to start that up with him now, not with him leaving town for two months."

"You were ready to a week ago," Georgia said. "Well, a little more than a week." She winked at Lily.

Lily took a deep breath. "He offered to stay. To sleep on the couch," she added quickly. "Just to be sure I was okay, but I told him to leave. I was fine."

"Gerald offered to sleep on the *couch*?" Georgia snorted. "Lord God, that man has no sense at all."

"I thought it was chivalrous," Lily said.

"And no doubt a relief," Georgia replied.

Lily cocked her head, suddenly wondering why

Penelope was not with them. Not that she expected *any* of them this morning, but if they'd been doing a group check on Lily, why wouldn't Pen have come? Could she be angry with Lily? Had she caught on to Lily's feelings? Lily even spent an irrational moment wondering if she could possibly know about last night.

Or maybe . . . had Georgia told her about the kiss with Brady?

"Where's Penelope?" she blurted. She had to know. "I mean, not that she needs to be here but . . ."

"Brunch with her ex, remember?" Megan said, shaking her head. "That can't be anything but bad news, if you ask me."

"You said it, sister." Georgia stood. "Okay, Lil. Time to get up. We've got to check on those muffins. Get yourself together and come on down; we'll have ourselves a good old-fashioned coffee klatch."

Georgia and Megan left the room, Megan closing the bedroom door behind her.

"I don't care what she says," Georgia muttered in a low voice to Megan as they descended the stairs. "Somebody had sex in that bed last night."

Megan laughed dismissively. "I don't even want to ask how it is you think you know that."

"It's nothing gross. I just have an instinct about these things." They reached the bottom of the steps and turned down the center hallway to the kitchen at the back of the house. The aroma of baking muffins scented the air.

"Those were sheets of passion," Georgia continued. "I'm tellin' you. There's a wrinkle pattern specific to a night of sex with which I am intimately familiar."

"I'm going to have to study mine the next time." Megan moved to the oven and opened the door, gazing in at the not-yet-golden muffin heads. "I'm thinking that pattern might also resemble the one made by a bedful of restless dogs, though."

"Nuh-uh. You think I don't know that pattern, too?" Georgia shook her head and sat on one of the stools by the center island. "Well, well, well, what's this?"

Megan turned, then looked where Georgia was looking, at the back door.

Brady Cole appeared in the window, carrying a grocery bag. He spotted them the moment they spotted him. There was no escape.

He knocked once, lightly, and opened the door. "Good morning, ladies," he said.

"Mornin' to you, Captain Cole," Georgia said, smiling wickedly. "Fancy meetin' you here."

Megan smiled. "Hi, Brady. Can I get you some coffee?"

He took a breath and looked around. "Uh, no. Thanks. Lily not up yet?"

"We just went and woke her up," Georgia said.

"Go on up, if you want." She waved her hand toward the stairs.

"Georgia!" Megan protested. "She's getting dressed, for God's sake." She rolled her eyes.

Georgia laughed. "I don't think that would bother Brady."

Brady wondered if he was blushing. "I just brought her some food. And wanted to see if she was feeling all right. No lingering effects from her, uh, faint last night?"

"There may have been effects," Georgia said, winking at Megan, "but nothin' bad. She seems all right this mornin'."

Brady nodded. "Good." His glance strayed around the kitchen. "Smells good in here."

"Blueberry muffins," Megan said. "Why don't you stay and have one? Lily will be down in a minute, and you can see for yourself she's feeling better. She certainly has a lot more color this morning."

He was sure she did. He could picture it, remembering vividly how she'd looked last night, just after they'd both reached their zeniths. Flushed and bright-eyed, tousled, and incredibly sexy.

He couldn't imagine sitting across from Lily this morning, the first morning after what he hoped was only the first time they'd make love, and trying to make conversation with her friends present. It would be awkward, and frustrating.

Not to mention that she'd kicked him out last night under less-than-agreeable circumstances, so the discomfort would be doubled. He'd been hoping to clear that up this morning.

Brady shook his head at Megan. "No, that's okay. I just brought by some bagels and cream cheese. Some orange juice. Coffee. Pretty much what you brought." He handed the bag to Megan and backed toward the door. "Just tell her I was asking about her."

"Sure," Megan said. "I'm sure she'll be glad to know you checked in."

"You come back now if you change your mind," Georgia said.

"Will do." Brady flashed them each a smile and went out the back door, closing it softly behind him.

"Mm-mm-mm," Georgia said to Megan when he was gone. "The plot thickens."

Megan looked at her speculatively and nodded. "It certainly does."

Fifteen

The trap was laid, the hiding place established, now all he had to do was wait.

Brady felt like the biggest fool under the sun, but he was not going to let this dog win. It was a resolution that was important for more than just retrieving his shoes, but for establishing a future that was not ruled by twenty-five pounds of canine hostility.

He settled down on his kitchen chair, one eye on the window through which he could see the tasty new loafer lying in wait in the center of the lawn. Brady was no fool. He knew Doug was not going to fall for something too obvious, but he'd see if things happened naturally. At first.

He inserted his iPod earplugs, then pressed the PLAY button. He could wait all day for the beast, if necessary. He wasn't flying until Wednesday, and this book he'd downloaded was actually getting kind of interesting, he could hardly believe it. When he'd started it he thought it would last him the rest of his life the way he kept falling asleep. Then he'd started running with it, and the plot had picked up.

Now he had to see whether Emma was going to fall for the double-talking Mr. Churchill or not.

He put his feet up on the windowsill and leaned back in his seat, the front two legs of the chair off the ground. Between his fingers were two thin strands of fishing line. He closed his eyes and listened.

His feet were just starting to tingle from being up too long when the line in his left hand twitched. He opened his eyes and gently eased the chair back onto all fours. He leaned forward, gazing out the window.

Sure enough, Doug was sniffing at the shoe, pawing it, making it move.

Brady had made sure it was one of the new ones he'd bought for the party. If Doug was clever enough to pick one shoe from each pair in his closet—which Brady had to admit was hard to believe, though he believed it—then he was clever enough to know if he had already taken the match to the one in the yard.

Doug sniffed again, then dipped a shoulder and rolled onto the loafer, sliding off the toe and rolling over onto it again. After a few minutes of this, he appeared to get bored and wandered away.

Brady was prepared for this. A few feet away from the shoe was a feather, a long sturdy feather onto which Brady had tied the second strand of fishing line. With the feather in what he thought was Doug's peripheral vision, he tugged at it.

Doug's head turned. Brady waited. Doug looked away. Brady tugged the feather again, and Doug lunged, trapping it between his front paws. Or so he thought. Brady gave another tug, loosening the thing from the dog's grasp, and moved it closer to the shoe. Doug gave a yip and lunged again. Brady couldn't help laughing. *This* was fun, he thought. And he had to admit, the little guy was sort of cute, in an ugly, pain-in-the-ass kind of way.

Doug got his teeth on the feather, and Brady pulled the string again. The now somewhat shredded-looking feather moved toward the shoe. Pulling the other line, Brady moved the shoe the moment the feather reached it, dragging it a few inches.

Doug looked exhilarated, snapping at the feather, then, when the shoe moved, leaping on that. He had just picked the shoe up in his jaws and turned toward the house, when Lily came out in the backyard.

"Doug, no! What have you got there?"

"Dammit," Brady muttered under his breath. He reached down and turned off his iPod.

"No! I said. Drop that," she continued, in a voice that would not have convinced anyone not to do anything.

Five more minutes with Doug carrying the loafer and Brady would have been able to follow the fishing line to wherever it was Doug had hidden the rest of his shoes. Now he was going to have to go outside and explain to Lily why he was tormenting her dog by dragging his footwear around the yard.

Unless she didn't notice the fishing line, he thought hopefully.

Lily reached Doug and bent down to pick him up. "Bad dog!"

Then she noticed the shoe. She straightened, shielding her eyes with one hand, and glanced up at his side of the house. He ducked away from the window. He was really getting deep into crazy territory now, but he couldn't help it. He'd thought she wasn't home. He wasn't prepared to explain what he was doing. Not only did the attempt show the embarrassing amount of free time he had on his hands, but it hadn't even worked.

"Just go back in the house, Lily," he muttered under his breath, "no need to look at the shoe."

She picked up the shoe. Then she tilted her head and felt the fishing line. He closed his eyes. Damn, damn, and damn.

She lifted the line and followed it with her eyes, straight to the kitchen window. He stood up slowly and waved.

Placing Doug on the ground, she gathered the shoe in one hand and the line in the other and reeled herself in. Doug bounced at her heels, delighted at this new element to the game.

Brady watched her get closer and closer to the back porch until she was standing in front of the open window, glaring at him. Doug stood beside her and gave Brady an ominous growl.

Lily looked Brady dead in the eye. "Catch anything?"

Brady sat down on the chair and put his feet back up on the windowsill. He smiled. He was toast.

"A girl, it looks like," he said. "Bigger fish than I was going for, but I'll take it."

She tossed the shoe in the window, followed by the wadded-up ball of fishing line.

"Do you know what might have happened if Doug had eaten any of that string? It could wrap around his intestines and kill him."

Brady scratched the side of his face. "I did not know that."

"Are you *sure*? Because I don't think you'd care if Doug died. I think you don't like Doug. And I know Doug doesn't like you. He doesn't necessarily accuse of you things you haven't done, however." She raised a brow.

"I'm telling you, Lily. He took my shoes. And if you'd have let him take that one, I'd have found out where he's hidden the rest."

She laughed. "Are you kidding? That's what this was about? You were trying to outsmart the dog?"

Brady took a deep breath. "Hey, it's harder than it sounds. Besides, I didn't have any other choice."

"Oh my God." She looked at him in amazement. "Brady, I told you, Doug doesn't steal shoes. Why are you so hell-bent on proving he does?" She put her hands on her hips.

He lowered his feet to the floor and stood. "I'm hell-bent on getting my shoes back." He held one finger up. "Hang on a second, I'm coming out."

"No don't," she said quickly. "Doug's here."

Brady sighed. "Lily, how long are you going to be ruled by who that dog likes and doesn't like? I swear, you coddle him like he's some old demented relative."

"Really?" she said archly. "Because I thought I was ruled by who Daddy liked and didn't like."

Brady stiffened. "I told you I was sorry about that."

"But you didn't say you didn't mean it."

"Lily, I don't want to fight with you. And I'm wondering if you want to fight with me because of what happened last night."

Her cheeks pinkened. "Let's see," she said, "you

are out here laying a trap for my dog, I discover it, and now I'm picking a fight because of last night? That is some impeccable logic, Brady. Besides, of all the people in the entire world, I would think *you'd* be the one to understand last night best of all."

"What does that mean?" But a sudden pounding in his chest told him he knew what it meant. She was trying to blow it off. She was trying to say that last night was exactly what he'd feared: a one-night stand.

"It means," she said slowly, "that we got carried away. Just like we did last time. Only this time it went further. It was nothing, I know that. Just a . . . a lapse, from your date diet. And an error of judgment on my part."

Brady put a hand on the window frame to lean toward her, then straightened. "This is stupid, I'm coming out there."

Lily looked down at her dog. "Don't say I didn't warn you."

Brady stalked to the kitchen door, opened it, and went out onto the back porch.

Doug was on him like a swarm of bees, growling and snuffling and nipping at the leg of his pants, jumping back as he lost his grip and nipping in again.

He never caught skin, but the message was clear: *I'd kill you if I were a Rottweiler.*

Brady moved toward Lily, half-dragging Doug along with him.

"I should never have told you about the date diet," he said when he got close.

Doug growled and braced himself with all fours as he tugged at Brady's jeans. Brady shifted his weight to that leg, so the dog couldn't pull his foot out from under him. "I thought we could be friends. If you remember, I wanted to be friends with you, Lily—"

"Sure, after you kissed me. So that I wouldn't become another Tricia and flip out on you."

He paused, staring at her. "Is that what you think?"

She threw out a hand. "It's obvious!"

"No it isn't. I wanted to be friends first so that I could do something right, for once. So that if you and I did get involved, it wouldn't be ruined by some stupid beginning." He crossed his arms over his chest and tried to ignore the bushwhacking going on at his ankle. "Why are you fighting me on this, Lily? Last night was . . . amazing. And don't try to tell me you didn't feel—"

"What?" she demanded, interrupting him. "What did I feel? Please tell me, Brady, because I honestly don't know."

She was suddenly near tears, he realized, and it shocked him. "Lily, please." He took a step toward her, his hands out, imploring. If he could just take her in his arms . . .

"No." She backed up, swallowing hard. "No, let's not cloud things up with what happens when we get close to each other. I don't think either one of us is thinking clearly. Especially not when we do things like . . . like we did last night. And we need to think clearly, get this thing straightened out. I don't want any repeats of what happened between us last night."

"Lily, I don't regret last night for a minute."

"Well, I do!"

The words were so adamant that even Doug paused from his work and looked at her, dropping Brady's now-sopping hem.

Lily blinked several times rapidly. "That's right. I don't mean to hurt you, but I do regret last night. Because I don't know what I'm doing. You and I . . . we're all wrong. Then there's Penelope to think about, and Gerald—"

Brady scoffed at the name. "Forgive me if I have no desire to think about Gerald. Besides, you aren't in love with him."

She gave him a look that made him wish he could swallow everything he'd just said. "I'm so glad *you* know my feelings so well. Between you and my father I'll be all sorted out in no time."

"I didn't mean what I said about your father," Brady said heatedly. "I'm sorry I ever said anything about him at all. So you want to make your father happy. You're close to him. So what? Who am I to second-guess that?"

"But you see you were right," she said, her voice rising. "You were right about all of it. I've been trying to do what Daddy wants me to for the last fifteen years. Who the hell am I that I can fall in love with a man just because my father wants me to? What kind of woman does that? And how could you want a woman like that, Brady, when all she can think is how bad you would look in that damn picture frame on Daddy's desk?" She turned half-away and put a hand to her face.

"You think I'd look bad in a picture?" he repeated, confused.

She dropped her hand and looked back at him. "I'm a mess, Brady. You don't want me. I'm a terrible friend, and I'm selfish and naïve and—and . . ."

Brady reached out and touched her arm, but she jerked away, backing up another step. She shook her head. "No. I'm sorry, but I have to go. You are . . . too confusing to me right now."

He sighed. "Lily, please—"

She turned fierce eyes on him. "I mean it. Don't tell me what I should or shouldn't do."

He put his hands up. "I'm not."

She brushed past him and went down the porch steps. "Doug, *come*," she said in a voice that brooked no argument. Sure enough, this time the dog obeyed.

Brady watched her go, wondering what on earth to do next.

Doug knew Lily needed him, but he'd had a hard time letting go of the New Guy's pants. He made

Lily unhappy every time they saw each other. It was too bad, Doug was starting to think, because that trick with the shoe and the feather was great. Nobody had ever done anything like that with him before, except Lily.

Doug followed Lily into the house and into the living room. She dropped into a chair and laid her head back against the cushion. Doug sat down beside her, where he could look up into her face and see what she needed.

Her cheeks got wet, and her hands clenched. Doug leaned over and licked her ankle. It usually got her attention, but this time she just sniffed. He wished she'd put the telephone on her face like she sometimes did, do some talking into it. That seemed to make her feel better. He went and got the receiver, trotting back to the chair and jumping with just his front feet onto the seat. He deposited it on the cushion next to her leg and sat back down on the floor, expectant.

She just took it, wiped it on her leg, and sighed. "Oh, Doug. How many times have I got to tell you we don't play fetch with the phone."

Doug sat down again, this time very close to her legs, and laid his head on her feet. He looked up at her, certain that she'd figure it out eventually. She was pretty bright, for a human. In the meantime, he'd make her feel better by being next to her, as close as he could get.

* * *

Lily woke in the middle of the night from a dream in which a woman—not herself—was screaming Brady's name. Lily had been running through the halls of her old high school, looking for him, hoping he was all right and fearing he wasn't.

She opened her eyes in the darkness and heard Doug whine. He was standing on his back legs, looking out the front window.

"Brady . . . " The voice sang out again, and Lily realized it hadn't been a dream, that woman's voice.

She threw back the covers and got out of bed. Pushing aside the curtains, she looked out onto the front lawn and saw Tricia, standing barefoot in the grass, brushing her flowing blond hair in the moonlight.

Lily glanced back at the clock—3:18. In the morning.

Tricia bent her head back and ran the brush down her hair in a lithe, sensual movement. Her hair looked silken in the pale light.

"Brady Cole, come out, come out, wherever you are! Come out and *get* me." Her laughter tinkled through the midnight air. One hand moved to the buttons of her blouse, a sleeveless white shirt that fell to her hips over a flowing white skirt.

Lily's eyes moved to the houses across the street, looking to see if Tricia had woken anyone else, but nothing stirred, not even a breeze. Tricia danced and spun on the lawn, one hand running the brush through her hair, the other unbuttoning her shirt. She got to the last button and shrugged off the garment, letting it drop to the ground. She wore a tiny, lacy bra that didn't appear up to the task of containing her voluptuous breasts.

Lily exhaled long and slow. Brady might have had terrible taste, he might have entangled himself with a grossly unstable woman, but it was sure easy to see why. The woman had a body like a Victoria's Secret model.

"Brady, look what you're missing!" Tricia's laugh bubbled out again as she pushed her skirt down her legs into a pile of white fabric on the grass and danced out of it. She spun in a circle in her tiny underthings, her hair flying out behind her.

Lily wondered if she should call him, wake him up. Though how he couldn't be awake by now, with this woman calling out his name and doing a striptease on the front lawn, was a mystery.

A second later Brady emerged from his house. He wore a pair of shorts and no shirt, and his hair was mussed from sleeping. Lily's heart climbed into her throat. He was so beautiful.

Unfortunately, so was Tricia.

Beside her, Doug whined and licked her hand.

"No, you're right," she said. "It's ridiculous to feel jealous of a crazy woman."

She watched Brady approach her on the lawn. His voice was low, but she could hear it because her window was open a crack.

"Tricia, what are you doing here? It's three o'clock in the goddamn morning. Did you know that?" He glanced furtively back toward the house, his voice much lower than Tricia's. But when you lived on a street with houses all around, sound tended to bounce, and Lily could hear almost every word.

Tricia gave a squeal of delight and threw herself into Brady's arms. Lily watched his hands grip her naked waist and felt a spasm in her stomach.

"I just called your parents. And Silverman," he said. "His service said he's going to call me back in a minute. You can't keep doing things like this, Tricia."

Tricia smiled and caressed his face with one hand. Brady pushed her back and away from him.

"You live a long way from all of them, Brady," she said, sultry as a cat, moving toward him.

"There are mental health facilities here," he said. "I can call them just as easily as Silverman."

Lily wondered what he meant. Would they actually send a paddywagon for her? Arrive with a straitjacket and cart her off?

"Brady, do you remember," Tricia began, moving closer and winding her arms around his neck. She murmured something in his ear, and Lily watched Brady's body stiffen. Was it from remembered desire? she wondered. Was Tricia recounting some incredible sexual feat they'd performed?

She should go back to sleep, try to ignore what was going on out there. It was none of her business, really. Brady had made this bed, she thought, literally and figuratively. She backed up and sat down on her mattress. Doug leapt up beside her. She put an arm around him.

Tricia's laughter cascaded up to Lily's window, and she had the awful sensation that Brady had decided it wasn't worth it to fight it, that he could just give Tricia what she wanted and be done with it.

Lily sprang to her feet and moved back to the window, pushing the curtain aside in time to see Tricia haul off and slap Brady across the cheek with her hairbrush.

His head snapped to the side, but he recovered quickly. He grabbed her wrist and spun her around, arm behind her back, so that he could talk low and fast into her ear.

They were facing Lily so she could see the look of ecstasy on Tricia's face—and the look of fury on Brady's.

She should help him, she thought. She spun for her closet and plucked her robe off the hook. Then she raced down the stairs to the front door, Doug hard on her heels.

Hand on the doorknob, she paused. This was none of her business. Brady wouldn't want her out there, would he? Would he think she was horning in where she wasn't needed?

Oh, to hell with it, she finally thought. They were out there on her front lawn and—

"Get your hands *off* me!" Tricia's shrill voice rang out.

Lily jerked open the door to see a completely nude Tricia standing in front of a kneeling Brady.

What in God's name had been going on? For a second Lily thought she'd interrupted something horrifyingly intimate, until she noted Brady's posture. She wasn't sure . . . but she thought . . . maybe . . .

She took a few steps forward. Brady was gritting his teeth. Good God, Tricia had kicked him in the crotch.

Lily ran down the steps, failing to close the door behind her so Doug ran with her. She reached Brady and knelt beside him. One glance at his face confirmed her suspicions. Tricia had racked him. Not only that, but when she'd hit him with the hairbrush the bristles had left a bright red abrasion on his cheek.

"Lily," he said in a tight voice, "it's all right. I can handle this."

Laughter of the hysterical sort threatened Lily's composure, but she squelched it. "I think that's pretty obviously untrue."

"Who the hell is this bitch?" Tricia said, advancing on the two of them.

Brady pushed himself to his feet, obviously in pain. "Don't take another step, Tricia. She has nothing to do with this."

Tricia's eyes narrowed. "Oooh, so protective. I bet she finds that really attractive."

"Don't you think you should put on some clothes?" Lily asked, rising to her feet as well but standing just behind and to the side of Brady.

"Why?" Tricia struck a model's pose, one hand on her hip. "Jealous?"

"Tricia, just put on your clothes before your parents get here." Brady's voice was hard.

Lily looked from him to the pools of white on the lawn that used to be Tricia's outfit. Two smaller ones lay nearby: her underwear. Lily thought about picking up the clothes and handing them to her, then decided she didn't want to touch any of them.

"Brady," Lily said, moving close behind him and putting one hand on his arm. "I know a guy on the police force. Do you want me to call him? They can keep her quiet until her parents come."

Brady turned halfway to her, looking at her askance. "No, Lily. Just, please, go inside. I can handle this myself."

His tone was so abrupt, so cold, she backed up a step.

"I'm just trying to help," she said.

"Well, don't." He kept his back to her. "Tricia and I have done this before. I can handle it."

Lily felt mortification form a lump in her throat. She looked from Brady—a muscle jumping in his clenched jaw—to Tricia.

Tricia smiled knowingly and swept a hand up her naked torso. "That's right. Brady and I *have* done this before . . ."

Sixteen

Lily sat with Doug next to her on the wooden love seat outside Hyperion Espresso in the heart of town, trying hard not to think about Brady and the strained scenes between them yesterday. Maybe she'd been hard on him in the afternoon, but the way he'd looked at her last night, with Tricia, like she was the last person on earth he wanted to see, had cut her to the quick. It seemed to her he looked more unhappy to see her than the crazy naked woman.

"So, Penelope, what happened with your ex-husband?" Megan asked.

Lily brought her attention back to the moment, telling herself she'd been way too self-centered lately; she needed to concentrate on her friends. Brady could just figure out his own life, without her help.

Lily shifted her eyes to Penelope. Their dogs lay at their feet. Penelope's Labrador retriever Wimbledon chewed on a piece of ice. Megan's Bernese Mountain Dog Peyton lay looking up at her mistress with adoring eyes, and Twister, the mutt that had gotten Megan and her fiancé together two years ago, sat up next to Megan's chair, giving a doggy grin and an air sniff in the direction of every passerby.

They sat under the shade of the awning on William Street, sipping iced coffee drinks and fanning themselves with their napkins.

Penelope had just sat down with her iced mocha and now looked at the two of them with a trace of guilt in her eyes.

"Wait," Lily said, "should we wait for Georgia?"

Megan shook her head. "I'm not sure she's going to make it at all. She had about seventeen thousand errands to run before she could even think about coming. We'll catch her up on it later." She looked back at Penelope and grinned. "So dish."

Penelope smiled. "You won't believe it. *I* couldn't believe it. First of all, Glenn was very apologetic for even being there, for imposing all of this on me. But he said he didn't have anyone else to talk to." She gave a one-shouldered shrug.

"What about what's her name? His new wife?" Lily asked. She pulled the straw from her mocha and licked whipped cream off the end of it.

They had all spent years being angry about Glenn and his new wife. After being with Penelope for ten years, and knowing from the start that Penelope had wanted a family, Glenn had finally divorced her because he said he didn't want children. Then, not even a year later, his new girlfriend was pregnant, and they had gotten married.

Now, just a year after that, he was popping up on Penelope's doorstep again. Lily could not think of one single reason that would be good enough.

"That's just the thing," Penelope said, leaning toward them, her voice hushed so that no one could overhear. Not that there was anyone on the busy sidewalk who would be within earshot long enough to hear anything of substance.

Megan and Lily leaned toward her, too.

"He can't talk to her because *she's* the problem. It turns out . . ." Penelope looked furtively around them. "Glenn's been having doubts about whether the marriage is going to work."

"Oh come on," Lily scoffed, poking the straw back into her drink.

"No, really. He said she's just awful to him. She even threw a plate at him one night. It nearly hit him in the face." She leaned back, eyes wide and amazed.

Lily and Megan looked at each other with identically skeptical expressions.

"Would it be awful if I said I wish it had?" Lily said.

Megan snickered.

Penelope frowned and shook her head. "I know, I know. He was awful to me, but he seems truly miserable now. He said the baby's really cranky and doesn't seem to like him. Takes after Abigail, he said, and gets upset every time he touches her."

"What an awful thing to say!" Megan protested.

Lily frowned. "Why was he laying all of this on you? I mean, why in the world should you care if he's unhappy or not?"

Megan laughed. "Thank you for taking Georgia's place. I was worried we wouldn't thoroughly examine the who-gives-a-shit side of things."

"Well, it's not like he was nice to Penelope when he left," Lily protested. "Why should she be anything but happy that he's miserable now? I know I am."

Megan tilted her head, nodded, and sipped her drink. "A good point," she said, swallowing. "What did you say to him, Pen?"

Penelope was looking at her mocha, stirring the whipped cream into the ice with her straw. "Well, I have to admit I felt a moment of satisfaction myself, until I thought about that little girl, the baby. But Glenn swears he's not going to abandon *her*."

"Like he did you," Lily said.

"But why *did* he come to you with this?" Megan persisted. "I mean, we all know you're a nice person and everything, but why would he think you of all people would sympathize with him?"

"Because," she said slowly, still looking at her drink, "he said he realized that he'd never stopped loving me."

Lily choked on her drink. Megan patted her on the back.

"He knew he'd never really loved Abigail," Penelope continued. "He only married her because of the pregnancy—"

"Does he think that makes him look *better*?" Lily asked. She placed her drink on the table at the end of the love seat and wiped her hands, wet from the condensation on the cup, on her shorts. "He married her, and he should have meant it."

"I know. But he said he doesn't love her, doesn't even feel like he can trust her, and that she doesn't love him either." She shrugged, then looked up at them almost shyly. She gave a little smile. "He said he realized how wonderful being a parent could be, though, and that he'd give anything to have a child with me, the one woman he ever truly loved."

Lily and Megan both stared at Penelope, speechless.

Lily, with so many emotions swirling, chose one out of the bunch and thought, *She's going to marry him, and I'll be the only one left. Alone. Single and childless.* Of course there was always Georgia, but she was rarely alone, and she certainly didn't want children.

But this wasn't about her, Lily reminded herself. She had to focus on Penelope, who did not deserve to be jerked around by that asshole Glenn. She deserved someone wonderful and caring, someone who would make her feel good about herself.

Brady would do that, Lily thought, wondering how she could be so sure of that. But she was.

Brady . . .

The very thought of him arrested her brain waves. She pictured his face above her as he'd entered her, his ember-colored eyes, his warm, strong body, his tenderness, his touch . . .

If Penelope wanted Glenn back, she thought suddenly, her heart lightening, then Brady was—

Right in front of her.

"Hello, ladies." He stood before them in running shorts and a tee shirt, his face damp with sweat along the hairline. His heightened color accentuated his golden eyes, and that ever-present iPod highlighted his well-defined biceps. She scanned his tan, muscled legs and remembered vividly the weight of them across hers.

She had to look closely to see the scratch from Tricia's hairbrush on his face. Without the fresh blood it was only slightly visible.

He gave Megan and Penelope a smile.

Lily couldn't help noticing that he didn't look at her.

Beside her, Doug let out a yip. She grabbed his collar and held tight. But while he rose to his feet, Doug did little more than snuffle at Brady, occasionally pulling against Lily's hand.

Brady looked as sexy as she had ever seen him. She couldn't believe Penelope would not be struck dumb by his overwhelming masculinity, all thoughts of Glenn vaporizing in the heat from his eyes.

"Brady!" Penelope said brightly. "How nice to see you!"

"You've caught us indulging in a little afternoon cake and caffeine," Megan said. "Care to join us?"

Lily was the one who was struck dumb. Could she sit here and watch Brady talk with Penelope? *Flirt* with Penelope? *Would* he sit here and flirt with Penelope, right in front of her, after what had happened Saturday night?

There'd be no reason not to, she reasoned. She'd made it clear yesterday that Saturday night was not to be repeated. So it wasn't as if she was supposedly falling in love with him.

"Lily?" Megan's voice interrupted her thoughts.

"Huh?" She looked over at her friend.

"Brady was just asking if you'd seen the doctor." Megan studied her with a bit more awareness than Lily would have liked. Or was she imagining that?

"No, ah, not yet. Tomorrow." She swallowed. "But I feel fine. All better."

Brady nodded. "Good. Oh, and I'm sorry about last night," he said casually, as if he'd been playing his stereo too loud and she had complained. But his eyes were guarded. "I hope you were able to get back to sleep."

"Yes, sure. I was fine. I hope everything turned out all right for you? And for, uh . . . ?" She didn't want to say Tricia's name, in case he felt private about it, but since he'd brought it up she had to ask.

She had heard cars pull up about an hour after Brady had made her go away, so she'd assumed her parents had come to get her. Or the therapist, Silverman. There'd been voices in the dark, Tricia's protesting, then crying.

Lily hadn't gotten up, however, not even to watch out the window. She'd just lain in bed thinking about Brady's tone when he'd told her not to help, to go inside, *Tricia and I have done this before.*

"Everything's fine." He nodded once. "I'd better get going. Nice to see you all." He smiled at Megan and Penelope, the wattage fading when he got to Lily, and went inside the coffee shop.

"What was *that* all about?" Megan asked. Then added, "Unless it's none of my business. Which I guess it pretty plainly is."

Penelope chuckled and said, "Mine, too, but I'm also dying to know. What happened?"

Lily sighed. "Remember that woman who showed up the day Brady moved in? The crazy one?"

They both nodded, and she told them the rest of last night's story, omitting the previous night's complications and all the ensuing emotions she'd been battling since then.

"It was strange, though, how adamant he was about refusing my help," Lily couldn't help adding at the end, glancing behind her to be sure Brady wasn't coming out the door of the shop. "I mean, I thought we were friends, but he treated me as if I was sticking my nose where it didn't belong. Do you think I shouldn't have gone out there?"

Megan shook her head. "I don't know how you could have stayed inside with all that going on. Especially after she kicked him in the crotch. I don't know why everyone talks about Achilles' *heels* when guys are so much more vulnerable in that area."

"I think I'd have been afraid to go out. That woman sounds dangerous," Penelope said.

"I do have to say, though," Megan continued, "that it's pretty obvious to me why he sent you back inside."

"It is?" Lily's heartbeat accelerated.

Megan was altogether too perceptive; had she

picked up on something between her and Brady? Would she say it in front of Penelope?

Of course she wouldn't. But still, the last thing she wanted was for Megan to figure out her feelings and realize what a horrible friend Lily was, to steal a guy intended for one of the women she was closest to.

Though she hadn't stolen him, exactly. More like borrowed.

"He was embarrassed." Megan's tone made it sound as obvious as if she'd caught him on the john.

"Oh absolutely," Penelope said.

Megan turned and looked in the window of the coffee shop behind her. "Did he leave? I don't want him to come out here and hear us talking about him."

Penelope nodded. "I saw him come out the door and go the other direction, up Princess Anne Street."

Lily's heart sank. He was avoiding her. Maybe it was too awkward, her sitting here with Penelope. Too many potential expectations all sitting at one table.

"So think about it," Megan continued. "You've got your biggest mistake stripping on your front lawn in front of your new neighbor—who is in fact quite close to your boss's, er, wife." She laughed, in a kind of amazement at how true that title would be before long. "Not to mention that you're also his landlord's daughter. And so your landlord's daughter comes out to help after you've just been whacked and racked by a naked woman . . . I'm surprised he could look you in the eye today at all." She sat back in her chair and sipped her drink.

"Whacked and racked!" Penelope laughed.

Lily thought about this. "I guess you could be right."

Could be even worse if you'd just slept with the landlord's daughter, Lily considered, the night before The Mistake showed up.

"But what I want to know is," Megan said.

Lily braced herself for one of Megan's famously blunt, on-target questions.

"What did Penelope say to Glenn?" Megan finished, turning back to Penelope.

Lily exhaled in relief. "Yes. What *did* you say?"

If she'd told Glenn she wanted to try again, Lily couldn't help but feel just a little off the hook for sleeping with Brady. After all, that would mean Penelope didn't want Brady after all, so no harm no foul, right?

Penelope smiled and shook her head, looking at her drink again. Lily's heart soared. She was embarrassed, Lily thought, because she'd taken her ex-husband back, because she'd said so many bad things about him over the years, because she'd vowed to have finally seen through him, and now she was going back to him.

Hey, everyone has a soft spot for a past lover or two,

Lily thought. She, Lily, would be compassionate. She'd understand how these things went. She wouldn't condemn her friend for going back to the man who had hurt her so badly in the past.

"I told him to forget it," Pen said.

Lily's heart dropped.

"I said that just because his life hadn't panned out the way he'd set it up didn't mean that I was going to repeat the biggest mistake of my life." She laughed a little ruefully. "I'm afraid I was pretty ruthless about it."

"Attagirl!" Megan said. Then, with a look at Lily's surprised face, added, "Well, *you* weren't doing Georgia's part anymore."

"But honestly, I felt bad about it afterward," Penelope said. "There's some part of me that still feels, I don't know, loyal, I guess. Does that sound crazy?"

"Not at all," Lily said. "Love is complicated. Messy. Nothing's ever clear-cut about it, even when you think it is. Or maybe *especially* when you think it is."

"That's for sure," Megan agreed. "Speaking of complications, did Gerald take off all right today? He did leave today, right?"

Lily nodded. "He called from the airport. He and Doris, the paralegal who was going with him, actually got an earlier flight than originally planned, so he called at six this morning to say good-bye. Again. He called last night, too."

"That's nice," Penelope said. "You see, he really does care. I can't wait to hear how much he misses you. I bet he flies home with a ring before the project's even finished."

Lily looked at Penelope in horror. "Do you think so?"

Megan laughed. "Wow, what's that look about? Is something up with you two? Don't tell me there's trouble in paradise."

Lily shook her head. Should she tell them about her change of heart? She wanted to, she was just so embarrassed. After going on and on about this guy for two years . . .

Once again she saw Brady's face above hers . . . had he looked so intensely into her eyes, or was she changing the memory in hindsight? What had he been feeling that night? Passion, certainly, she had felt that from him, so much that it seemed to generate energy between them, electricity, fusion. She had felt that night as if they were more than the sum of their bodies, as if they were combustible, like Georgia had said: a constantly exploding supernova.

"I . . ." She sighed. "It's so strange. I hate to even say it out loud, and I feel so foolish." She looked down at the top of Doug's head and scratched between his ears.

Penelope leaned toward her and squeezed her arm with one hand. "What is it, Lily? You know you can tell us anything."

Lily smiled at her. "As soon as Gerald started talking about marriage, I . . . I don't know. Suddenly it seemed as if . . . as if that was the *last* thing I wanted."

Lily shifted her eyes from Megan to Penelope. Pen looked shocked, but Megan was nodding slowly.

"But *why*?" Penelope said. "We just met him, and we all liked him so much! Did he *do* something?"

"I . . . just don't think he really loves me," Lily hedged.

"Oh now that's just paranoia." Penelope sat back, looking assured, and somewhat relieved. "It's cold feet. Of course he loves you. Why else would he be talking marriage?"

Lily met Megan's eyes but couldn't hold the contact. She said to Penelope, "The thing is, I don't think I really love him either." She shrugged. "It's strange, but I guess I had to reach the point of almost getting what I wanted before I knew I didn't really want it. Gerald was sort of a figment of my imagination, I think. A dream. Apparently I didn't want him to come true." She laughed morbidly. "Now it's my turn: Do you think *that's* crazy?"

"Absolutely not," Megan answered immediately. "You have to trust your feelings. You're not committed. It would be foolish to continue the relationship just because it was something you always *thought* you'd wanted. I say dump him."

"What did you say to him?" Penelope asked, still gazing at her wide-eyed. "Did you break up?"

Lily grimaced. "Not yet. I thought I'd let him go on this trip, give ourselves this break, then talk to him after we've both had time to think. I want to be sure of my feelings before I do anything. I just don't know how to *get* sure! It's like my feelings change from day to day, hour to hour."

"Are you saying that sometimes you still think you're in love with Gerald?" Megan asked, with an all too knowing look.

Lily shook her head. "More like sometimes I don't want to let go of the dream. I'm so used to having it. It's the reality I don't want. How sick is that?"

"No sicker than the rest of us," Megan said.

"Which isn't saying much." Penelope laughed.

Brady avoided Lily for the next few weeks. It was easier than he thought it would be, which clued him in to the fact that she was also avoiding him.

Not that he thought she'd come running after him. She'd made it pretty clear that any contact she had with him was a mistake. An opinion that was no doubt confirmed by the episode with Tricia the night after they'd slept together.

The more he thought about it, the less he could blame her. The situation had gotten ridiculous.

Who could overcome the obstacles to a normal relationship that he'd manufactured in his life? He'd come to town hoping for a fresh start, but that had been blown the moment Tricia had shown up, the very first day he was here. Then, not long after that, he'd broken all promises to himself and kissed Lily. Then he tried to back off and explain how he wasn't doing that sort of thing anymore, then he'd slept with her and Tricia had shown up again.

It was obvious, the writing was on the wall, they were not meant to be. Tricia was like an evil omen, a personal reality check that appeared whenever he committed the same mistake he always did.

Not that Lily was nuts like Tricia. But she was clearly not any woman he should be falling for. The date diet was supposed to help him make wiser decisions in cases like these. He was supposed to make friends first, then move into intimacy. Instead, he chose someone who was in love with someone else and jumped into bed with her.

That probably hadn't done anything positive for her either. She was probably torturing herself with guilt over Gerald, now, too.

No, the whole thing was a mess, making it a perfect situation to run away from.

So run he did. With the aid of his boss, Sutter

Foley, who had a series of meetings and conferences across the country from New York to LA and a couple of cities in between, he flew off into the sunset for days at a time, hoping to expunge the idea of Lily from his mind and heart.

Flying had always been a relief for him. Something about getting up in the air released Brady from the tensions of his earthbound life. Up above the clouds, his worries seemed tiny and manageable. He had long considered flying his therapy, the sky his shrink.

Not very poetic, but there you had it. He was a man in search of space, and the sky was the only freedom from himself he could find.

"How long have we got?" Honey Miller, his copilot, asked from the seat next to his as they touched down on the tarmac.

Too bad it was ninety-two degrees in Chicago, Brady thought. Not much to do outside with the weather so crappy. Maybe he'd take in a movie, now that he'd finished his audiobook.

He'd liked the ending of the book, liked that Emma ended up with Knightley and not that charlatan Churchill, but Lily was crazy if she thought Gerald was anything like the gentleman all the other characters admired so much. Knightley was not the self-centered egotist Gerald was, and he genuinely had Emma's best interests at heart.

Gerald appeared to like only what Lily would do for *his* best interests.

Brady focused on the task at hand, taxiing the plane down the runway and picking up the radio handset. "I'd say about six hours. Maybe seven. They're having lunch out, but coming back here after the last meeting. Keep your cell phone on. I'll let you know departure time when I know it."

"Should we get the fixed base operator to take a look at the flight director?" she asked.

"I'm about to do just that," he said.

He radioed the tower. After identifying himself and the plane, he asked, "Where's the nearest FBO? I need catering and maintenance."

The tower radioed back, gave him the particulars.

"Have you got an avionics mechanic here?" Brady added. "Yeah, the flight director's acting a little screwy."

The voice on the other end instructed him where to go, and he signed off. He took the plane toward the hangar they'd indicated as Honey undid her seat belt and began gathering her things.

In the cockpit, the part-time stewardess—Brandi, with an 'I'—was preparing the aircraft for the passengers' deplaning. Foley had flown with two VPs and his director of research and development for this meeting, and they were only here for the day.

"You going for a run?" Honey asked, once he'd stopped the plane. She rose from the seat and grabbed her bag from the compartment behind the cockpit.

"Nah. Too hot. I might see a movie."

"They having dinner on the plane?" Honey asked, jerking her head back toward the passengers.

"I don't think so, but I want to have something for them to eat. Tomorrow's double meetings in New York and Boston, so they want to get home tonight quick." He shook his head at their schedule, but he was glad for the airtime. "Busy week."

"I'll say. So I'll wait for your call."

Brady looked at Honey. "Yeah, but plan on being back about eight-thirty for the walk around. We'll probably leave by nine-fifteen."

"I don't know why they don't just stay here and go straight to Boston tomorrow morning," she said, hefting her bag onto her shoulder.

Brady gave her a sly smile. "You were at the party a few weeks ago. I'm thinking the boss wants to get back to his new fiancée."

She laughed and rolled her eyes. "Whatever. I'm going to the gym."

He gave her a short salute with his pencil. "Sweat some for me."

She nodded once. "Will do. Have a good day."

"You bet." Brady turned back to the instrument panel and made sure everything was in order, then sat back in the cockpit seat.

A second later, he heard Honey say, "Oh, excuse me, sir. I thought you were already gone."

"Not at all," Sutter Foley's voice replied. "Just want a word with Captain Cole."

"Yes, sir," she said.

Brady heard her exit the airplane and turned in his seat to see Sutter duck into the cockpit.

"What can I do for you, sir?"

Sutter looked distinctly uncomfortable and Brady felt a moment of trepidation.

"Just wanted a word." He came into the cockpit and looked around.

"Should I come out there, or would you like to sit here?" Brady asked, gesturing toward the copilot's seat. "Or is this something I should ask the FBO if they've got a conference room we could use?"

"Oh no, no. It's nothing like that." Sutter came over and folded his long body into the copilot's seat. "Look, this is awkward, and I promised myself I wasn't going to do it, but Megan's been after me . . . you know how it is."

Brady exhaled. Not something about work, then. He wasn't being fired, on top of everything else he'd screwed up lately.

He grinned. "Not really. Been a while since I've been in a relationship. Never been in one like yours."

Brady liked his boss. Sutter was formal when they were working, which made Brady's job that much easier, but laid-back when business was off the table. Not that things ever got too personal. Those conversations consisted mostly of things like "Got good weekend plans?" or "Hope you didn't imbibe last night, we've got a last-minute flight this morning."

"It has its moments," Sutter said, grimacing. "Look, I don't want to pry, but Megan's wondering about Penelope. You should know she's very protective of her friends, very involved with them. I don't quite understand it, but it seems to work for them."

"Women are always plotting and scheming together," Brady said. "We don't stand a chance."

"Now you see that's exactly the kind of thing you should never say to Megan," Sutter said, running a hand down his tie and looking out the cockpit windshield. "I learn that lesson about once a week."

"But it's worth it, right?" Brady said.

Sutter sent him a dubious look, then laughed. "It is, but don't ever tell her I said so. I'll lose the only edge I've got."

"Keep 'em guessing." Brady nodded. "Listen, I know they've had a plot or two involving me, and I'm pretty sure I've screwed up my end of the effort."

"It's the only way to keep them from trying again," Sutter said, chuckling. "Look, you don't have to tell me anything. I just wanted to give you the heads up that she's on the scent of this thing and wants to figure you out. For her to try to put me on the case is unusual. So let me apologize for the whole situation right now. I'd stop her if I had any control over her at all."

Brady smiled and unhooked his seat belt. "Nah, that's okay. I mean, I don't know what to tell her, but it's flattering that she's interested in me at all. Makes me think maybe I'm not so obviously bad for people, if she's willing to set me up with a friend."

"You're being a bit hard on yourself," Sutter said, then gave him a sly look. "But you know yourself best. Here's what I was thinking. I can tell her now that I've brought it up with you— which will get me off the hook—and I'll say that you think Penelope's a nice girl but you're taking your time, playing the field, as they say, and don't want to rush into anything. That will give her enough to think about, but get you off the hook for anything definite, at least temporarily. And we'll leave it at that. All right with you, then?"

Brady narrowed his eyes, with a wise-guy smile. "You think she'll leave it at that?"

"Absolutely not. She'll think I didn't ask the right questions. But she's used to my incompetence in these areas." Sutter smiled.

Brady laughed. "I do believe you're ready for

marriage, Mr. Foley. But here's what you can tell her about Penelope. Great girl, *gorgeous* girl, but I'm not dating right now. I told her that before, so she'll believe you heard the party line."

"Deal." Sutter nodded and rose from the seat. He moved toward the cockpit door, then turned a shrewd glance down at Brady. "And did I hear the party line? Not interested in Penelope, are you?" He raised a brow. "Just curious, you know. I learned from an old maiden aunt of mine that you can't watch part of a soap opera without wanting to know the rest."

Brady chuckled and pushed himself out of the pilot's seat. "Nothing against Penelope, and frankly I don't think she'll be all that heartbroken if I don't ask her out, but to be honest, I'm waiting for the right girl to become available."

Sutter chuckled. "I thought so." He started to leave, then paused at the door. "It's none of my business, of course. But if the right girl is Lily Tyler, you won't have long to wait, I don't think."

Brady's mouth dropped open. He started to reply, but he had no idea what to say. How had Sutter known? Had he been that obvious? And if he had been, *when*?

And what did he mean, he wouldn't have long to wait?

Sutter read his face and chuckled again. "See you tonight," he said, and left.

It just went to show, Brady thought, the girls

had nothing on guys when they were paying attention.

Unless, he thought suddenly, that last bit of information was the *real* tidbit Megan had been after . . .

Seventeen

Lily sat in her living room, drinking an iced tea and writing up lesson plans for summer school when she saw Brady running up the street, iPod strapped to his arm. He slowed when he was still two doors down and disconnected the earpieces, then pulled his tee shirt over his head as he reached the driveway to the house.

He'd been gone a lot lately, flying, and it felt good to see him back, even if they weren't exactly talking.

Lily paused, watching him. Her breath caught at the sight of his bare chest, legs pumped and sinewy from running, sweat leaving a sheen on his tanned skin. His hair was dark with the damp, his stride long and loose from the exercise.

She swallowed hard, feeling him on her skin, hearing his voice in her head, reaching for him with her mind.

They hadn't spoken more than two words to each other in more than three weeks. Occasionally they passed each other on the street while driving. She'd see him on his motorcycle, and he'd hold up a hand. Or she'd catch a glimpse of him going inside as she was going out, but they said little more than hello.

For her part, Lily couldn't help following him with her eyes, but he barely looked at her.

Between her outburst the day after they'd slept together, and his reaction to Tricia's appearance on the front lawn, they both seemed lost in mortifications of their own that kept them apart.

The most interesting thing to Lily, however, was the fact that in all that time Brady had still not asked Penelope out. Lily had found this out from Megan because she was too afraid to ask Penelope, too afraid to hear disappointment in her friend's voice and feel responsible.

Megan, on the other hand, didn't seem very worried about it. Lily would have asked her why, but she didn't want to appear too interested in Brady's actions. Megan was too close to figuring things out as it was.

Brady reached the front stoop and took the steps two at a time, not even glancing at Lily's side of the house. Did he never think of her at all? she wondered. He'd probably decided she was too much work. Too confusing, sending mixed messages all the time. And it was true. She'd sent mixed messages to herself, too.

She sighed and looked back down at her papers.

Next to her on the couch, her cell phone rang. She picked it up and looked at it. *Gerald.* At one time that name on her phone would have made her heart leap. Now it just made her tired.

She hadn't heard much from him recently. Maybe he'd picked up on her tone of polite disinterest. Then again, he'd sounded pretty disinterested himself, going on mostly about the work and responding with generic platitudes like "oh really?" and "good for you" to whatever she said about herself or what was going on in her life.

It seemed that since they hadn't been able to forge much of a relationship before he left, they weren't left with much to maintain long-distance. They certainly didn't have anything to talk about on the phone except their completely disparate and personally unrelated activities.

Lily picked up the phone and said hello.

"Hello, Lily, it's me," he said, his standard greeting. "How are you?"

"Fine, just sitting here grading some final exams. How are things in Hawaii?"

Gerald answered with his standard joke about another day in paradise, and they talked about nothing for several minutes. Since he usually called on the cell phone, she'd had no trouble seeing how far their relationship had dwindled. In the beginning their conversations had lasted half an hour or so. Now they were down to approximately seven minutes.

Sure enough, before long the conversation ended because of a knock on Gerald's hotel-room door. But this time, as he'd hung up the phone, promising to call her again soon, Lily could have sworn she heard a woman's voice in the background saying something that sounded distinctly like *was that her? Did you tell*—And then the line went dead.

Lily looked at the phone a second, then put it back on the couch. She stacked her papers on her lap and placed them on the coffee table in front of her. Taking a long sip of her iced tea, she became dimly aware that Doug was barking, shrilly, relentlessly, from some distant part of the yard.

She got up and went to the kitchen, looking out the back door. He was nowhere to be seen, but she could hear him barking. It was muffled, as if he were caught somewhere and couldn't get out. She opened the back door and went onto the porch. The barking was coming from the shed.

But how could he have gotten in *there*? It was always locked from the outside; in fact it couldn't be *un*locked, as the mechanism was old, and the key only good if you held it all the way to the right as you pulled the door open. The windows were all painted shut, and it was full of Aunt Vivien's old furniture, packed so tight you could barely get inside.

She walked down the steps and headed for the shed anyway. Sure enough, the barking got louder.

"Doug?" she called.

His barks became more frantic, as if the devil himself had hold of his toe.

He was definitely inside the shed.

Lily blew out a breath and checked around the three sides of the shed she could see. The fourth side bordered Nathan's lawn so she couldn't see it without climbing the fence. In any case, she could see no holes, no obvious places where Doug could have gotten in.

"Doug! Stay there, Doug, *stay*. Good boy! I'll be right back." She turned and ran back into the house, grabbed the shed key off the hook near the back door, and returned to the outbuilding. Poking the key in the rusty lock, she cooed to the dog, reassuring him that everything would be fine, she'd have him out in a jiffy.

Finally, the door opened onto the cool, musty space. Aunt Vivien's furniture had been in there for years. Lily had been meaning to go through it since she'd moved here, pick out what could be saved and refinished, but she had yet to do it. The more years that passed, the more daunting the task became. With the furniture now covered with dust and spiderwebs, and the occasional dead mouse carcass, she hated even coming into the shed.

"Doug? Where are you?" She propped the door open with the stone she kept next to it for just that purpose. The light from outside illuminated the broken dining table, the seventies-era sideboard, and an enormous console television. Against one wall was a blanket chest, on top of which was a chest of drawers, on top of which was a mattress from the four-poster bed whose headboard and footboard were leaning up against the back wall. On the left was a wall of boxes and an armoire with a split door blocking the side window.

The only places Doug could be were underneath the piles of junk and stacked furniture, in some crevice that could not be accessed by a person. Lily got down on her hands and knees, peering into the darkness. She hated to think what else might be in there.

"Doug!" she called. "Come on, boy. Come here!" Surely he saw the light from the door. "Head for the light, boy!" She laughed.

Doug whined from the back left corner of the shed.

"Doug, come on! You got in there, just come out the way you came in." She patted her hands on the dusty cement flooring. Life with dogs would be so much easier if they just spoke English, she thought.

Something shifted off to her right, and Doug started barking again. Lily sat up. What could *that* be? A rat? A human? No, there was no way a human would fit in there.

"Doug, just come!" she called over his frantically growing barks.

He must be caught, she thought, trapped behind or under something. She stood up and gingerly put her weight on the console television. From there she crawled back over the sideboard. Beside her, the mattress from the four-poster, which had been canted at an awkward angle, tilted ominously toward her. Lily pushed it until it righted itself against a rafter on the ceiling, then crawled forward again.

She'd gone only a couple feet when, with a great groaning noise, the mattress slipped onto the sideboard and the chest of drawers crashed down behind it.

Lily shrieked and thought she was about to be crushed, but the chest forced the mattress onto her back, then caught at an angle on the armoire as it fell, creating a cave under which Lily and the mattress lay, the base of the chest pinning the mattress against her with its weight.

Doug barked furiously, and Lily yelled back at him to stop. The whole expedition was suddenly intensely irritating. He'd gotten in here, surely he'd have gotten out on his own eventually. Why did she feel like she had to rescue him? Brady was right, she did coddle the dog.

"Doug, no! Dammit!" With effort, she turned over onto her back and tried to slide herself out from under the mattress, but she couldn't bend her knees, and there was nothing to grab hold of. She was pinned.

Good God, she thought after trying to slither like a snake and failing, she was going to die in here. Suffocate under Aunt Vivien's decaying furniture.

A few feet to her left, now that she was on her back—the opposite direction from where Doug was—she heard movement, and she let out another involuntary yelp. What the hell *was* that?

A second later she heard a larger noise near the door of the shed.

"Lily?" Brady's voice.

She simultaneously breathed a sigh of relief and cringed. Of all the times for him to finally choose to talk to her, he had to find her trapped in the shed, with spiderwebs and dead things no doubt hanging in her hair and squished on her back.

Not to mention a mattress flattening her to the television set.

"Under here," she answered morosely.

She heard him approach, heard a loud *thud*—his voice muttered *shit*—then the door slammed shut.

She froze. "Oh my God. Brady, you didn't shut the door, did you?"

More mutterings could be heard, along with the sounds of someone picking himself up and brushing himself off.

"Shit," he said again, low. "No, I didn't *close* it. It closed itself after I damn near broke my foot on that rock."

"That rock," she said, closing her eyes, "was keeping the door open. It locks on its own. From the outside."

Silence greeted this remark. Then she heard a hand on the door, rattling the catch against the ancient lock with considerable force.

Silence descended again, and he said, "Well, that sucks."

She gave a humorless laugh.

"Are you stuck?" he asked.

She leaned her head back and exhaled. "Good guess. Yes, I think I might be."

Brady's hands encircled her ankles, and she jumped. His palms were warm, his grip firm.

"Sorry," he said. "I think I can pull you straight out. You're not actually caught on anything in there, are you?"

She shifted and groaned as the edge of the mattress settled against one hip. "No, it's just . . . this stuff is so heavy."

He pulled on her legs, and she slid about four inches before feeling the mattress move a little. He stopped and let go. Immediately, she missed the feel of his hands.

"Damn, Lily. One false move, and this bureau's liable to flatten you. Or me." His footsteps crossed the cement floor from one side of the shed to the other. "Maybe I could get up there and push it back. I don't know. If I do that, then these boxes will fall over . . ."

"I do have this mattress, you know, in case you hadn't noticed. I can't imagine getting hurt under here. Just maybe suffocating."

"What the hell were you doing out here, anyway?" he asked.

"It's Doug. He's trapped back in the corner. I could hear him barking. And there's something else, I think. Something on the other side that keeps moving, too. I kind of don't want to run into that."

"Maybe it's trapped, too. And you're trapped. And I'm trapped, though less than you and the dog and the mystery beast. So . . . it's another fine mess you've gotten me into." She heard the smile in his voice.

"Glad you're enjoying it."

"It's not often I get to do my Laurel and Hardy imitation."

"Is that what that was?"

"You're obviously not a fan. You know, I think

if I just pull you straight out, fast, then that stuff can fall where it wants. It doesn't look like it'll come this way."

Lily turned her head. "Whatever you think. I just . . . something's digging into my side, so let's do this quick."

His hands went round her ankles again; she felt her skin come alive.

"Ready?" he asked.

"Yep."

He pulled. Her shirt rode up, her hair covered her face, her back scraped as it crossed from the sideboard to the console television. Whatever had dug into her side ran up her rib cage and poked her shoulder, but she felt herself come free from the mattress. As she did, Brady fell backwards, and she landed hard on her butt on the cement floor.

Behind her something shifted and the sound of falling objects made her lunge forward. Brady grabbed her arm and pulled her up, nearly jerking her shoulder out of its socket. Then she was hit in the back, pushed to her knees, and the mattress and bureau came crashing down behind her.

Lily was thrown against Brady's body, and the two of them were pinned against the front wall.

"Well, that's better," Lily said, after a moment.

Fortunately for Lily, the mattress protected her from the bureau, padding her back, and her legs were under her enough that it hadn't crunched them. Lily's chin pressed against Brady's belly. Just a few inches below her face was his fly.

She started to laugh. "Are you okay?" she asked. She could feel his belly moving up and down with his breath, so she knew it hadn't killed him.

"Yeah." He groaned and the mattress shifted. "It just knocked the wind out of me a little."

She pushed herself to her feet, still pressed up against his body. Every nerve ending was alive with the feeling. She wasn't sure where to put her hands, finally opting for his rib cage.

Skin touched skin along their legs as they both wore shorts. Brady had on a freshly laundered tee shirt, and Lily's cropped top revealed an inch or two of her stomach, along which she could feel the waistband of his shorts.

Brady moved his hands to her hips. She felt his cheek on her hair.

"I think I can . . ." He moved slightly, objects shifted weightily behind them, and her body pressed against his.

It was dim in the shed. A filthy square window in the door let in a little light, but she couldn't see his face, could not even move her head in that direction. But that only made the current situation more sensual. They were just bodies, hands, skin, pushed against each other. No eye contact, no reading each other's expression, no misunderstanding.

"Maybe that was a bad idea," he said, low.

A moment later she felt a hardness grow under his shorts along her abdomen. An answering heat flared within her.

"Sorry," he muttered.

"Quite all right," she said, her voice coming out higher than usual.

From outside the front of the shed, Doug barked. Once, twice, then silence. They heard him snorting along the bottom of the shed door.

"I thought you said he was trapped in here," Brady said.

"I thought he was!" She couldn't believe it. Somehow, he'd gotten out and she and Brady were now . . .

If she didn't know better, she'd think the dog had planned this.

Brady moved slightly, shifting his hips in an obvious effort to relieve his sudden constriction, and the contact sent heat shimmering up her body. She tried to move her hips in return, to ease his discomfort, but he groaned.

"Don't do that, Lily. Please," he said, laying his head back against the wall behind him. "You'll only make it worse."

Laughter tickled the back of her throat. "Oh I don't know," she said lightly. "I'm kind of enjoying it."

"You are, huh?" He pressed his hands against

her hips in an attempt to move them away from the evidence of his arousal.

"Yes, I am. You haven't spoken to me in weeks, and now you have to. So yes, I'm enjoying this."

"We might be talking here for the next month if nobody notices we're missing. I don't know how we're going to get out of here if I can't push this mattress back. But it's blocked by the junk behind it." He shifted again. "This is a fire hazard, you do know that."

"I thought you said if you pulled me out, the stuff would fall the other way."

"Yeah, well, that's why I'm not an engineer."

She laughed.

"Besides," he added, "I'm not the one not talking to you. You're avoiding me. That's why we haven't talked."

"Brady, we haven't talked since the night Tricia showed up and I tried to help and you sent me away. In my book, that means the ball was in your court." She moved her hands a few inches lower, resting them on his hipbones, as he had his resting on hers.

"Actually, I thought the ball was still in your court from the day you told me not to tell you what you felt. Which, by extension, I took to mean not to tell you how I felt."

Lily stilled. "How do you feel?"

He snickered once. "*Now* she'd like to know.

Maybe I'm not in the mood for saying anymore."

She couldn't help it—she smiled and pressed one hip ever so slightly forward. "Not in the mood, you say?"

"I think I made clear a long time ago that that operates independently of my mind."

Lily paused, considering. Was there any point in avoiding the subject any longer? Maybe it was the darkness that made her so bold, but she steeled herself, and said, "And your heart?"

She had made up her mind about Gerald. It had been easy since he'd been gone and all she'd been able to think about was Brady. In fact, whenever she talked to her father she had to remind herself to ask about Gerald.

And Brady hadn't asked Penelope out, making that situation a little less loaded.

Could she dare hope there were actual emotions behind his actions? Or was she just a binge in the midst of his date diet?

"At this moment," he said slowly, "it seems to have the same sentiments as my heart."

Lily stood still, her hands lightly on his rib cage, afraid of breaking the spell of the moment. Had he said what she thought he'd said?

He began to chuckle. "And if that's not the most romantic way of saying that, I don't know what is."

She moved her hands to his hips, her fingers tightening. For the moment, she was glad she couldn't look into his face. It made her braver.

"Saying what, exactly, Brady?" she asked, her voice soft.

Her cheek against his chest, she could feel his heart pounding fast. The heat between their bodies seemed to ratchet upward exponentially.

He blew out a breath of air slowly, carefully. "I'm in love with you, Lily."

Lily held her breath.

"Sorry," he added, at her silence.

She tried to move, tried to shift her head so she could look up at him, but she couldn't.

"Brady, I—"

"Hang on a second," he said. "I'm going to try . . ." He snaked one hand up between them, then over her head. She felt his chest muscles contract, and with one great push she felt the mattress behind her give way a few inches.

Beyond that boxes crashed, and with an old-wood creak and the slamming of drawers, the bureau tilted backwards far enough to create about a foot of space between them.

Lily leaned back and gazed up into Brady's face, searching his eyes.

He looked down at her with sadness in his expression, and an almost shy deference to the set of his normally cocky shoulders.

"I'm sorry," he continued. "I know all about Gerald and how perfect he is for you, how much your dad likes him, and all that. I know I don't even have a college education, and I'd look awful in that picture you talked about. I know that you—"

"Shut up!" she said suddenly, taking his face in her hands. "Brady . . . I'm in love with you, too."

With that she pulled his head toward hers and planted her lips firmly on his.

It took Brady a second to absorb the meaning of her words, but her lips reached into his consciousness immediately. When he realized what she'd said, his arms went round her waist, and he pulled her close, as close as he could. His mouth took over the direction of the kiss, and she yielded to him.

He pressed her back against the mattress behind her. It tilted now in the same direction as the bureau, toward the back of the shed. Lily leaned and pulled him into her, her hands reaching his hips and one leg rising up to curl around his waist.

Their mouths opened frantically against each other, tongues searching, their breathing hard. Brady pushed his hips into hers, the pressure at once releasing and increasing his desire.

Lily's hands grabbed for his shorts, moving to the waistband and undoing the button. Brady found the hem of her shirt and slid his hands up under it, her skin silk and cream against his fingers. He released the bra clasp quickly and moved his palms to her breasts, thumbs and forefingers finding the nipples and making her gasp.

She shoved his shorts down. He backed away from the kiss and pulled her shirt over her head, the bra coming with it, and there in the dim light of the shed he saw her clearly. Her eyes shone bright with desire—and something else. Something like . . . *love.*

Her hair was mussed, her skin bare and pale, her body lithe and his for the taking.

Emotion welled up within him, threatening to choke him.

"I love you," she breathed.

He couldn't help the smile that curved his lips, the drumbeat in his chest, and the heat behind his eyes. He was loved, by the first woman he himself had ever loved.

How had he gotten so damn lucky?

"Lily," he said quietly, calmly, the eye of the storm, "I love you, too."

With that, they shed the rest of their clothing, and their bodies came together. His lips found her neck as she guided him inside of her, and he pushed upward hard, pinning her, pinning *them,* joining their bodies and hearts in a matrimony of passion, desire, friendship, and love.

He had found it all. And he could hardly believe it.

He thrust into her, a confirmation of every emotion he had. His nerve endings tingled from his toes to his scalp. He felt her everywhere, enveloping him, holding him, urging him onward. They joined each other again and again, their bodies in sync; their hands, mouths, breaths gentle yet strong, together yet separate, euphoric yet sure.

They were together now. They were, he thought in amazement, as one.

Sometime later, from outside the shed, they heard Doug barking again. Not frightened, this time, but aggressive. Someone had come into the yard, Brady guessed. Despite himself, he'd learned to interpret some of the dog's language.

He untangled himself from Lily's arms, chuckling as she threatened not to let him go, and stood from their reclined position on the tilted mattress.

He reached down and picked up his shorts and underwear. "We probably ought to think about trying to get out of here."

She sighed. "Really? I was just starting to like this shed, for the first time since I moved here."

He looked at the beautiful creature before him. Could it be? Could he really end up with a woman like this? The kind who looked at you like you hung the moon and made you feel as if you could.

He smiled—couldn't help but smile—turned around, and picked up his tee shirt; when he did he caught sight of Nathan through the small window in the door. He was crossing the yard, making his way slowly toward Lily's back door.

"Hey," he said, "Nathan's in the yard. If I get his attention, he can get us out of here."

Lily rose and moved to stand beside him. He looked down at her, and that smile hit his face again. He snaked an arm around her naked shoulders. She leaned into him and stood on tiptoe to look out the window.

"Wait, let me get dressed before you do anything," she said.

She moved away and started gathering her clothing. It hadn't gone far. They only had about two square feet to move in. In fact every time she bent over she bumped him with her hips. He let his hands trail over them, appreciating all over again her lithe, shapely body, the newness of her comfort with him. Reluctantly, he turned back to Nathan and watched to be sure he didn't disappear before they could get him to let them out of there.

"What's he got in his hand?" Brady said, leaning toward the dirt and spiderweb-smeared glass. "It doesn't look like he's knocking on your door. It looks like he's . . ." He tilted his head as if it would help him see around Nathan's body.

Lily pulled her shirt over her head and moved back beside Brady. "It looks like he's smearing something on the door! What in God's name . . . ?"

After a minute or two, Nathan turned and headed back across the lawn, more quickly this time. His path toward the gate would take him near the shed, but Lily and Brady were more intent on what he had in his hands.

"It's a jar of peanut butter," Brady said. "Why was he was smearing peanut butter on your back door?"

"I have no idea," Lily said grimly. "Maybe there's something else in the jar."

"Why would he smear *anything* on your back door?" Brady smelled a rat.

Lily shook her head.

But Nathan's path wasn't taking him toward the gate. It was taking him toward the shed, without their having yet made a sound.

Lily raised a hand to pound on the door, but Brady grabbed her wrist, lowering it and taking her hand as he did so.

"Wait just a second," he said. "Let's see what he's up to."

"Where's Doug?" Lily whispered as Nathan got closer. "I'm surprised he hasn't cornered him."

Brady craned his neck to see more of the yard through the tiny window.

"Over by the opposite fence." He paused. "It looks like he's eating something. Jeez, it looks like a steak."

"Steak!" Lily stood on her tiptoes again to look out the window. Brady put both hands around her waist and lifted her slightly to make it easier.

"That's a bribe," she whispered harshly. "I'm surprised Doug fell for it."

No sooner were the words out of her mouth than Doug spotted Nathan's path toward the shed. He jumped up from his gourmet treat and raced toward Nathan, snorting and growling as he came.

Nathan's face registered shock, then panic. He raced toward the shed, making odd kissing, hissing sounds. "Kitty! Here, kitty!" he said, his voice several octaves higher than usual and completely at odds with his trademark all-black attire. "Kittykittykitty!" he shrieked.

Brady and Lily watched in shock, their mouths open.

Nathan hit the side wall of the shed, and they lost sight of him. But they could hear him, calling for "kitty" over the sounds of Doug's growls and barks.

When the barks became solely growls, Brady knew the dog had hold of Nathan's pant leg.

Two minutes later, however, Doug turned tail with a squeal and headed back toward the house like a bat out of hell.

"What—?" Lily's fingers gripped the edge of the window as she jumped to her toes again.

A second later a large gray cat took off after the dog.

"Hey, that's the cat I found tied to a tree a few weeks ago," Brady said.

Doug just made it through the dog door when the cat reached the back stoop. For a second it looked as if the cat was going to follow him through, but the door swung back and hit it in the face.

Brady couldn't help it. He started to laugh.

Lily elbowed him in the ribs. "Stop it. Cats are the only thing in the world Doug's afraid of. This is so mean."

Seconds later the cat was licking the door, and Doug's panicked yips could be heard inside the house.

"That's just how he's been sounding lately when he's scared," Lily said. "Has Nathan had that cat licking the door to scare Doug?"

Nathan rounded the corner of the shed, just in front of them, looking furtively up at the house.

"Nathan!" Brady yelled.

Nathan let out a scream the exact pitch of a six-year-old girl's and spun toward Brady's voice.

"Hey, Nathan! In here! We're stuck in the shed!" He waved a hand in the window. "Let us out!"

"The keys are in the lock!" Lily called.

Nathan's eyes widened, and his face colored a deep, dark red. "What?" he said.

"Let us out!" Brady said, rolling his eyes. "We're stuck in here."

But Nathan didn't move.

Eighteen

It took Nathan a moment, but he finally seemed to come out of whatever state of astonishment he'd been in. He tossed the jar of peanut butter into the bushes by the fence, then came to the shed, turned the key, and pulled the door open.

Lily burst out of the dusty room, breathing in the fresh air as if she'd been caught in a coal mine. But Brady's attention was centered on Nathan.

"Thanks, buddy," he said, sauntering out and clapping the guy on one bony shoulder with a comradely hand. Then he gripped it hard. "Why don't you come on up to the house, let us thank you properly?"

Nathan looked nervously from Brady to Lily.

"What were you guys doing in there?" he asked, looking simultaneously confused and appalled.

Lily's face flushed, and Brady grinned at the sight of it. His little wanton, blushing at the impropriety of it all. Emma would be proud.

"We got stuck," she said, a tad defensively. "Doug was caught in there, and I had to get him out. Though I have no idea how he got in there."

She frowned and looked along the sidewall of the shed again. From where he stood, Brady could plainly see that she was looking at a distinct opening between the rotting wooden clapboards and the ground. Something had dug out a pretty generous entryway.

Brady went to her side. "Looks just about big enough for Doug to get into."

"Followed by a cat," Lily said, glaring at Nathan. "He must have been chased in there, scared to death."

"He probably got out through a similar hole on the other side," Brady said, looking back at Nathan. "Care to tell us what you know about that cat, Nathan?"

Lily's hands went to her hips as she stood before her neighbor. "And what were you doing painting peanut butter on my back door?"

Nathan's expression changed instantly to the proverbial deer in the headlights.

"I think it's obvious what he was doing," Brady said. "Scaring the hell out of Doug. Not that I

don't think that's an understandable occupation,"
Brady added, patting Nathan on the back while
guiding him up the lawn toward the house. "But
you do realize that when you scare Doug, you
scare Lily, don't you? And *that* we just can't have."

"I, uh . . ." Nathan said.

Lily looked profoundly disappointed. "I thought
you were my friend, Nathan. Why would you want
to scare my dog?"

"I, uh . . ."

"Come on in the house," Brady said, realizing
the futility of trying to make the stunned man
talk at the moment. "Let's get some iced tea and
talk about this."

An hour later the story had come out, and Brady
had to work hard to keep from laughing. Not that
it was a particularly laughable occasion. It was
just that Nathan had somehow made him feel better about some of his own problems. Brady had
been so humiliated by Tricia and her staggeringly
bizarre behavior, he'd missed the fact that Lily
had a stalker of her own, right next door.

It turned out that Nathan had been carrying a
torch for Lily for years, ever since she'd moved in.
But he could never get past Doug. It wasn't until
Lily had mentioned that the one thing Doug was
afraid of was cats that it occurred to him he could
find a cat—a mean one—and use it to scare Doug
out of the way.

When it scared Lily, too, he got another idea.

That if Lily got frightened enough, she could come stay with him and his mother until the "prowler," that he had invented, disappeared. By that time he figured he would have had a chance to convince her of his love for her.

And, of course, she would realize how she felt about him, too.

During this confession, Lily had been compassionate, if initially incensed that Nathan had tormented her dog, and had let Nathan down as gently as she could. He was just a friend. She didn't think her feelings would ever change. She was sorry, but the fact was she was in love with someone else.

At that she had smiled at Brady, and Nathan's mouth had gone slack with comprehension. His eyes strayed back and forth from Lily to Brady.

"*Him?*" he said, aghast. "But we hate him! He's the cocky asshole pilot."

Brady raised his eyebrows at Lily.

She blushed. "Nathan, you know I never said that."

"Not in so many words, maybe, but we agreed he was a jerk—"

"A lot of time has passed since then," she said, cutting him off.

"Only a couple of months," Nathan insisted. "And what about Gerald? Huh? I thought he was the one you wanted. I don't think you know what you want, Lily. I've watched you a long time, and—"

"That's enough questions out of you," Brady said. If Gerald's name was never mentioned again it would be too soon.

"Sorry," Nathan said, shoulders hunching. He shot Brady a resentful look. "Though this *is* between Lily and me."

"Maybe so." Brady sat back, sorry for the guy more than anything else. "Just call me an interested bystander."

Nathan ignored him. "Lily, I didn't mean for it to really scare you," he said, looking miserable. "I just wanted to get Doug out of the way. I couldn't even *talk* to you when he was around."

Lily put a hand on his arm, and said, "Nathan, I understand. I don't approve of what you did, and I'm still shocked that you'd be so mean to my dog, but we don't have to talk about this anymore. Just . . . don't ever do anything like this again."

"No, no, never again," Nathan said sincerely, shaking his head and looking at his lap.

"Okay," Brady said, rising. "And on that note, I'm going to go take a shower. I feel like I've got bugs crawling all over me. See you later?" He winked at Lily.

She smiled, and her entire expression softened with it. "Come back tonight," she said. "I'll cook you dinner."

He looked into her eyes, warming under their spell, and felt his lips curve in that perpetual smile. "You got it."

*   *   *

Lily had talked to Nathan for a long time, consoling and chastising him, treating him as if he were one of her students who had failed, but who could make up the work if he tried.

It was disturbing that she'd missed what was going on, especially after that night he'd offered to let her stay with him and his mother, but she'd been so focused on her issues with Gerald—and Brady—that Nathan had been little more than background noise. Which was part of the problem, she realized. She needed to start treating her friends better, not be so wrapped up in her own affairs.

Not tonight, though, she thought, with another burst of happiness. She'd been having them all day, bursts of happiness like fireworks going off in her chest. Blossoms of realization that Brady felt about her the way she felt about him, and that maybe, just maybe, they could make a relationship that would work.

First, though, she had to call Penelope, just to be sure. Later, she'd figure out what to do about Gerald.

After that she'd start cooking dinner. Something special. Shrimp Louis, maybe. Or lobster rolls.

Lily and Penelope chatted for a while before Lily got the nerve to bring up Brady.

"So," Lily began, "I guess after the Glenn thing you're still, uh, thinking about . . . Brady?"

That sounded bad, she thought, putting a hand over her face, like she thought Penelope might be waiting for the guy that she'd stolen. But how to ask?

As luck would have it, Penelope's call waiting beeped just after Lily had asked the question, so she had to sit on pins and needles waiting for her friend's reply.

When she came back on the line, Pen said, "What were we talking about?"

Lily steeled herself again. "Brady?"

"Oh right—"

"Penelope, listen," Lily interrupted. "Before you begin, there's something I have to tell you. A confession, really. And before I tell you, I want you to know how terrible I feel about this, how I know I've been a bad friend, and I'm going to make it up to you, I swear. I'd never do this kind of thing ordinarily but it just happened, and I didn't know what—"

"Lily, stop!" Penelope said, laughing. "If this is about Brady and you, then I know already. You guys are perfect for each other."

"Wha—? You *know*? What—how—did Megan tell you something?"

"She didn't have to! Though we did talk about it some after I figured it out. As usual she knew what was going on far earlier than the rest of us."

"Oh my God, how did you *know*?" Lily exclaimed. "I can't believe I've done this awful thing."

"What's so awful about it?" Penelope objected. "I think you guys are great together. That's how I knew. I could tell how you looked at each other, how you talked to one another, and mostly, how you looked when his name came up. But—oh—is this about Gerald? Is that why you feel so bad?"

"No," Lily said, "well, yes. But mostly it's about *you*. I feel like I've betrayed you, because, you know, we meant Brady to be for you and got your hopes up and all."

Penelope laughed gently. "Lily, honey, we were only just *introduced*, for goodness' sake. We didn't even go on one date. It's not as if you stole a boyfriend or anything."

Lily exhaled hugely. "I know. I just felt like I had. Because we'd been talking . . ."

"I know," Penelope said, consolingly, "but that's not how it was. I mean, I liked Brady but I really hadn't thought about him much, what with all the Glenn stuff. And honestly, I think he's more your type than mine." She laughed. "I guess that's obvious now, huh?"

They laughed together, and Lily felt better than she had in weeks. The fear that she'd been betraying her friend had weighed on her more heavily than she'd even realized.

They chatted a while longer, smoothing over all the strangeness that Lily had felt and reassuring each other of their closeness, then they hung up.

Lily went upstairs, showered, and came down to begin cooking dinner.

At five-fifteen the doorbell rang. Lily jumped up from the stool in the kitchen and smiled hugely to herself. He was early. Maybe he couldn't wait to see her again, just as she couldn't wait to see him. She needed to confirm for herself that what had happened in the shed that morning had really happened. That she and Brady had said they'd loved each other; that they'd embarked on something wonderful.

She ran to the door and opened it wide, smiling broadly.

Her elated expression turned to one of disbelief, however, when she saw her father in his Armani suit standing on her front porch, black limo parked in the street behind him.

"Daddy!" She couldn't contain her shock, could barely register that it was him there on her doorstep. She felt as if the two were so incompatible she must be experiencing some kind of synapse misfire.

"Honey, I'm glad you're home," he said, stepping into the house past her stunned figure. "I would have called, but I didn't want to alarm you by telling you I was coming." He turned back to her in the hall and leaned in to kiss her on the cheek.

At the sound of his voice, Doug's bark erupted from the kitchen and his sturdy body came racing down the center hallway. Lily scooped him up before he could get near her father. God forbid he should shred an Armani leg.

"Oh yes," her father said dourly. "You still have Doug, I see."

"I'll be right back," she said, hastily returning to the kitchen to put Doug in his crate. She barely had the presence of mind to pat him on the head before closing the door, so bewildered was she by her father's unexpected arrival.

She returned quickly to the hallway. "What were you saying, Daddy? Something about alarming me? Is something wrong? Is—are you all right?" She looked him up and down from head to foot, satisfying herself that he was not in any obvious distress.

"I'm fine, but why don't we sit down together?" He motioned her toward the living room as if he were the one who lived there.

"Okay." She proceeded him into the room.

"The place is looking good," he said. "You've done a nice job with it. It looks much better than it did when Aunt Vivien was living here."

Lily was still gazing at him in stunned incomprehension. "Daddy, you're kind of scaring me. Why are you here? Not that I don't love having you here, of course, but . . . it's just so unexpected."

He sat down gravely on the couch. "I know, Lily. And I'm sorry, but it can't be helped." He clasped his hands together in front of him and gazed down at them. Lily had never seen him so subdued, so careful of what he said or did.

She sat gingerly on the edge of the armchair next to the couch.

He slid over on the sofa and patted the cushion beside him. "Come sit here, why don't you?"

Panic flooded through her. She rose on wooden legs and planted herself next to him on the couch. He took her hands in his. Hers were suddenly frigid, his warm and comforting.

"Daddy, what's this all about?" she asked, barely breathing.

She could not even imagine what he might be about to say. Was he sick? Was it cancer? Had he lost all his money in the stock market? What? It wasn't as if they had a lot of friends in common that he might have terrible news about.

"It's about Gerald," he said finally.

"Gerald!" Her surprise came mainly from the fact that he hadn't even occurred to her as a possible source of news.

"This is very difficult to say," he said, looking her solemnly in the eyes, "so I'm going to say it quickly. He's gotten married. In Hawaii. To the paralegal, Doris."

Lily's mouth dropped open. "In Hawaii?"

She didn't know why those were the words she repeated. They didn't mean anything to her. They were just the ones that happened to emerge from her mouth.

She blinked.

Gerald.

Married.

Doris.

She could hardly put the idea together in her head.

Then, slowly, the pieces began to fit. She and Gerald had had nothing but uninspired conversations almost since the first week he'd arrived there. She hadn't been thinking about it much because she hadn't been thinking about *him* much. But there he'd been, with the model-perfect Doris, who Lily had no doubt had had her eye on the *uber*successful and *GQ*-handsome Gerald for years. They were working together, staying together, talking about all that business stuff that Lily had only been peripherally interested in, in one of the most beautiful places in the world, and they'd eloped. It made perfect sense.

Was that her? Did you tell—? She heard the words again, clearly this time. It had been Doris in the background of Gerald's call, she knew now, jealous of his conversation with *her.*

And here Lily had been worrying about what she was going to say to him about her feelings, or lack thereof, afraid she was going to hurt him, shock him, and he hadn't even had the courage to tell *her.* He'd sent her father!

She began to laugh. She did not have even an ounce of regret at losing Gerald.

Her father frowned. "I know this is something of a shock. And people react differently to shock. But you do understand what I said, don't you, dear?"

"Yes." She nodded, wiped mirth-teary eyes with her fingers. "Gerald got married in Hawaii. To Doris."

"I have to say that I'm very angry with both of them. In fact I'm considering speaking with the partners about his promotion. This type of shadiness, this infidelity and impulsiveness, well it speaks badly to his character. Very badly. And Doris . . ." He shook his head. "Honestly it doesn't surprise me about Doris. She was something of an opportunist, though that isn't such a bad thing in the context of a law firm."

Lily sobered slightly. "Did he say . . . was he seeing her before they left? He wasn't actually cheating on me here, was he?"

She'd been so sure of Gerald's loyalty. She hated to think she could be that wrong about somebody.

"I asked him the same thing," her father answered. "He swore it was something that happened suddenly, to both of them, while they were in Hawaii. In fact he said I could even ask you about that, because he'd invited you to come to Hawaii for a weekend, and why would he do that if he was planning to elope with Doris?" He gave her an inquiring look.

She nodded, remembering. "That is true. He did invite me to come." She considered a moment, musing how strange life's twists could be. "It's funny, I wouldn't have thought Gerald could be so . . . spontaneous."

"I call it irresponsible." He shook his head again, looking down at their clasped hands. "I'm so sorry, sweetheart. I hated to have to tell you this."

He looked so miserable, Lily's heart went out to him, and she leaned over and gave him a hug. He squeezed her in return.

"Daddy, don't worry," she said into his shoulder. "It's not as bad as you think. Gerald and I . . ." She pulled back and looked into his eyes. He looked tired, she thought. Older. Maybe it was because he was outside of his office and in *her* environment now, without his power and authority behind him, that he looked so much more human, so much more vulnerable.

He'd come all the way down here, south on I-95 during rush hour, which was an unmitigated nightmare, to tell his daughter the bad news in person. In case she was upset. In case she needed him.

She had never loved him more than she did at this moment.

"Gerald and I decided before he left to leave things casual, Daddy," she said, embellishing a little. "Don't be angry with him. He's been calling, and we just haven't been connecting. I mean, the calls have been connecting, but *we* haven't. The bottom line is we don't have much in common, and I think we were both figuring that out." She paused, let loose another relieved laugh. "Well, clearly *he* was figuring that out."

Her father was frowning at her, confused. "You aren't upset with him?"

She thought about that. "I guess maybe, just a little. Only because I wish *he'd* said something to me."

Then she realized how completely hypocritical that was considering what she and Brady had just done and how she hadn't given a thought to telling Gerald, not yet anyway. Though she believed she would have mentioned something had she eloped.

"But I understand completely why he didn't," she continued. "*Completely*. And I don't blame him a bit." She squeezed her father's arm. "Really, Daddy, please don't worry about me. To tell you the absolute truth, I'm relieved."

He still looked confused, but he smiled. "Then I am, too. But I have to say this is quite unexpected. I believed you would be devastated."

She nodded. "And a couple of months ago I would have been. But things have changed. A lot."

As if on cue, there was a brisk knock on the back door, it squeaked open, and in walked Brady, carrying a bottle of wine and a bouquet of flowers. Lilies.

She smiled at him.

Then she glanced at her father.

He raised his chin and glanced from Brady to Lily. "Ah," he said coolly. "I begin to understand."

Her father stood, pulling his shoulders back and giving Brady his most imperious look.

Brady stopped in the doorway, surprise evident on his face. Then he placed the wine and the flowers on the dining-room table and strode into the living room.

"Mr. Tyler, good to see you again." He walked right up to her father, his hand held out, his eyes direct.

Her father had no choice but to offer his own hand and shake. "Brady, how are you?"

"I'm very good, sir. And you?" Brady stood comfortably, as if her father were just another associate.

"I'm well," he said ominously, and gave Lily a dark look.

Lily straightened. She was a grown woman, she could make her own decisions. It was nice of him—*wonderful* of him, really—to be concerned for her about Gerald, but she had done nothing wrong by starting this relationship with Brady.

Well, nothing that he knew of, anyway.

"Daddy," she said firmly, "Brady has come for dinner. Can you stay too? I've made shrimp Louis; that's one of your favorites, isn't it?"

Her father was frowning at the floor. After a

moment he lifted his head and looked her in the eye. Then he turned to Brady.

"I'm sorry, Brady, would you excuse us for a minute? I'd like to speak with my daughter. Alone."

Brady's eyes became guarded. "Of course."

"Why don't you open the wine," Lily said to him, with a look that she hoped he interpreted as *don't go anywhere*. "We won't be long."

Brady flashed her a smile. "Sure."

She and her father stood silent while Brady crossed the living room, moved through the dining room, picking up the wine and flowers as he went, and disappeared into the kitchen.

"I thought he was going out with your friend," her father said. His tone was conversational, but she wasn't fooled. That was how he lured witnesses into revealing more than they intended.

"I thought he was, too," she said. "But he decided not to ask her out."

"He asked you out instead," her father said.

Lily met his eyes, thought *sort of*, but said, "Yes."

"Lily, I don't know what you're doing," her father said intently, his voice low. "Did you break things off with Gerald for *him*?"

Lily's insides quaked, the way they always did when her father was angry. And he was angry now, there was no mistaking it. She should have known. He had been almost as anxious for her to marry Gerald as she had been. Gerald was a known quantity to him, a man not unlike himself, and he was right there in the office where her father could guide him, groom him, make sure he was the son-in-law he'd always wanted.

But Lily was the one this was all about, she thought. She was the one at the heart of the matter, and with Brady she was happier than she'd ever been. Granted, it was early, very early, in the relationship, but she already knew that it was special.

"I did," she said. "And it wasn't because Gerald was gone, either, Daddy. My feelings for Brady have been growing for months, but I only just discovered, after Gerald left, that he felt the same way about me."

The least she could do was get Gerald off the hook, because really he'd done her a favor by marrying Doris. She had no guilt, no regrets, nothing to feel bad about now that she knew she hadn't hurt him.

"I don't know what else to say, Daddy," she continued, "except that I've fallen in love with Brady. And he has with me."

Her father scoffed and turned away from her, pacing to the other side of the room before turning to face her.

"And yet a few short weeks ago you were miserable because Gerald was leaving for so long. How fickle, Lillian. I'm surprised at you."

Lily blushed, aware of how bad it all looked

from her father's point of view. He didn't understand the turmoil she'd been in, the fear she'd had of falling for Brady, before she knew who he really was, the way she'd deliberately twisted her own feelings to maintain the status quo.

"It's complicated," she admitted.

Her father glanced back at the kitchen, where Brady was not visible, and lowered his voice again. "No it's not. It's simple. You traded in the difficult path for the easy one. Gerald was going to be gone for a few weeks, and so you turned to the man next door. How could you do it? And for someone like *him*!" He threw a hand out toward the kitchen. "I thought you'd learned *that* lesson with the plumber, Lillian. How could you trade a man like Gerald for a man like that?"

Lily's back straightened, and she glared at her father. "I just said I didn't turn to him because Gerald left. I was confused about both of them for a long time before that happened. In fact, it was because of my feelings for Brady that I didn't want Gerald to go away. I was afraid . . ."

She took a deep breath and ran her hands through her hair.

"Daddy, this is too hard to explain to you. You'll never understand. I don't think you could unless you've been in the same situation. But you have to trust me when I say that this is not a whim. I'm in love with Brady. And there is absolutely no comparison between him and Duane.

They are completely different people. Please don't humiliate yourself by showing your prejudices."

Her father's face went red, and they glowered at each other a moment. He had withered her with this look on any number of occasions but she would not be felled by it this time. This was too important.

"Daddy, I know how things must look to you," she continued, trying to keep the conversation reasonable, "but this is what's real. Brady and me. Gerald and I were never right. We were more of an idea than a reality."

"Don't give me that mumbo jumbo," Jordan Tyler said heatedly. The high-powered lawyer being bested by the public defender. "Gerald was going to offer you *marriage*, Lillian. A good home, a promising future. What has this fellow got? Nothing! Nothing compared to what Gerald could offer you. And how do you know he's not just playing around? Gerald was a serious person with a serious job and serious intentions. This Cole fellow could be nothing but a fly-by-night!"

"He is *not* a fly-by-night. He's a good person, Daddy. The best man I've ever been with. You don't even know him."

"I *don't* know him," her father said, nodding. "You're right about that. But I know men, and I know he's not the type to offer marriage."

"Just how do you know that, sir?" Brady's voice, calm but firm, questioned him from the doorway to the dining room. "Believe me when I say that I hated to listen in, but I was only about fifteen feet away, and your voices got pretty loud."

"This is none of your business, young man," her father said, scowling at him in a way that had wilted many an adverse witness.

"I disagree with you, sir. Since you're talking about me, I believe it *is* my business."

The way he stood, so tall and straight, so composed, Lily felt her heart swell with pride. But this was her battle. He didn't need to hear all of this.

"Brady, it's okay," Lily said quietly.

Brady glanced at her, his expression softening. "No, it's not okay, Lily. This is about me, about you and me, and I'd like to clear up a thing or two." He shifted his gaze back to her father. "Maybe I'm not a high-powered lawyer making a lot of money, Mr. Tyler, but I have a good career, an enviable career, I believe, and I have had it for twelve years. I make good money, as you should know from my credit report, though I haven't felt the need to spend it on a closetful of expensive suits or a Jaguar. But the important point that I believe you're missing is that I am in love with your daughter. And while it's early yet to be talking about it, I can say with complete conviction that if things continue the way I hope and believe they will, there is every reason in the world to think I *will* offer marriage to Lily. At which time I only hope *your daughter* will see fit to accept me, or not, on her own terms and for her own reasons."

Lily stared at him, respect for him and joy for herself blossoming in her heart. She smiled, her heartbeat fluttering and her mind racing with the knowledge that he felt the same way she did. They loved each other! They had a future! And he was even standing up to her father for her.

She beamed at him.

"Now, if you'll excuse me," Brady said with a polite inclination of his head, "I will go set another place at the table. I hope you'll accept Lily's invitation to dinner. I think you and I have some getting to know each other to do, because I plan on being around a long, long time."

"My God, Brady, you impressed him!" Lily exulted, later that night, in her bedroom. "You impressed him like nobody I've ever seen before. It was incredible!" She laughed and fell back on the bed, arms wide.

Brady moved to the bed and knelt over her, pinning her arms to the mattress with his hands and leaning down to kiss her. "But did I impress you? As much as you impressed me? She cooks, she cleans, she defends her boyfriend to her father!" He grinned.

Lily laughed and reveled in the simple fact of his calling himself her boyfriend.

He kissed her again, then sat up.

"So old Gerald got married, eh?" he asked, running a finger down the side of her neck, making her skin tingle.

"Evidently." She shivered under his touch, and smiled. "And to Doris, who'll be perfect for him. She'll make certain he makes partner, that's for darn sure."

"Ah, that type."

"Yes." She nodded. "That type."

"Interesting," he mused, still tracing that finger along her skin.

"What's that?" she asked.

"Well, with Gerald going off and marrying someone he's known for a while, with none of you the wiser to what was going on between them, even though he was acting as if he was going to marry you . . ."

"Does this humiliation have a point?" she asked dryly.

"In fact it does," he answered with a sly smile. "The point is, that makes him something of a Mr. Churchill, doesn't it? I mean, he couldn't be your Knightley anymore, not with his underhanded ways and unchivalrous behavior. Not to mention his secret girlfriend."

Lily gaped up at him. "Did you get all this from the movie?"

He gave her an insulted look. "No. I read the book."

"You read the book!" she repeated. "*When?*"

He smiled. "Just about a week ago. The way you talked about it, I wanted to see what it was all about. Does listening to it count? I got the unabridged version."

She grabbed his hand and pushed herself up so she was sitting across from him on the mattress. "Are you telling me you listened to *Emma*? By Jane Austen. *That Emma?*"

He gave her a bemused look. "Yes, that *Emma*. The one with the lying Mr. Churchill and the admirable Mr. Knightley."

Lily's smile had to be blinding. She could not have been more surprised. Brady had read her favorite book—to please her! Or understand her. Either way, it was wonderful.

"You know, I think you might be right," she said, thinking about it. Gerald hadn't been her Knightley—*Brady* had. He was the one who'd been true all along, almost without her noticing. And Gerald—well, running off and marrying someone else was pretty Churchill-esque. "Gerald's behavior does put him in a league with Frank Churchill. But I wouldn't call you Mr. Knightley, if that's what you're getting at."

Brady frowned and crossed his arms over his chest. "You wouldn't?"

"No." She shook her head, smiling, realizing with amazement that despite her own bunglings she'd ended up with exactly what she'd wanted.

She echoed one of her favorite lines from the movie. "I'd call you *my* Mr. Knightley."

Brady grinned and with that they leaned together at the same time, meeting in a kiss both tender and heartfelt, a kiss that promised everything.

As they kissed, Doug jumped up on the bed and squeezed between them, lying down as they separated, laughing. Almost at once he began to snore.

Epilogue

Doug didn't think of him as the New Guy anymore. Now he was the Good Guy, this guy that Lily called Brady.

There were many reasons for Doug's conversion on the issue. For one thing, there was that game with the feather, which he occasionally repeated, though the shoe never made another appearance. But now he even lifted Doug up onto the brand-new seat of his big shiny toy and drove him around.

Doug was refreshed to discover that the seat was much better for sitting on than consuming, and happily jumped up onto it even when the thing wasn't moving. It made a nice warm spot to lie down on sunny days.

Lily had put a stop to the rides the moment she'd seen one, however, so now they only did it when she was at work, and only in the backyard. But that was okay. It scared the kibble out of any cats who passed by.

Shortly after the Good Guy started spending so much time at the house—after Lily realized how hard the Good Guy worked to make Doug happy with special treats and games and whatnot—Doug decided it was time to start returning his footwear.

One by one, Doug went to his secret spot—behind the big metal cylinder in the basement—and picked out a shoe, bringing it back upstairs to lay it, like an offering, on the altar of Good Guy's front mat. Sometimes he was even able to bring it up to Lily's bed, where the Good Guy was often to be found these mornings. The first time Doug had done this, he'd received the heartwarming benefit of loud laughter, first from the Good Guy, then, after some coaxing, from Lily herself.

This made Doug happy. The Good Guy was the first male to inspire Lily to laugh so much, making it easier for Doug to let him do things for him.

Now they were planning some kind of big party, for which Doug would get to wear a special collar, one with a big black bow tie on it. Lily kept calling it his "tuxedo" but Doug thought of it as his black bone collar. Someday he'd get it off and bury it, as it deserved.

After that, it looked like the Good Guy would be bringing all his footwear over to Lily's house to put in the little side room with hers.

This was perfect for Doug, as he could use some help keeping all the other males away from his Lily. The Good Guy was most effective at that. Doug wasn't sure how, exactly, since he never peed outside, and certainly had never secured the perimeter with it the way Doug had.

But still, Good Guy turned out to be such a fun and useful presence, that Doug decided to let him stay.

Next month, don't miss these exciting new love stories only from Avon Books

And Then He Kissed Her by Laura Lee Guhrke

An Avon Romantic Treasure

Hired to train young ladies in proper etiquette, Emmaline Dove knows not to put a single toe out of line. But all her rules were much easier to follow before she met the handsome older brother of her latest charge. It may be time for Emily to learn that some rules are meant to be broken . . . especially when it comes to affairs of the heart

Arousing Suspicions by Marianne Stillings

An Avon Contemporary Romance

Detective Nate Darling has seen a lot of things over the years, but so-called dream interpreter Tabitha March is in a class all by herself. And when terrible dreams start to come true, Nate must decide if Tabitha is the prime suspect or the woman who's going to turn his well-ordered world on its ear.

Thrill of the Knight by Julia Latham

An Avon Romance

When the brave knight, Sir John, rides to rescue the maiden trapped in a tower, he doesn't know that Lady Elizabeth and her maid are one step ahead of him—and have switched places! Now both must struggle to focus on the task at hand while battling a powerful attraction.

Too Wicked to Tame by Sophie Jordan

An Avon Romance

Lady Portia Derring has to marry for money—lots of it. But agreeing to marriage and actually going *through* with it are two very different things. Of course, Portia hadn't counted on her betrothed being as reluctant as she, and now she's thinking besting him in battle may be worth "till death do us part."

DISCOVER CONTEMPORARY ROMANCES *at their*
SIZZLING HOT BEST FROM AVON BOOKS

Avon Romantic Treasures

Unforgettable, enthralling love stories, sparkling with passion and adventure from Romance's bestselling authors